Graham took tw
and peered dow

"They look as if they

Fanny snorted and Graham turned toward her.

"Settled from exhaustion, Mr. Staddler." She sank further into the spindled chair. "I must confess my fear of failure is beginning to invade my determination to see those babies have a proper home."

He reached out and lifted her chin with the tip of his finger. He searched her eyes and she prayed he did not find her weak and lacking in some way, even though she'd just boldly admitted her fears. This man was larger than life. Every word she'd read about him, every tale she'd heard, lived and breathed before her in the flesh. He had purpose and drive, a goal worth chasing. He hunted wanted criminals or hired on to protect folks from thieves. He was a hero to many and, as he'd been to her prior to encountering him today, a tall tale to others.

Christina Rich lives in northeast Kansas. Her passion for stories comes from a rich past of reading and digging through odd historical tidbits, where she finds a treasure trove of inspiration. She loves photography, art, ancestry research and, of course, writing happy-ever-afters.

Books by Christina Rich

Love Inspired Historical

The Guardian's Promise
The Warrior's Vow
Captive on the High Seas
The Negotiated Marriage
The Marshal's Unexpected Bride
A Family for the Twins

Visit the Author Profile page at LoveInspired.com.

A Family
for the Twins

CHRISTINA RICH

LOVE INSPIRED
INSPIRATIONAL ROMANCE

LOVE INSPIRED®
INSPIRATIONAL ROMANCE

Recycling programs for this product may not exist in your area.

ISBN-13: 978-1-335-49850-2

A Family for the Twins

Copyright © 2023 by Christina Rich

For questions and comments about the quality of this book, please contact us at CustomerService@Harlequin.com.

Love Inspired
22 Adelaide St. West, 41st Floor
Toronto, Ontario M5H 4E3, Canada
www.LoveInspired.com

Printed in U.S.A.

Suffer little children, and forbid them not, to come unto me: for of such is the kingdom of heaven.
—*Matthew* 19:14

This book could not have happened without a wealth of people.

Rhonda Gibson and Tammy Trail, thank you for being sounding boards during this story as I worked my way through the pages. To my editor, Emily Rodmell, thank you for another opportunity to write a great story. To the editors who worked on this book, you ladies ROCK! To my agent, Tamela Hancock Murray, thank you for your constant positivity. To Carolyn Bolen, you're always a wealth of information when it comes to the Flint Hills and Morris County, thank you.

To Brian Bolen, a hero among heroes, and the inspiration for my stories, thank you for the million and one things you do every day to support me, but especially all you did while I worked, earned my bachelor's degree and wrote. You made dinners, did dishes, did laundry, took care of our kitties, helped me make up names and answered off-the-wall questions that may or may not have been story related. Mostly, thank you for the thankless job you do each day. You stepped into a role when you didn't have to, and you choose each day to take up that role and be a dad. Thank you for being a hero to that young man. He may not have the words, but his selfless heart and constant smile are evidence of how great a job you did in raising him, and his love for you shines through his smile. To Jeremy, you may not be able to read this or even fully understand the words, but you have taught me a lot about communicating outside the box, kindness, giving and thoughtfulness, things I know you learned from your dad. This one is for you, Young Man.

Oak Grove, KS
1868

Chapter One

"Fanny Ellis, you are a right dim-witted addle-brained fool for leaving your pistol tucked beneath the mattress," she told herself as she stared at the gaping door. Why, she didn't even have the gun belt she'd made by sewing a few of Mama's old apron strings together to keep the weight of her pistol held by Daddy's holster from sagging the fabric too much. She'd dyed the strings in coffee to lose the floral effect, but now that she was older, she wished she hadn't. Those two items, Mama's fabric and Daddy's steel had kept their memories alive for her. If she closed her eyes tightly, sometimes she could still see the tiny yellow string of flowers dancing down Mama's back and smell the bacon frying up in a pan for when Daddy and her brothers returned from chores. Twenty some years was a long time to hold precious memories tucked in her heart like a locket.

The creak of a door brought her back to the here and now, and she pulled her bottom lip between her teeth. The door to her sewing establishment swung open and closed with the breeze, waving at her as if to invite her into her own place.

Gracious, if her brothers discovered she'd ventured into town without her pistol, they'd be as downright blustery mad as the north wind in a frigid rage. Good thing they wouldn't find out about her little slip of forgetfulness. They'd be gone a few weeks at best on their cattle drive. She should ease right out of the alley, walk around front to the mercantile and bother Mr. Taylor for assistance. She could ring the buzzer to his upstairs quarters if he wasn't stirring around, yet. Of course, the general store proprietor just might add a slight fee to her weekly rent, but that would be better than making Oak Grove's headlines if she encountered a rascally thief.

SPINSTER FANNY ELLIS SHOT DEAD IN A ROBBERY OF HER FABRICS.

She covered her mouth to stifle a giggle. The dead part wasn't funny, but who'd steal her cut fabrics when they could break into Mr. Taylor's and steal everything he had? Bolts of fabrics, candies, flour. Sugar and coffee. Frilly ribbons and the silver brush and comb set she'd been eyeing ever since it arrived.

"Oh, bother!" No use woolgathering over something she'd never have. Not when the door to her establishment lay wide open for all and sundry to peep inside. A chilly gust peppered her with little bits of dust, stinging the bare flesh between her riding gloves and the sleeves tapered against her fore-arms. Shuddering, she huddled into herself against the chill assaulting her. "You're being a ninny," she said. "Chuck up your chin and act like an Ellis."

She weighed the worth of having a sense of caution versus being a ninny. If it turned out nobody lurked inside her little shop and she cried wolf, she'd be the laughingstock of Oak Grove and her brothers would not allow her to leave home and make her own way in the world. Something she should well have done years ago.

A ninny, she was not. Nor was she a damsel in distress. That title could be saved for Miss Eunice Gilbert, the light of Oak Grove, according to Fanny's brothers Nathan. And Seth. Fanny snorted. If Eunice was what good men wanted, she didn't have a chance of ever finding a husband. None whatsoever.

She dragged a breath into her lungs and looked over her shoulder one way and then the other. There was nothing but a line of crude buildings casting shadows over the back thoroughfare of Main Street's businesses. Nary a single soul walked about, not even a bird or a stray dog. The entire town must be out seeing the cattle drivers off, which made what she was about to do even more foolish, but she couldn't allow her door to stay open, and if she was getting that close, she might as well look around to make certain everything was right as rain.

She climbed the two steps and stilled. Darkness swallowed the little space she rented from Mr. Taylor, but she didn't hear hide nor hair from inside, not even the brush of her frilly curtains against the windowsill. But what if someone was inside?

This time, she didn't hold back her laughter. It was utterly ridiculous to think someone had broken into her sewing shop. There wasn't even a sign declaring the establishment as a shop, and she didn't keep a money box since most of her orders were barters for eggs, apple pie, fried chicken and the like. Her fabrics were nice enough and of good quality, but they weren't made of gold, and nobody was likely to covet them. So why in tarnation was the door ajar?

Perplexed, she tugged off her riding gloves and tucked them into her pocket as she replayed her actions from yesterday afternoon in her head.

She'd pulled the door tight and locked it before she left. Didn't she? She was certain she had. Habits were hard to break. One misstep in her exacting schedule and the rest of her day was out of sorts leaving her unable to think outside her habitual tasks. She seriously doubted the early spring winds had forced the door open. It was then that she noticed the splintered wood near the lock.

Sweet maple syrup!

Someone had broken into her little sewing shop. Perhaps the potential thief hadn't realized they were breaking into an establishment with very little value.

Her cheeks flared with anger, her worry and fear replaced with indignation. She clenched her fists until the edges of her nails pricked the callouses on her hands. Who would dare do such a thing?

Well, she really should bother Mr. Taylor now. As

a woman, she knew it was wise to use caution, even if she despised the need for protection in dangerous situations, and this situation spoke of danger.

"Gracious, the dilemma." She rested her chin on her hand. "What would Hiram do?"

Hiram was the most sensible of her brothers. Still, he wouldn't go running for help at the sight of an open door. There was no reason she couldn't use caution without Mr. Taylor's help. If she bothered him now, he'd no doubt charge her another small fee. A fee that would be reoccurring along with her weekly rent payment. A fee that would be better served to pay Mrs. Wheelwright for room and board upon her brothers' return from their current adventure. If she was going to move out of their home, she would need to learn to see to such matters herself.

Decision made. She drew her palms down the front of her skirts, pulled back her shoulders, and reached deep to the toe of her boots for every bit of Ellis courage she could muster. She was an Ellis, after all.

Fanny stepped across the threshold and peered into the shadows. The lantern was five steps into the room. The curtains on the window were even farther away. She tried not to be overly fearful, but after witnessing the death of her parents as a small child while she hid behind Mama's dresses in the chifforobe, there were some habits honed deeply into her blood.

Once again, she internally chastised herself for leaving her pistol at home tucked neatly beneath her mattress, wrapped in Mama's delicate shawl, yellowed from age. She never usually left home without it, not even while being escorted by all three of her brothers. She'd like to blame her shortsightedness on her brothers leaving for such a long period of time. However, their leaving had not been the only thing that occupied her mind. She'd been wondering how she would tell them upon their return that she was moving into Mrs. Wheelwright's boarding house.

She needed a weapon of some sort. A large branch would suffice. "Fanny Ellis, don't be dim-witted. You need trees to find branches, and there are no trees to be found in town."

Weaponless, Fanny pulled in another breath, rolled her shoulders and took another step inside. She let out a yelp at the soft shake of a rattle and darted back outside. Heart pounding, she smacked her palm against the thudding to settle it. The rattle softened, but Fanny wasn't inclined to go back inside without a hardy stick.

She snagged the broom Mr. Taylor's shop boy had left by the back door and tiptoed back into her sewing shop. She stilled, waiting for the noise to begin again. This time, a soft gurgle met her ears, followed by a coo. Cocking her head, Fanny attempted to identify the sound, but she couldn't place it. The renewing of the rattle thrust fear back into her limbs, freezing them in place until she heard a distinct clunk on the floorboards. Fanny's eyes widened at the enormous wail that followed.

"A baby?"

She craned her neck toward the small corner behind the stack of empty crates Mr. Taylor kept for deliveries. It was a dark dank corner, and nobody ventured toward it without a shovel in their hand in the event a rattlesnake sought a cool dark resting place in the heat of the day. It was still early spring, though, and the air remained cool, much too cool for the slithering serpents.

The cry came to an abrupt halt, and Fanny half wondered if she'd fallen prey to the prairie madness that plagued some of the Plain's womenfolk. Was it possible her mind was imagining babies crying in her place of business? No doubt the madness was spurred by her longing for a babe to warm her arms.

The sound of a soft sneeze echoed in the small room. Jumping, Fanny gripped the broom handle tighter. Her desperation for a purpose in her life would see her in an asylum. She'd best not speak a word of this to anyone, not even her brothers. Still, it would serve her well to see with her own eyes the empty space behind the crates. The floorboards creaked with each of her tentative steps. She didn't know what she feared more, finding the space empty or finding a baby.

Gathering her courage, she peeked around the crude crates and gasped at a single crate on the floor. A tiny pale fist batted the air. The infant was wrapped in scraps of fabric Fanny had set aside for a quilt when she had enough. The baby locked its gaze with hers, and its face lit up with a toothless grin. Fanny's heart fluttered in delight. She leaned the broom against the wall and knelt beside the box crate.

"Hello, little one. How did you make your way in here? Where are your parents?"

The infant's coo echoed, and Fanny shifted her attention to another box crate where a second infant blinked at her. "Babies?"

What on earth were they doing in her sewing shop? Fanny touched a finger to the baby's little fist, and it kicked its legs. She lifted the crate and sashayed toward the sunlight streaming in through the open door.

"You've the most unusual eyes. Not quite blue, not quite gray. They remind me of a lady who worked here for a time, Clea Anderson."

Clea had left months ago without so much as a word and several unfinished dresses. She'd also stolen what little cash Fanny had earned from her customers, leaving only an apology behind. Fanny didn't hold a grudge. She suspected Clea had her reasons, and she often wondered about her and prayed for the young woman whenever she crossed her thoughts.

Fanny returned the crate to its resting place and glanced at the second baby. The babies weren't much bigger than Marigold the calico cat. She scooped her fingers around the baby's middle and held it out in front of her. Its little head wavered, propelling Fanny to lay the child down in the crook of her arm. It was sort of like cradling Marigold, she mused. "Hmm, this isn't so bad, is it?"

Heat seeped against Fanny's arm and stomach, and she squealed and held the baby away from her. "Oh, my! Seems you need your nappy changed."

She didn't know much about babies, but she'd seen

the hostler's wife change her youngest once after a fitting. Fanny glanced toward the other baby. "I suppose you both need changing."

Crouching next to the crates, she contemplated how best to gather the second infant without dropping the first. She also had at least one wet nappy to deal with. Fanny glanced around the small room. The fabrics were neatly organized and already spoken for by the ladies of Oak Grove. The scraps in the crates the infants had been nestled in were far too small to cover their wee bottoms, and she was hesitant to lay the baby in her arms down. It wouldn't do for the makeshift bed to become soaked, too.

"I wonder if Mr. Taylor has what we need. However, will I carry you both? The crates are too small for both of you, and I wouldn't dare leave you two alone." She didn't know who'd left the babies or why, but she had a good bit of finger shaking to do at the wretch. How dare someone act so irresponsible and abandoned such precious gifts!

Against her better judgment, she settled the baby back on the pile of scraps and cooed at the whimpering infant while she drew her fingers over the downy fluff covering the baby's head. The baby hiccupped. Fanny squeaked, and both babies began to cry.

"Shh, all will be well." She smiled as their cries softened. "Give me a moment."

"Hello."

Fanny squeaked, again and both babies threw their arms into the air. Had their parent returned for his charges? She jumped to her feet and rose before thrusting her hands on her hips. A man peeked through the curtain dividing the general store from her shop. "Oh, you gave me a fright."

"Are you all right, miss? I heard you scream."

"It was hardly a scream. A mite of a noise is all."

His head bobbed as if to pacify her without a verbal response, which in her way of thinking was his way of arguing without actually arguing. She darted her gaze along the height and breadth of him before settling on his face. Shadows cloaked him like a second skin. She was certain she'd never seen him before, but it was hard to tell given the dim light. Was he the one who'd broken into her shop? Had he left the babies? Uncertainty trotted over her.

"Nonetheless, I heard you from inside the mercantile."

She supposed she could have been a bit louder than she thought.

"I am well," she said, shifting her weight to keep the infants from his view and to get closer to the broom. It wasn't her preferred weapon of choice, but it was something.

He snapped the curtains wider and light streamed in from Mr. Taylor's store. She scanned the stranger again. The red kerchief around his neck complemented high cheekbones that must have spent long days beneath the sun. His eyes were dark, and it was difficult to ascertain if they were threatening. Were they blue like the midnight sky? Brown like freshly churned dirt?

"You certain, ma'am?"

The genuine concern in his voice softened her a little and eased her anxieties. He didn't seem the sort to rid himself of babies. At least not without ensuring they were cared for first. "Startled is all."

"Alrighty, then. Mind if I asked what startled you?" He slipped his hat off his head, revealing a wealth of golden curls.

"I mind a great deal. Wouldn't do to tell a stranger what startles a gal, lest he take a fancy to go about startling her for his own enjoyment." She had brothers who teased her incessantly. They knew what frightened her most and used the knowledge to their advantage. Like frogs nestled in her stocking drawer. Besides, she didn't know this man from Adam. Experience forced her to be cautious, even if she thought he might be the good sort. There was something about him that reminded him of her brothers, and they were as good as men came. "Besides, wouldn't it seem reasonable that you startled me?"

He dipped his chin. "I suppose you're correct. I don't usually scamp about, but I was looking for Mr. Taylor. When I heard your scream, I thought someone might be in trouble."

"Well, as you can see, I am perfectly fine. Now, if you'll excuse me." She wanted him to leave, needed him to leave, so she could investigate her new charges. Why were they here in her shop? And how did they get here? Folks didn't just go around leaving babies behind. "I have business to attend."

"I had hoped to speak with Mr. Taylor."

One of the babies let out an ear-piercing squeal,

like Violet the pig, and Fanny just about jumped right out of her skin. The stranger's eyes widened. He strode toward her, leaned over the makeshift workshop table and inspected the noise.

He was so close that she could smell him. Oh, bother, he smelled like he'd ridden through every hidden treasure along the prairie. Wildflowers, tall grasses, churned earth and a whole lot of open sky. Not to mention horse and leather. Those were some of her favorite scents. She liked them better than coffee and Mr. Taylor's sweet candies in the glass jars on his countertop.

The stranger smelled like freedom, and probably nothing like she did. This morning, she'd attempted to send her brothers off on the cattle drive in a grand fashion. The scent of burnt eggs and charred biscuits still clung to the fabric of her dress. She only hoped the brisk wind flowing through the windows she'd left open at home would dispel the awful smell before she returned there.

"You certain everything is all right, ma'am?"

Another wail pierced her ears, and she dropped down near the crates and scooped up one of the dissatisfied bundles.

"Shh, little one." Fanny held the baby out from her and swayed. She raised her voice to be heard over the crying. "I'm not certain where Mr. Taylor's gone."

The cowboy held out his hands. "May I?"

At her hesitation, he said, "I won't drop the baby. I promise."

The second baby cried louder. Fanny wasn't certain what to do, but she couldn't very well hold both babies at the same time. She nodded and passed the fussing bundle over to him. The cowboy's large hand cradled the baby's head while the other held its bottom. He gently bounced the baby up and down while making shushing noises.

The man began to sing to the infant. His rich baritone lifted to the rafters and bounced off the walls. Fanny gasped, and the baby grew quiet. The sound emanating from the cowboy mesmerized her, lulling her into a sense of wonderment. It was like a siren's call. Only she'd imagined the voices of women luring sailors into the sea. The nighttime stories told to her by her brothers had been meant to bore her to sleep, but they'd always left her with one thought, beware of the sirens for they'll lure you to your own death.

She quickly cut the strings mooring her attention to the man and picked up the other baby. She mimicked the cowboy's cooing noises but didn't dare join in the song lest she risk becoming enamored with him. She rocked her hips back and forth, swaying with the infant in her arms and did all she could to block out the voice filling the nooks and crannies.

"It's all right, little one," he crooned, breaking the verse. "I am looking for someone and was told Mr. Taylor knew just about everyone in these parts."

"I believe so." She bounced the baby lightly in her arms and rocked side to side, speaking in soft, soothing tones. The baby settled a little, as did Fanny's nerves. After all, she couldn't completely settle with her pulse thundering the way it was.

Gracious, was it warm in here? She started to fan herself but thought better of it. It wouldn't do for her to drop the baby. "Some folks don't stick around long, but everyone heading west stops here for supplies, so he typically knows them, too. Has a memory like a daguerreotype. Never forgets a face."

She giggled at the silly way she was speaking and moving because of the infant, but the handsome man was doing the same. If anyone had entered her sewing shop at that moment, they might have thought the two had gone mad. "He never forgets a story, either. Mr. Taylor always has a tale to tell. Some as wide as the Mississippi."

"What time you expect him back?"

"I don't rightly know. Mr. Taylor takes lunch at Moore's at noon."

The man snuggled the infant against his chest as naturally as any woman blessed to have her womb filled with one. He slipped a gold watch from his vest pocket. "It's a quarter to nine now. Guess I'll take lunch at Moore's when it's time." He dropped his watch back into his vest pocket, turned to leave and then stopped. Holding the baby out, he asked, "What should I do with this?"

Fanny tilted her head. The cowboy suddenly seemed uncomfortable with the baby, which made her curious at the change. Not having any experience with tiny creatures other her animals, she felt uncomfortable, too, but she was warming to the motions. "Wait, did you say it wasn't even nine in the morning? Why, Mr. Taylor doesn't open the store until ten."

Why was the door to the mercantile open? Had someone broken in there, too?

"Mister?"

"Yes, ma'am?"

"Did you say the door was open?"

"Wide as a barn door in the middle of summer."

Just like hers. Her brow rippled. "Would you mind holding the baby a moment more?"

"I suppose," he said, cradling the baby against his shoulder.

Fanny emptied one of her sewing baskets and layered it with scraps of fabric before tucking the baby inside. She handed the basket to the cowboy, readied a second basket and did the same with the second baby. She took up the baskets, skirted around the stranger and strode into the mercantile. Her steps slowed as she approached the front door. She glanced over her shoulder at the handsome cowboy as caution straightened her backbone. Was he the one who'd broken into the mercantile?

Lots of folks rode through Oak Grove, very few remained, leaving it near impossible to know if someone intended harm. She liked to think she'd learned how to recognize a scoundrel, but if he made to close the distance between them, she would try to make it out the door before he stopped her.

She shook off her reservations about him. She didn't sense a threat from this man. None whatsoever. He had a good deal of goodness about him. At least she'd like to think he did. After all, he'd offered to hold one of the babies until they calmed. And what sort of scoundrel sang the way he did? None that she knew of. The fact she hadn't known many scoundrels didn't count.

"You didn't notice the splintered wood when you entered?" she asked him.

He froze, his gaze moving along the lines of the frame, halting where the wood had split. His hand slid to the ivory hilt on his hip. Fanny flinched. Had she misjudged his character?

"I admit I didn't." His fingers danced on the handle of his gun.

"Are you going to shoot me?"

Chapter Two

The man's brow bunched up like fabric when Fanny gathered it in her hand against the wooden embroidery hoop to lessen the bulk. He seemed to realize the threat he posed and dropped his hand to his side, his brow smoothing as he did so.

"No, ma'am. A little on edge, is all."

She nearly laughed. The entire morning had held her on the precipice of a fit of vapors. First, she'd fallen into the creek and had to pull herself back up the back up the bank. Her simple brown skirt had become soaked, leaving her the bright yellow gown suited for social gatherings that had been hanging in the kitchen when she nearly set the house on fire. Thankfully, she'd only burnt the eggs, the biscuits and the tips of her fingers when she'd attempted to rescue the skillet. After breakfast, Daisy the horse had decided she wasn't too keen on carrying Fanny to town. Fanny had had to hitch Bellflower, her other rescued horse, to the buckboard. Then there was the break-in. And the babies.

The cowboy shifted his stance, drawing her attention to the leather chaps hugging his long legs. A blue linen shirt having seen better days cupped his wrists and fluttered about his forearms when he moved. He towered over her a good deal, but most men did. However, this man would tower over Hiram, the tallest of her brothers. She looked back at the door. "Do you think I should be concerned over Mr. Taylor's well-being?"

A dark eyebrow arched. "You think he's been robbed?"

"I don't rightly know." She shrugged. "Could be, I suppose."

She pressed her lips tightly together. She was unsure how much to share with this man, but she sensed he appreciated straightforwardness, even from a lady. Besides, if he'd broken the door, he would certainly have rummaged through Taylor's supplies instead of *scamping* about her sewing room. She glanced around the store and noted nothing seemed out of place, not even a lid was cockeyed on any of the candy jars, which would have been the first thing she would have taken if she were stealing. "The back door that I use to get into my store was open when I arrived, too."

"I see." He pulled the white ivory handle from his holster, his brow dipping curiously low. "I'm guessing you sauntered in without a care?"

"Now, just you wait a minute, mister," she said,

adjusting the handles of the baskets near her elbows so she could shake a finger at him. "I gave it a lot of consideration and weighed my options. And I did not *saunter* into my place of business without a care." She really wanted to harrumph and stomp her foot. Instead, she growled.

"Very well, you didn't saunter. I certainly hope your husband takes you to task when he finds out you took an unnecessary risk, entering a place that had obviously been broken into."

Oh, the audacity. This time, she did stomp her foot. She realized her mistake when one of the infants let out a mewling complaint. "For your information, I do not have a husband."

His gaze shifted from her to the baskets, and his brow quirked upward as if to call her a liar. She waited for him to speak his thoughts aloud, but his jaw ticked in silence. "Is there a door leading upstairs?"

She skirted around the shelves and began to push the door leading to Mr. Taylor's upstairs quarters open with her foot.

The cowboy wrapped a gentle hand around her upper arm and cleared his throat. "Ma'am, will you oblige me and take your children to a safer place?"

No wonder he hadn't believed her when she said she didn't have a husband. The man's gentleness and sense of reason softened her prickly nature. There were babies to consider.

She nudged away from the door leading to Mr. Taylor's home with the swiftness of a rabbit chased by a fox. She tucked the baskets beneath the counter, dropped to the floor and peered above the rough wood. She'd thought to push the door with her toe. He kicked it. Wood cracked like lightning. The door banged against the wall with a resounding boom. The cowboy disappeared, his footsteps echoing off the narrow passage. Fanny scooted the baskets farther beneath the counter and slid as much of herself as she could into the hiding spot.

She kept silent, listening for shouts and the sound of gunshots or windows shattering. Trembling, she squeezed her eyes shut and reminded herself she was no longer a little girl hiding from bad men. She waited with her lip clenched between her teeth as memories thrust her back to that awful day when her parents were killed and to the sounds that had often plagued her sleep.

The quiet tore at her ears, pushing and rumbling.

"Is this Mr. Taylor?"

The stranger's voice released her from the fear terrorizing her. She slipped from beneath the counter and peered over the wooden top. She sucked in a breath when Mr. Taylor appeared in the doorway with the cowboy behind him, his gun at the store owner's back.

"I told you already who I am." Mr. Taylor's nightcap hung precariously on his balding pate. Bare feet peeked from beneath a long white night shirt.

She drew in a trembling breath and released it out in a huff. She rose to her feet, grabbed the baskets and settled them on top of the counter. Fanny nodded, and the cowboy holstered his gun. He slipped through the curtains into her sewing shop.

"Would you explain what is going on, Fanny?" Mr. Taylor righted his nightcap. "And what on earth are you doing with those babies?"

"Both our doors have been broken, Mr. Taylor."

His eyes grew wide. He looked around her to the front door and then over his shoulder. "I've been robbed?"

"I don't think so. All looks to be in its place."

The cowboy stomped up the walkway and through the broken front door. "I went out the back and checked the area. I don't see anyone lurking, but that back door will need to be replaced, as will this one," he said, touching the dangling knob.

She shifted her weight and mentally calculated the cost of repairs. If her brothers hadn't left this morning, she would have asked them for help. Maybe it was better they weren't here. When they found out what happened, they wouldn't allow her to work in town anymore. They'd tie her to a chair and lock the doors if they had to, just to keep her from danger.

"Thank you," Mr. Taylor said.

"Are you a lawman?" Fanny asked.

"No, ma'am." Heavy boot steps ate up the distance between them. The cowboy stuck out his hand. "Graham Staddler."

Graham Staddler! The gunslinger? She perused him from head to toe and back again. She'd heard tales of his prowess with his Colts, lots of tales. Why, she'd read an account in Oak Grove's paper that he could shoot a flea off the tip of a hound's tail. When she'd asked her brothers Seth and Nathan if that was possible, Hiram had laughed. Her brothers were the best shots in the state, and she wasn't far behind them, but this was Graham Staddler. He was the best anywhere.

She looked him over once more and tried to merge the picture she'd painted of him in her mind with the man who stood before her. Yes, he was tall, but she'd believed the man from the stories to be much taller. The honey-blond curls springing from his hat weren't quite the color she'd imagined, either. She pursed her lips. No, she'd imagined the gunslinger as someone much more intimidating, and not as someone who'd miss a splintered door when he walked through it.

She shrugged, uncertain if he was who he said he was. If he stuck around long enough, she supposed she'd find out. She clamped her hand around his, noting the hard callouses on his hand. "Fanny Ellis, but you can call me Fanny. Everyone around her does."

She bit her teeth down on the inside of her cheek to keep from rambling. No need for her to get all starry-eyed over someone who may not be who he said he was. But gravy, if he was Graham Staddler, she'd like to set her shot against his.

His eyes raked over her like a man inspecting a horse, but he seemed to quickly dismiss her and shifted his attention to Mr. Taylor.

"Mr. Taylor, there doesn't seem to be anything amiss. I assume there is a blacksmith in town who can fix both locks."

Again, his attention settled on her. Concerned he'd see fear and worry in her eyes, she flicked her gaze to the front door. The store and her sewing shop had provided her with a sense of independence and security. It'd been her safe place. Was it no longer? Would she ever be able to come to work again without looking over her shoulder, wondering if someone was going to break into her business? "Thank you."

Those two words were all she could utter. She wasn't prone to tears, but she sensed them churning up the backs of her eyes. It had taken a lot of convincing on her part to get her brothers to agree to her owning a business and riding to and from town on her own to see customers. She suspected older brothers were overly protective in general of their younger sisters, but she sensed hers were even more so due to the fact their parents had been killed. One of them usually said they had an errand of some sort to tend to and rode along, but it had been the only way she could have a bit of independence, so she'd accepted it. Now, she feared all that would disintegrate like a snowflake on a flame.

"Would you like to see if anything was taken?" He drew his thumb and index finger down his dark mustache, the color a sharp contrast to his honeyed curls.

"Yes, of course." She nodded. "Mr. Taylor?"

The mercantile owner shook from his shock and glanced around. "It will take a while to consolidate the merchandise against the ledgers, but it looks as if nothing has been stolen."

"If you'd like, I can help take inventory," she offered.

"No need," Mr. Taylor said. "I have my methods. Don't need a gal coming in and messing things up."

She stiffened at his words. Mr. Taylor wasn't fond of women stepping outside their expected roles. It was only by the grace of the good Lord, and the rent she paid him, that he allowed her to use his back room for her sewing business. He had grumbled a great deal before they shook hands on their agreement and still took every opportunity to tell her she should be caring for a husband and a family, not working. Once Mr. Staddler was out of earshot, she supposed Mr. Taylor would bend her ear some more on the matter. It wasn't like she didn't want to be a wife and a mother. She just hadn't had any suitors who weren't old enough to be her granddad.

"Very well. I'll be in the back if you change your mind." She took up the weighted baskets and swished past Mr. Staddler. She entered her shop and scanned the room, her skirts spinning about her. Nothing was out of place that she could tell, but she was so angry after hearing Mr. Taylor's insensible words that she barely saw anything beyond red. A creak sounded behind her.

Mr. Staddler leaned against the doorframe, looking finer than sunshine after a week's worth of stormy weather. "Is all right as rain, Miss Ellis? Do I need to get the sheriff?"

"Marshal," she corrected, half realizing she'd done so because she was distracted by the cowboy's handsomeness. He wasn't like the local farmers and cowpokes she knew. Mr. Staddler was genuine. She still wasn't convinced he was the famous gunslinger, though.

Kissed by the sun, his tanned face spoke of hours spent outdoors, but he didn't smell like a barn. He smelled of horse sweat and adventure, and he looked like the sort of man she'd conjured up in her mind while reading those dime novels Mr. Taylor sold in his store. The sort of man she hoped would one day see her, Fanny Ellis the spinster, and decide she was worth a moment of his time. *Now, Fanny, quit that jabbering.*

"Marshal, then. Would you like me to fetch him?"

"That won't be necessary. Whoever broke in here must have been mighty disappointed to find nothing but sewing bits."

She was surprised his feathers hadn't ruffled at her correction. Most men were quick to cut her down and put her back in her place, subservient and quiet. Arms aching from the weight of the baskets, she held one out to Mr. Staddler. He scooped the infant out and held it against him.

"If I'd had a sign on the door, the thief would have known and been saved some trouble."

"You're certain?" he asked again as he held the infant close.

"I don't think—" she stammered to a halt. Her heart warmed at his actions. He didn't seem nervous over holding the tiny human. He also didn't seem like a gunslinger with Graham Staddler's reputation.

Mr. Taylor pushed into the sewing room. "Fanny, what is going on here?"

The cowboy held the baby out in front of him and the bits of fabric covering its bottom drifted toward his boots. A stream then arched from the child, landing on the cowboy's muscular chest, and the blue linen darkened.

Fanny laughed. "Looks like that's a boy in your hands, Mr. Staddler."

"Fanny," Mr. Taylor said as he chuckled. "Wherever did they come from?"

"I don't rightly know," she replied.

"Wait a minute. These babies aren't yours?"

"No, Mr. Staddler." Fanny adjusted the handle of the basket with the baby to her other arm, wishing with all her heart she had been blessed with such a gift. "They don't belong to me. They were here when I arrived."

"Then whose are they?" Graham asked. "They aren't very old to be away from their mother. Maybe a month or so."

Fanny didn't know a thing about babies and she marveled that a man of Mr. Staddler's reputation would know.

"Well, they aren't mine," Mr. Taylor said. "I reckon whoever broke my doors decided Fanny here would make a fine mama for them, though."

Fanny gasped at Mr. Taylor's words. *Fine mama* was as close to a compliment as she would probably ever hear from the proprietor, but why would he ever think such a thing?

"I grant you're correct in that assessment, Mr. Taylor."

"What?" she stammered, her tongue tangling against her teeth. "I don't know the first thing about being a mother. Why, I didn't even know how to hold one until I saw you do it, Mr. Staddler. I don't even have a husband yet." She'd nearly burnt the house down this morning making breakfast. No matter how many attempts she made or recipes she read, she could not cook. Having lost Mama when she was little, she never learned except what her brothers had taught her, and that wasn't much. The babies would starve.

"I don't think it takes much to be a mother. You're a woman, after all," the cowboy stated.

Blood rushed to her ears. The comment was something she'd expect from Mr. Taylor. Not from this man. But he was a man, after all. She could give as good as she got, though. Living with three obstinate brothers had taught her a thing or two. "That is a rude thing to say. Just because I am a woman, does not mean I know the first thing about mothering." She pierced him with her sternest glare and swept back into the mercantile with an emphasized sway to her hips. "The audacity."

The whimpering infant in the basket tugged at Fanny's heart. She gazed down into the most beautiful pair of eyes and softened her tone. Settling the basket onto the countertop, she scooped the baby up and held it close to her chest, just as she'd seen Mr. Staddler do. "To think any woman would make a decent mother. It takes much more than gender to make a woman a mother. Why, I don't even know whether you're a boy or a girl."

Not that it mattered. Fanny would've gladly accepted either into her life. She'd seen people fuss and worry over whether their baby would be born a boy or a girl, witnessed abandoned children or parents who had so many children without seeming to care for them. The sight of such situations had put a strain on her relationship with God. Why would the good Lord bless people unable or unwilling to care for their young ones properly and leave her longing?

Mr. Staddler's comment had added kindling to the fiery ache in her heart. She tucked the hurt spurred by envy deep inside her soul, lest she find herself sinning against God.

"My apologies, Miss Ellis." Mr. Staddler interrupted her musings. "I meant no offense."

She turned on him with a pointed finger and noticed he was about to wrap the babe in his arms in a piece of fabric from her sewing table. An expensive piece of brocade Miss Eunice Gilbert had already purchased. As much as Fanny disliked making beautiful gowns for the perfect Miss Gilbert so all her brothers could sing the young woman's praises, she also needed the funds, and Eunice was her best paying client.

"No!"

Mr. Staddler's hand stilled in the air at her shout, and the baby in her arms startled. Tiny limbs flung into the air before settling once again at its side. "It has pins in it," she said.

"I suppose that wouldn't feel good against his skin. Here." He placed the fabric on the edge of the counter, shrugged out of his vest and wrapped it around the baby.

"That will not do, either." Mr. Taylor pulled a gray sweater from a hook and handed it over.

"Thank you, Mr. Taylor." The cowboy spread the sweater onto the counter with one hand and then laid the infant gently in the center of the material. Fanny watched, mesmerized as he tenderly wrapped the baby in a clean cloth. "Is there an orphanage in town, or a home for babes such as these?"

"No," Mr. Taylor said. "Closest one is near a week's ride from here."

Fanny gasped, recalling the time she'd spent in a place like that filled with other children of all ages. After her parents' death, the authorities had decided her older brothers could not care for her. She'd been another face without a name. That was before Hiram had rescued her, stolen her out of the field in the middle of the day. She shook her head.

"That is not an option."

It wasn't as long as she had a roof over her head. Her brothers wouldn't be too keen on having the little ones invade their home, they already complained about all the animals she brought home, but they would have to get used to the idea. Maybe the babies' mother would return before her brothers came back.

"Again, I meant no offense. I only offered a solution."

"A solution that will be quickly forgotten." She sighed and softened her expression at his look of dismay. She wasn't typically surly, but the day had been taxing, and it wasn't even noon yet. "It is I who should be the one to apologize, Mr. Staddler. You are only trying to help, and for that I should be grateful, not barking like a dog taken over by madness."

"Graham, please." The corners of his mouth drew upward.

Fanny's pulse kicked up a beat, and a warm sensation spread through her midsection. It took her a moment to realize the infant had once again wet itself. No, not itself, but rather her. She held the baby away from her body and then settled the sweet thing back against her.

"Then I beg you to call me Fanny. Everyone does. Mr. Taylor, would you happen to have flannel on supply?" She gave the proprietor a questioning look.

"I believe I do." Mr. Taylor fished around one of the shelves until he pulled a stack of squares down.

Fanny took the cloths from the proprietor, lay the baby beside its brother and unwrapped the fabric to change it. "A girl. How could a mother give such sweet little ones up?"

"I understand your hesitation about the orphanage. Any other suggestions?" Graham asked.

"None, I can think of." She would figure it out, though. She would take them home and formulate a plan. One that kept them out of the orphanage.

"Fanny," Mr. Taylor said, snapping his fingers. "All of Oak Grove knows you long to be a mother. Maybe God is granting you your heart's desire."

Could Mr. Taylor be right? She didn't think so. These babies may have been deposited in her sewing shop, but they did not belong to her. They belonged to another. "What about their mother? She must certainly be worried about them," Fanny said.

"Could be," Mr. Staddler agreed. "Maybe their mother is the one who deposited them here. Someone went through a lot of trouble breaking the doors. I'm guessing whoever it was wanted you to have them."

"I'm not certain who that could be. There haven't been many women heavy with child in Oak Grove."

Mr. Taylor cleared his throat. "It might be someone from one of the camps outside of town."

"I don't recall any of the railroad wives being heavy with child," she said and then glanced at Graham. "It's not a place I frequent, but I do offer to mend their clothing when needed."

"You are the epitome of virtue," Mr. Taylor said. "An example to every young woman. You have shown charity by offering to keep their items in repair and their children clothed."

More compliments from Mr. Taylor? Had the Earth turned upside down? Too bad virtue and grace didn't go hand in hand, right along with a good dose of beauty. She could use some grace and a whole lot of beauty.

"You think these children belong to one of the railroad workers?" Graham asked.

"I am not certain," Fanny said. "They're poor and most depend on their husbands to do right by them and not gamble or drink their coin away, but I cannot see any of them ridding themselves of their babies."

"None of the ladies in town has been with child, Fanny. It is likely this pair belong to one of the families from out of town. They'd be more likely to dump children than the respectable ladies of Oak Grove," Mr. Taylor offered.

Fanny was taken back by Mr. Taylor's harshness. His prejudice against the poor had been bandied about, and she'd even seen him refuse credit to some of the railroad ladies for necessities, but lack of money did not make them less than human. She'd seen the hopelessness staring at her when she'd visited. Somewhere along the way, hard times had grabbed hold of them and beaten them down.

"If that is the case, the babies are better with you anyhow," Graham said and snagged a flannel square. He unwrapped the sweater from the infant in front of him and tied the cloth around the baby's bottom just as Fanny had done.

"You're a quick learner, Mr. Staddler. You must have children of your own or nieces and nephews."

"Graham," he said, fishing a yellowed paper from his vest pocket. "Thank you. I nearly forgot about my business here. Mr. Taylor, I'm told you have a memory like a daguerreotype."

Fanny blushed at the repeating of her words.

"I do. I try to note everyone who comes into the

store. It is helpful when the marshal comes inquiring about an outlaw looking to get lost out west."

Graham's Adam's apple bounced as he handed the sheet to Mr. Taylor. Fanny sensed Mr. Taylor's words had somehow upset the cowboy.

"Have you seen this woman?" Graham asked.

Fanny peered over Mr. Taylor's shoulder and stifled a gasp at the image sketched on the wanted poster. She glanced at the baby in front of her and then to the baby in front of Graham before settling her gaze back on the poster. The image was only a picture drawing, but it was an exact depiction of the woman who had the same color of eyes as the babe's she now held. Fanny swallowed and wondered if the babies were somehow related to the woman she had called friend before she'd stolen from Fanny and left Oak Grove without a word.

Fanny glanced back at the wanted poster in Mr. Taylor's hand and knew there had to be some sort of mistake. She scanned the writing above and below the picture. The name in bold black letters was a Stella James and different than the woman Fanny knew but unless her friend had an identical twin sister, that was Clea Anderson on the poster. Clea might have stolen from her, but she was not a bank robber as the wanted poster claimed.

Clea had lived at the camp with her husband. She'd been different, though. She was smart and clearly had a genteel upbringing. Clea was the reason Fanny continued to visit the camp and mend clothing. She'd seen the bruises marring Clea's skin and known her friend had had few choices in life. It made Fanny wonder how many of the wives living in the camp were in the same position. She did what she could to help them. Mended clothes made a woman stand a little taller.

Oh, Clea, what have you done? Was this man a bounty hunter looking to cash in on her capture? Maybe even hang her for a crime she hadn't committed. Fanny didn't know why her former friend was pictured on a wanted poster, but for whatever reason it was, Fanny was certain Clea was incapable of any mischief warranting her arrest, and she would not partake in her capture, especially since she suspected the babies in her care belonged to Clea. After all, they had the same strange colored eyes. If she could find Clea and discover whether these babies were hers, she would. "Who is she, Mr. Staddler?"

"Fanny," Mr. Taylor said, glancing over his shoulder at her. "Don't you know her?"

Of course she did. However, she would not reveal such information until she was certain the cowboy wished Clea no ill will.

"You've seen her recently?" Graham's countenance grew anxious as he pierced her with an intense gaze.

"No," Fanny said, shaking her head. It wasn't an outright lie. She hadn't seen Clea since before the fall harvest festival nearly eight months ago.

"Isn't this the gal who used to help with your sewing?"

She nibbled on the inside of her cheek. She could

box Mr. Taylor's ears for his unfailing memory. She couldn't very well lie to Mr. Taylor, could she but this Stella James sure looked a lot like Clea? Fanny leaned closer in the pretense of inspecting the picture closer. "Could be, but the name is different. The lines of her cheeks are fuller, not as sharp, but you know I'm not very good with faces, Mr. Taylor, and with the creases wrinkling the paper, it's a mite hard to tell."

"I think it's the same woman," Mr. Taylor said.

"What happened to this lady? Where can I find her?" Graham shot off questions like her brothers shot their pistols when they practiced shooting random objects from the fence posts. "I'd like to see her for myself."

"I can't honestly say, Mr. Staddler." Fanny's cheeks flamed with embarrassment as she'd spoken with a little more bite than she intended. She took the little boy from Graham and adjusted him in the crook of her arm. His feet rested on his sister, who nestled in her other arm. She tightened her grip a little to keep from dropping them, but not so tight as to crush them. "Now, if you'll excuse me, I need to tend to these babies."

She also needed to find Clea Anderson before this imposter did. How dare he claim to be Graham Staddler. The gunslinger she'd heard tales of wasn't the sort to go after ladies. Her shoulders sank a little. The woman she knew pictured on the wanted poster wouldn't have robbed a bank, either.

Fanny needed to find her before it was too late.

Chapter Three

Relief washed over Graham when Fanny took the baby from him. Relief and a great deal of disappointment. He'd feared holding the little fellow would dredge up bad memories, but Miss Ellis—Fanny—had seemed out of sorts with the babies, so he'd offered. Now he knew why. She wasn't their mother. He found it perplexing anyone would leave the infants in her care when she didn't even know how to hold a baby properly. She'd held the babe like a cat with sharp claws, but it wasn't his place to instruct her on the matter.

His arms felt the loss of the baby more than he expected. So much so it nearly felled him to his knees. For a moment, he was back at the cabin he'd built with his two hands, cradling his infant son, Jacob, as he whispered all his hopes and dreams for their family and the land he'd hoped to cultivate. All that had vanished when his wife and Jacob succumbed to cholera. He'd promised to protect them, and he'd failed. He hadn't felt the will to smile or live outside a day-to-day existence until he'd seen Fanny trying to soothe the infant while holding a conversation with him. That moment had brought back memories. Good ones. Painful ones. He pushed the guilt gnawing at his insides away and brought his focus to the woman in front of him.

"How do you intend on caring for these babies, Miss Ellis?"

She snapped her glittering green gaze to his. The softness of adoration hardened as she glared. "I have two arms, Mr. Staddler, and as you previously mentioned, I am a woman. As such, surely I know how to care for a baby."

The gal was full of spit and venom, and he kind of liked that she challenged him. She grabbed his interest. He couldn't remember the last time he'd felt anything besides numbness and the need to get through the day.

The fire in her eyes sparked a desire to provoke her, but he'd vowed to avoid women. He was also desperate to find his sister. He needed to find out more about the woman who used to work for Fanny and see if the gal was his sister. He needed to remain focused. Getting distracted by a beautiful woman and her charges could see Stella killed, but his tongue got away from him like a runaway coach. "Have you forgotten there are two babies?"

The rosy hue high on Fanny's cheeks illuminated the green of her eyes, and her burnished brassy curls framed her heart-shaped face and snaked down her back to rest against the curve of her hips. The adoring look she'd given the babies made him itch for a woman to once again look at him that way. No, not just any woman. Miss Fanny Ellis. There was the fire of irritation in those eyes now, not any great adoration.

"I have not, nor have I forgotten you have business to attend to, which I shall leave you to."

He moved in front of her to keep her from passing by him. "About that business, Miss Ellis—"

As if she knew he was about to ask about the woman who'd worked for her, she said, "We agreed to call each other by our Christian names. However, I now do not believe we'll have an occasion to speak with each other again. If you'll excuse me."

He motioned toward the baskets she'd obviously forgotten about and did all he could to contain his laughter when her lips pursed into a crooked line of frustration. He was certain she would have tossed something at his head if she hadn't been holding the babies.

"Thank you," she said.

Those two words of gratitude had more bite than most dogs he'd encountered. She laid the infants in their baskets, threaded her arms through the handles, raised her chin and disappeared behind the curtain.

"She's a fiery one," Graham said. He admitted he may not be the sharpest tool in the barn when it came to women, and he may not always recognize folks' cues during the course of conversation, which was one reason why he preferred horses to men for company. But one thing was for certain, Fanny Ellis was piqued, and he was the cause of her annoyance.

He couldn't quite discern the reason for her frustration, and he was tempted to follow her and convince her to tell him all she knew about the woman who'd worked for her and decern whether she might be his sister Stella. However, the veil of mourning cloaking his heart cautioned him to steer clear of Fanny. Something told him she was dangerous to his self-imposed isolation.

"That she is, Mr. Staddler. She leaves most men quaking in their boots. A shame, too, as she'd probably make some man a decent sort of wife out here in the wilds. She don't care much about clothes and the finer things."

Graham scratched his chin at that. The dress she wore was finer than the everyday clothing he saw women wearing, and he wondered if she'd been given the dress by one of her clients in exchange for sewing. When he'd first entered her sewing shop, he'd been stunned by her beauty. By her wide-eyed gaze and the dusting of freckles draping the bridge of her pert nose. By the burnished locks, vibrant against her bright yellow dress.

He'd appreciated her frank speech with him. He'd judged her as being honest and straightforward. She didn't play the games he'd come to know were part of a woman's nature. Even his sweet, innocent wife had played a part to capture his attention.

Fanny hadn't batted her eyelashes or played a damsel in distress, not even when she'd discovered

who he was. Most folks followed him around with
wide eyes and silly grins, begging him for his latest
feats. Feats that were nothing more than tall tales
spun by overimaginative observers.

He'd been surprised when Fanny had thought
to check on Mr. Taylor's well-being in light of the
break-in. She hadn't shown a hint of vapors. Her
behavior made him rethink all he thought he knew
about women. She was quite different.

He dug his fingers into his beard. Her straightforwardness seemed to rush right out of town like
a tumbleweed on a strong gust of wind when she'd
seen the wanted poster. He couldn't help wondering
if she was in cahoots with his scheming, conniving
brother-in-law. Her reaction to the poster told him
she knew more than she was letting on. Much more.

Even if Mr. Taylor hadn't been adamant about
Stella looking like the lady who'd worked for Fanny,
Fanny's attempt to avoid the conversation would've
confirmed his suspicions. Something he'd said had
rubbed a nerve. He was certain it had nothing to do
with his assumption that someone of the softer gender would know how to care for an infant and everything to do with the image of his sister sketched on
a wanted poster. However, his suspicions were only
that, suspicions, and they did not warrant a verbal
accusation. He didn't want to risk complete isolation since he might need to question Fanny further.

Graham turned to Mr. Taylor. "Are all the ladies
of Oak Grove as stubborn as she is?"

"Yeah they are," Mr. Taylor said. "Fanny's different, though. She's likely to chew your ears off or shoot you. Not sure what's worse." Before Graham could ask more about Fanny's stubbornness, Mr. Taylor asked, "About this lady you're looking for, Stella James, what's she done to grab your attention?"

If his sister had burnt bridges in Oak Grove, his association with her could ruin any chance he might have to apprehend her safely. "Seems she robbed a bank down south."

Mr. Taylor perused the wanted poster before handing it back to him. "You intend to cash in on the bounty?"

"Not exactly." He wouldn't take money for turning his own kin into the law, but he would turn her in. However, he had to admit that he'd thought about kidnapping her and stealing her into Mexico. "I want to see my—er, the gal," he corrected himself, "have her day before the judge, not hung or shot before she's had the chance."

Mr. Taylor scratched his forehead. "Not many women end up with their faces on a wanted poster."

Graham thought back to his last job at a ranch near the Oklahoma border owned by Mr. Conners. The cattle thieves had been led by a wily woman by the name of May Hughes. She'd been shot and killed. Not by him, but by an anxious young bounty hunter looking to earn his reward. The hunter, unable to read, hadn't realized Mr. Conners wanted her alive and wouldn't pay the bounty for a dead thief. Graham didn't want the same thing happening to Stella. She was all the family he had left in the world. "More women are taking up the life of crime than you know, Mr. Taylor. Some out of destitution."

Then there were women like his sister, who'd been coerced into doing things they normally wouldn't because their husbands were the worst kind of rascals known to man. Mr. Taylor's belief that the gals married to the railroad men deserved living in squalor rubbed Graham raw. His sister had been courted and wooed by Cal James properly. Graham had believed Mr. James had good intentions and would provide a good life for his sister. Graham disliked blaming his blindness on grief, but he'd been so eaten up with it that he'd been satisfied when Mr. James asked for his sister's hand. Stella was sweet and gentle, and as Graham had followed her trail, he'd heard tales of a broken arm and black eyes. His shoulders tensed.

"Don't make it right."

"No," Graham said, knowing Mr. Taylor spoke the truth. "It doesn't. I would like to find the lady who worked for Miss Ellis. It seems you think she looks like Stella James."

"That she does, right down to the little freckle near her left eye, but she didn't go by Stella."

"Do you happen to recall her name?" Graham dragged his hand over his prickly jaw. "Any information could be of help."

"I understand, Mr. Staddler." Mr. Taylor pulled a large book from beneath the counter, flipped through the pages and drew his finger down the columns. "I recall it was unusual. Not a common sort of name."

between some fabric. She pulled it out and un-
ed it.

Why, the rotten scoundrel." The scrawled rough
told her immediately who'd written it. The pen-
ship was distinctive and could only belong to one
on this side of the Mississippi—Mr. Davies, the
oad foreman. She scanned the lines again, dis-
ving what she was reading. *Fanny, please take*
of these waifs. X.

he clenched her teeth together. If Mr. Davies
e the note, as she was certain he had, did that
these babies were his and not Clea's? She rose
r full height and looked from one baby to an-
. "Seems as if you two are supposed to belong
e now. We'll see about that," she said to the
-eyed babies chewing on their fists. "Not that I
dn't mind having you. I just don't have the keen-
ea of how to take care of you." Especially, if the
s had a parent capable of meeting their needs.
oved the paper into her pocket and tried to ig-
e ache gnawing in her heart. She really didn't
eans to be a mama. Did she? Not when she
d to move out of her brothers' keeping and
s. Wheelwright's boarding house. And she
rtainly would not shoulder the burden of Mr.
responsibilities. At least not without a good
tion. If he wasn't their father, he certainly
o was. Finding Clea to warn her about the
unter trailing her when she'd been gone so
d wait another day.

aded the infants into the buckboard, and

Graham leaned his elbows against the counter.
"What is it you're looking for?"

"Her name. I'm certain she signed for supplies for
Fanny." Mr. Taylor scanned the pages. "Ah, here it
is, but she marked an *X*." Mr. Taylor closed the book
and placed it back beneath the counter. "I apologize
I can't be of more help, and I'm afraid Fanny won't
offer any more information than she already has.
The gal's pretty tight-lipped around strangers, especially when her ire is up. However, if you give me a
few days, I might be able to get the name out of her."

Graham speared his fingers through his hair. The
hope he'd felt at Mr. Taylor's recognition of his sister
faltered. "Unfortunately, I don't have a few days."
He had no time to spare if he was going to save his
sister from the same end May Hughes met.

"You can talk to those living in the camp outside
town. If I remember rightly, that's where she lived."

Among the ruff and rowdy rail workers? Were
things worse than he'd thought for his sister? Had
Cal sold her out? Determination set his teeth against
each other. Graham dropped his hat on his head. "My
thanks, Mr. Taylor."

"Follow the river north. You'll find the camp easily enough, but if I were you, I'd take the marshal
along, or Miss Ellis. Don't want to see your name
etched in a pine box."

"Miss Ellis, huh?" He raised an eyebrow.

"She's a right fine shot in a gale storm. Besides,
the folks there like Fanny."

Fanny Ellis did have a charm about her, but he'd

do well to stay as far from her as possible. She made him forget the image hidden in his inside pocket. "I appreciate your concern, Mr. Taylor, but I think I'll go it alone."

Graham glanced toward the curtain concealing the woman who'd sparked his curiosity. She was a conundrum. Perplexing his thoughts and emotions. If he had time to dally, he might consider hanging around Oak Grove just to see Fanny Ellis's green eyes spark with fire again. It was just as well that he had matters to attend to, because it seemed the lady was in want of a husband, a father for the children it looked like she was taking in. Those were roles he never intended on filling again. Once he found Stella, he'd be taking his sister back to Fort Scott for trial, and then he'd head west as far from Kansas and the memories it held.

"You might want to check with the marshal, first." Mr. Taylor rubbed his earlobe. "Seems I recall the gal's husband causing some trouble."

That bit of information tickled his ears. Trouble clung to Cal James like stink on a dog after a close encounter with a skunk. Or at least it had since he'd taken off with Graham's sister, right along with the inheritance set aside for her by their parents. The more Graham came to know about his brother-in-law, the more he'd understood that his sister's money, what little there'd been of it, had been the attraction. Not that his sister wasn't pretty, mind you. She was, but Graham had a sinking sensation her inheritance had made her all the prettier.

"He might know where they've least give you a direction. I'd hate your time riding out to the camp if y more right here."

"Thank you, Mr. Taylor," Graha his head. "I appreciate the help."

"Gracious, that man is the mos I've ever had the misfortune to enc the baskets on her worktable and le against the smooth surface. She l baby to another.

"Now, don't be getting too comfo work to do." Like finding Clea And imposter did. After all, a man like C the one she'd read about in the ne she'd heard gossiped about among mercantile after he'd apprehended or saved another farm, would n not hunt down a lady.

"Oh, bother," she sighed as bon hanging from a basket. O ribbon Clea had tied on the ha ket for scraps. "I do not eve for her. I am as helpless as t I should see if you have any

She knelt down and rum to see if the intruder left deposited the infants in the handle of a wooden r with as much calm as she could muster, she drove the half mile north of town. The ride was slow and bumpy, but she could not exactly wait any longer to find out if Mr. Davies was the father of the twins. The sooner she returned them to him, the better.

She pulled the brake in front of a billowing tent painted with Flint Hill dust and jumped to the ground in a swirl of yellow. She wasn't feeling too bright and sunny, though. She was feeling downright roaring mad. She thrust her hands on her hips and bellowed, "Mr. Davies! Mr. Davies, you no-good, yellow-bellied coward, I know you're here. You better come out before I start shooting."

The railroad boss, a spindly man, stumbled from between the flaps of a mud-splattered tent. He tugged his suspenders onto his shoulders while tucking in a dingy long-sleeved undershirt. "No need to make threats, Fanny."

Fanny thrust the piece of paper into his chest. "No? What sort of scoundrel breaks into an establishment and leaves two babies unattended in a cold dark room?"

His jaw opened and closed like a fish on the bank. "It weren't me."

She narrowed her gaze and held the paper at his eye level. "You, Mr. Davies, are the only person in Oak Grove who writes *like this*. I should know because of all the unpaid IOUs you owe me. See?" She pointed at the bottom of the note where the scoundrel had started to write his name and then must've thought better of it. "If you didn't want me to know who left the babies, you shouldn't have left a note, Mr. Davies. And you shouldn't have left your mark."

"You needed to know they're yours." His cheeks turned a deep crimson, and he held his lips tightly together.

They weren't hers. They belonged to him and to a woman blessed enough to have children, unlike her.

"I'm not taking your babies, Mr. Davies."

His cheeks grew crimson. "They aren't mine."

"Where'd you get them, then? And why did you bring them to me?" After holding them, how could anyone give them away? "I would know the truth, Mr. Davies, so you best start spilling."

"They ain't mine," Mr. Davies stuttered. "Honest."

An older woman she knew as Dora slipped from between the tent flaps. She wiped her hands on her apron and swiped at her damp brow. By the looks of things, Mr. Davies had her working alongside the men laying rail ties and making him lunch. "They're not his, Fanny."

Fanny's shoulders fell, and all the anger that had been building up since she'd found the note was snuffed right out of her. Her gaze shifted between Mr. Davies and Dora. "Then whose are they? Where'd you get them?"

Dora's long slender fingers gripped Mr. Davies's shoulder. "Might as well tell her, Jim."

"I promised I wouldn't." Mr. Davies hung his head.

She understood what it meant to men to keep their word, but Mr. Davies often fell short of the keeping. She crossed her arms. "Look, Mr. Davies, I'm not going to shoot you, but all of Oak Grove knows how solid your word is."

Her sarcasm brought the man's gaze to hers. She quirked an eyebrow, daring him to deny the fact that his word was as solid as a hastily built shanty facing a cyclone. "I know you have good intentions, but now is not the time to keep your trap shut. I'd like to know who their mother is."

Mr. Davies looped his thumbs behind his suspenders and rocked back on his heels. He narrowed his eyes as if to challenger her. Dora tapped him on the shoulder again. His gaze slid sideways to his gal and he spat near his boots.

"Why you have to go making me honest, Dora?" He spat near his boots. "They're Clea's."

Clea Anderson? So, Fanny had been right. They'd looked too much like Clea to not be hers.

"She's here?" Fanny sucked in a sharp breath. The color of the infants' eyes had brought to mind Clea, and now she had confirmation. It had been so long since Clea had been around Oak Grove. Fanny had hoped she'd moved on. She'd hoped Clea was far from here and the gunslinger looking for her. Please, God, don't let her be here. "I thought she'd moved on with Cal after he was caught cheating at cards."

Dora shook her head and took Fanny's hand in hers. "I'm afraid not. That man of hers rode in last night with the babies."

"Dumped 'em right and proper, too." Mr. Davies spat on the ground.

Dora soothed her hand down Mr. Davies arm until

she grabbed his fingers. "He said they couldn't raise the whelps and Clea wanted you to have them."

"Where is she, though?" Fanny asked.

"Where is who?"

Graham Staddler's deep timbre hammered through her like a horrific thunderstorm. She'd been so focused on Mr. Davies that she hadn't even heard him approach. She turned, and his dark gaze settled on her. "Why, Mr. Staddler, are you following me?"

"Following a lead, Miss Ellis."

His short response positioned her on the edge of panic. She had yet to ascertain if Clea was in the camp. For her friend's sake, she hoped not, and she inwardly prayed Mr. Davies and Dora would keep silent. Of course, the folks around here rarely spoke to strangers, but given the way her morning had gone so far, she wasn't taking any chance by not asking the Almighty for help.

"Who is it you're looking for out here, Fanny?" He moved a step closer with each word. After all he'd done for her this morning, she knew he wouldn't harm a hair on her head, but she still took a step back.

"Why don't you threaten to shoot him like you did me?" Mr. Davies asked.

Fanny noticed one of Graham's eyebrows shoot up beneath the rim of his hat. She glanced at Mr. Davies. "Threats only work on you, Mr. Davies."

"Fanny, have you come to warn Stella James about me?"

She shook her head. "I don't know who Stella James is, Mr. Staddler."

"Graham. We agreed you would call me Graham."

"What I call you, Mr. Staddler," she bit out, "is of no consequence. I'm here to discover who the mother of these babies is."

Besides, she wasn't certain he was who he said he was.

"*The* Graham Staddler? The gunslinger?" Mr. Davies asked as he pulled Dora behind him. "Whatever it is you're looking for, you won't find it here."

Mr. Staddler crossed his arms, and his blue eyes—oddly similar to the infants left in her care—didn't even acknowledge Mr. Davies. Instead, his gaze bore into her, daring her to tell another lie.

"It is the truth. I've come to find the babies' mother." She tossed her hands in the air at his grunt and shoved the note against his firm, muscular chest. "I found this in one of the baskets, seeing how I'm familiar with Mr. Davies's IOUs, it was only natural for me to come here."

"And?" he prodded.

The wind battered the white tents, thundering in her ears and mimicking the beat of her pulse. She stunted the urge to wipe her damp palms down her skirts.

"And what?" she asked, sensing Mr. Davies's and Dora's gazes bouncing between them. No doubt the rest of the camp had stopped their digging and their hammering to watch them, too.

"What did you discover?" he asked in a low calm timbre that rattled her nerves.

She huffed. "Well, I've hardly had a moment to discover a thing with you accosting me."

"Accosting you?" Graham leaned his flushed face toward her.

"Now, no need to threaten the lady, mister." Mr. Davies stepped between them, holding up his hands. "I don't need no trouble from my bosses, and if you end up shot by Fanny, I'll have all sorts of trouble."

Graham rose to his full height and stepped back as he rubbed the back of his neck. "My apologies. Finding Stella James is of great importance, and time is not on my side."

She caught a glimpse of the gunslinger she'd painted in her mind, but the fact remained, he was hunting a woman.

"So you can cash in on the bounty before another bounty hunter does?" she snapped. "I won't allow you to earn a dollar on another's misfortune."

Especially since that person looked too much like Clea to be anyone else.

"And what about the unfortunate souls Stella James stole from down in Fort Scott?" He flexed his jaw as he blew out hot anger. He massaged the back of his neck and seemed to calm. "You've got me all wrong, Miss Ellis." Pain etched the corners of his mouth. "I need to find her before she gets hurt." His gaze pleaded for her understanding. "She's my sister."

Of all the things Mr. Staddler could have confessed, that had been the furthest from her mind. The man she'd read so much about, the man she'd daydreamed of riding from town to town with, doing good deeds for the settlers in Kansas, took form right before her eyes, and her anger was doused with a cold bucket of water.

She held his gaze, looking for any falsehood. The color of his irises were so familiar and yet so very different. Where Clea's were clouded with worry and hopelessness and sometimes framed with the deep colors left from her husband's fists, Graham's were full of fire and light.

She opened her mouth to speak, but the words caught in her throat. She didn't know what to say. What could she say? She'd certainly had a mouthful of words for him when she'd believed he was an imposter seeking monetary gain for the capture of the woman who'd worked for her, but this... This was unexpected.

And if what he said was true, and Stella was Clea, that meant the babies rightly belonged to him until their mother could be found.

Her heart ached a little. She'd only held them a short time, but they'd soothed a place deep in her soul while spurring a battle there, too. She'd decided to leave home and make her own way so as not to be a burden to her brothers any longer, or to anyone for that matter, but the thought these babies might need her had sparked hope within her chest and stirred the desire to be a mama that she'd buried deep in her heart.

She wasn't ready to give up on that. She wasn't ready to give up the babies. Not yet. Still, she couldn't hold the truth from him, even if it meant he insisted on sending them to an orphanage. If he did, she'd fight him on it until he allowed her to keep them. And if that didn't work... Well, she just might shoot him.

"Clea."

His entire body jerked as if someone had shot him. He froze. "What did you say?" His words were slow and clipped.

"Clea Anderson. She's the babies' mother."

He dropped his arms to his sides and clenched his fist. "That's—that's impossible."

"How could that be impossible?" Dora asked. "Cal deposited them babies here only last night."

Graham's coloring faded like the sun slipping beyond the horizon. His jaw tensed, the curly beard rippling like a swollen creek. "It's impossible because Clea Anderson is dead."

Chapter Four

Miss Ellis paled at his words and visibly choked back emotion. "H-how do you know she's...d-departed?"

"She's been gone a few years now." He slid his hand beneath his hat, tangling his fingers into his hair. He turned away, breathing in the scent of churned earth from the digging of the railroad men. He allowed the distant clang of hammers to pull him back from the past.

He'd been running from grief for so long he hadn't expected it to meet him head-on. Not here. Several hundred miles away from where he'd left his little family cold in the ground. Certainly not like this in the midst of strangers. He'd thought when he was tired of running, he'd go back to the spot he'd buried Clea and Jacob, lie down and stare up at the wide expanse of nothingness. He'd lie there and wrestle with God like his son's namesake until he no longer felt the pain of loss.

A small hand touched his shoulder. He looked down, and bright green eyes blinked up at him. Tears escaped over the edge of Fanny's lashes. Moved by her compassion, Graham nearly swept his finger over the freckled curve of her cheek, but he sensed the tears were for the woman she'd believed was Clea, the woman who was in fact his sister, Stella James, whose crimes were mounting against her. Those tears filling Fanny's eyes weren't for Clea, his sweet, delicate, beautiful wife who'd never committed a crime. Nor were they for him.

"You're saying Clea wasn't Clea, but your sister, Stella. The lady on the wanted poster?" Fanny asked.

Not trusting his voice, he nodded.

"Then who was this Clea?" Mr. Davies asked.

"And what's this Stella done that's so awful she's a bounty on her head?" Dora asked.

Graham shook his head. He couldn't bring himself to answer the questions. He wouldn't allow these strangers to rip off the scabs he'd worked so long and hard to keep in place. He strode away from the tents and mounted his horse.

He turned his horse, Turnip, in a wide circle and halted when he caught sight of Fanny's pale face. "Thank you for your time, Miss Ellis. Fanny."

"Wait," she said, holding up her hand.

A wave of emotion filled his throat like it hadn't since he'd held his wife's hand in his as she took her last breath. It was so big he couldn't swallow it back. Fanny's wide green eyes beseeched him to stay, and he was tempted to do so. To accept the healing

salve to his soul she offered in her beautiful, com-
passionate face. He clamped his hat low on his brow
and turned from temptation to find peace. He wasn't
ready. Not now. He certainly didn't know if he'd ever
be. He had a sister to apprehend and haul back to Fort
Scott, else he might be curiously tempted to remain
in Oak Grove for a spell.

He allowed Turnip his head, and they flew over
the landscape, chasing the wind and drying tears. It'd
been years since he'd cried for Clea and their son.
He came to a rise and spotted a lone oak rebelling
against the strong Kansas spring air, its branches
bowing and leaves dancing. Two white markers
in the shape of crosses poked through the golden
grasses, one on either side of the majestic tree.

Graham eased Turnip to a stop and leaned against
the saddle horn as he worked to catch his breath. The
markers held him hostage as effectively as someone
with a shotgun. He dismounted, draped the reins over
Turnip's neck and paced a bit, his mind reeling with
all sorts of thoughts.

Hearing Clea's name for the first time since he'd
knelt on the grassless mound whispering the vows
he'd spoken to her before God in their small church
had shaken him. He'd halted at the "death do us part,"
not ready to declare their separation. That had been
the last time he'd told Clea he loved her.

Fanny speaking Clea's name years after he had
removed it from his vocabulary had been like a can-
non ball to the gut. It felt like his heart had been torn

from his chest and was held in the palm of a red-haired green-eyed woman.

Now this. He swiveled on his heel and glared at the crosses, daring them to take their best shots. As long as he kept moving from town to town, working as a hired gun, he had little time to recall what he'd left behind. Not when other folks' problems took precedence. The markers were shrouded in prairie grass and had been left to fend for themselves in the elements. They forced him to face his past and all he'd neglected. Were Clea and Jacob's graves over-run and forgotten as these were?

Graham trudged through the tall grass until he reached the shade of the big oak. He leaned his palm against the trunk and allowed the bark to bite into his flesh. He couldn't bring himself to look at the names, if there were any. He was afraid he'd see Clea's in his own hand. It was a foolish notion, since his wife and son were buried outside Fort Scott, near the Missouri border. Still, the images were too much alike.

Kneeling, Graham blindly yanked the grass from around the crosses. When he was done, he sat back on his haunches, rested his arm over his knees and stared at the ever-changing shadows darkening the crags and crevices of the landscape. White puffy clouds interrupted the sunlight, and Graham moved back into a state of peace.

He dropped his gaze to a freshly covered mound under the tree. There was no cross to mark the grave. Only a few rocks. Curious, he rose and strode through the grass. The grave was large enough to indicate it belonged to a grown person, but the stones remained bare. There was no name etched into the limestone, not a single marking made by the sharp blade of a penknife to give a clue as to who might be held by the earth or when they were laid to rest.

Kneeling, he speared the dirt with his fingers. It was soft, freshly churned with a shovel. The sun had yet to dry the moisture. If he had to take a guess, it'd been dug only yesterday, maybe even overnight. Closing his eyes, he bowed his head and allowed the dirt to sift through the creases between his fingers and drift back to the mound.

He needed to keep moving. To keep ahead of the grief-filled memories. Problem was his mission was here in Oak Grove. Stella had dared use Clea's name, a name he'd forbidden to be spoken in his presence. He wanted to be angry with his sister. To leave her to her fate and the mercy of the bounty hunters, but his love for her and his own sense of guilt at not recognizing the danger Cal James posed overshadowed his anger.

Stella was a victim of Cal's duplicity. A victim of Graham's grief. He could not hold any offense against her when he'd forced her hand. She'd had to use another name, even if it was Clea's. All that was important now was finding Stella, and it seemed she, or at least her scoundrel of a husband, was in Oak Grove.

He picked a wildflower and twirled it between his finger and thumb. The periwinkle color somehow reminded him of Miss Ellis, and he wasn't certain why. Maybe it was because the color would suit her fiery-red hair and sun-kissed skin.

When he left Fanny, he'd had no intentions other than to outrun the memories he'd fought so long to keep buried. Leaving for the next town was optimal for his sense of well-being but not conducive to finding Stella. And what about the twins? He'd nearly forgotten all about them. Only now did he realize the implications of Fanny's words. Those babies were Stella's. They were his kin. His niece and nephew.

He stood and swept his hat off his head. "Burnt beans in a frying pan," he said out loud as he fisted his hands. Fanny was right. They couldn't be sent to an orphanage. Yet he didn't know what he could do with them, either. Maybe she'd hold on to them a bit. At least until he found Stella. His gaze fell to the freshly dug grave.

And what if you don't find Stella? The question came unbidden and sent cold ice through his veins.

Fanny watched Graham until he disappeared on the horizon. She wondered exactly what had caused him to ride away in a flurry. Was it the babies? The fact his sister had been so close only to disappear? Or had it been the mention of Clea Anderson? Given his reaction, she had a feeling it was the latter. The woman must have meant a great deal to him to sway on his feet as he had.

Fanny was familiar with loss. She'd mourned her parents a long time and felt responsible for their deaths. She'd always thought she could have done something to stop their murders. It wasn't something that went away easily. She'd had to resign herself to the knowledge that she'd been a little girl when it happened. Coming to terms with his past was something only Graham could do. She couldn't help him there, but she might be able to help find his sister.

She turned to Mr. Davies and Dora. "Was Clea— Stella with Cal?"

Mr. Davies shook his head and then glanced to his feet, giving her the sense he wasn't telling the whole truth. "If she was, I didn't see her."

"Well, do you know which direction Cal rode in? Maybe he's made camp not too far?"

"That man is right deadly," Mr. Davies said. "He ain't no business of yours. You best leave him be and hope he won't be coming looking for those little ones." Mr. Davies shifted his fear-filled gaze away from her. "If'n he changes his mind, that is."

Fanny knew he was right. Even if she did find Cal, what would she do? Give the twins back? Not likely.

Dora touched her arm. "Just leave him be, and take the gifts he gave you. Stay as far from the scoundrel as you can, Fanny, and don't let your guard down."

She sensed Dora was trying to tell her something, but Fanny wasn't quite certain what that was. Both her and Mr. Davies were warning her about Cal, but she wasn't sure why, especially since he'd willingly given up the twins.

"Thank you," she said after climbing onto the seat of the buckboard. She took the reins in her hands. "I won't tell Mr. Taylor you broke the mercantile door trying to leave the babies in the sewing shop."

"What are you talking about, Fanny? Why would I go through the mercantile when I know darn good and well your shop is in the back?"

"You didn't break into the mercantile?"

He shook his head. "Just your shop, Fanny. I waited until right before I thought you'd arrive."

"I was with him. Helped him make sure the babies were safe as could be," Dora said. "We drove straight around the back. Had nothing to do with the mercantile."

"Then who did?" she asked.

A look passed between Dora and Mr. Davies, the latter turning a sickly shade of white.

Curiosity prodded her. "Who?"

"I can't say as I know," Mr. Davies finally responded. "Now, go on home with your babies, Fanny."

She flicked the reins and clicked her tongue at Bellflower. The buckboard jerked into motion. Fanny glanced over her shoulder to find the twins still sound asleep.

The Ellis family farm was on the south side of Oak Grove, and the ride was long. Fanny was thankful Bellflower knew her way home since she kept losing her thoughts in all the questions roving around in her head. Where had Graham gone? Would she ever see him again, or had he moved on to find his sister? She wouldn't blame him if he had. After all, she'd thought to find her and warn her against the gunslinger hunting her down.

She thanked the Lord Graham had said who he was, and that he meant Stella no harm. His feats of chivalry were known all over Kansas, and it was nice to know he really existed. If only men like Cal didn't. Her mind rolled to Mr. Taylor's door. If Mr. Davies hadn't broken the door, who did? And why?

It wasn't as if anything had been taken. Whoever splintered the door had had an agenda, and it wasn't stealing. One of the babies whimpered, and Fanny cast a look over her shoulder. Had whoever broken into the mercantile been looking for the babies? A shiver went down her spine. Mr. Davies and Dora's stern warning to leave Cal be pounded in her chest. The man was pure evil. She'd seen it colored on Stella's face, which is why Fanny would never hold the theft of her hard-earned funds against her friend. Stella was a good sort caught up in the talons of a wicked man.

Home came into view, and she released the tension knotting her neck as she pulled down the lane. Traveling so far with precious cargo without her pistol had set her on edge, especially knowing Cal had been in town only last night. She told herself that she had nothing to worry about. He'd willingly given up the twins. He wouldn't come back for them, would he? She bit the inside of her cheek. One thing she knew about Stella's husband was that he didn't willingly give up anything unless he was compensated. That meant one of two things. Either Mr. Davies was lying about where he got the twins, or Cal could be coming for what he believed belonged to him. Maybe both.

* * *

Several hours later, Fanny collapsed onto the kitchen chair and buried her head in her hands. Whatever had she been thinking keeping the infants? She didn't know the first thing about being a mama to anything other than animals. Daisy the horse and Bellflower, Violet the pig, Marigold the calico, and Rose the barn cat. Of course, there was also Pansy the milk cow, Sunflower the goat, and a few chickens. They were all easy enough to care for. Much easier than these two, but then when caring for the animals, she wasn't always alert to her surroundings and jumping at every little noise, wondering if Cal had shown up to seek his compensation.

She lifted her head and gazed at the babies nestled together on her mama's quilt on the floor. They were near enough to the fire to keep them warm on this cool spring evening, but far enough from any sparks that might crackle out of the logs.

It'd been a harrowing day to say the least. By the grace of God, Dora had arrived and shown Fanny how to properly heat the cow's milk. The milk had soothed the twins' grumbling bellies. After Dora helped spoon-feed the pair, she'd returned home, leaving Fanny with no idea of how she would proceed. She lifted up a prayer of thanksgiving that the two were finally sleeping. Her body ached with exhaustion. Her arms burned, and her back throbbed from carrying the unfamiliar weight of the twins. She was also quite certain the barn smelled better than she currently did. Unless God answered her silent prayers for help she'd be smelling a mite worse by the time her brothers arrived back from their cattle drive.

Her heavy lids were falling when a knock sounded on the door. She jerked awake and snagged the rifle lying across the table. She glanced at the babies and relaxed a little when she saw they hadn't moved. Another knock had Fanny scooting from the table and pulling herself from the chair. She pulled the hammer back and used the barrel to push the curtain aside. She nearly melted at the sight of the man standing on the other side of the door. Fanny leaned the rifle against the wall and pulled open the door. Holding her finger to her lips, she motioned for him to enter.

Graham nodded but waved his hand for her to come outside.

"I cannot leave the twins," she whispered.

He nodded and said, "I'll be right back."

She watched him stride to where his horse was hooked to a buckboard. Graham hefted a crate from the inside and strode back toward her. She stepped back as he climbed the steps to allow him entrance. He ducked beneath the door and slid the crate onto the table. "I figured you kept the babies."

The smell of roasted chicken and vegetables emanated from the box, drawing Fanny to dig through the contents. She pulled back a cloth, and her knees wobbled in sheer delight. She licked her lips and lifted the plate to her nose and inhaled long and slow. Bread. A nice tender loaf of bread. She couldn't wait to sop the chicken juices up with the bread and sink her teeth into the moistness. Her stomach rumbled as Graham's words registered. She settled the plate of bread on the table.

"Keep the babies." Fanny narrowed her eyes. She was tired, which made her prickly. And she was certainly hungry, which made her pricklier than a cocklebur bush in full bloom. "And why wouldn't I have?" She held her hand up between them. "Do not answer that, please. As you can see, I have kept them. I intend to keep them until their mother is found."

"Figured as much," he said and swept his hat off his head before hanging it on a hook beside the door. He turned to her and held her gaze. His irises were as blue as the evening sky as the sun begins to slip beyond the horizon. "Thank you."

She hadn't expected a thanks—another apology, perhaps. He had ran off and left her to tend to his niece and nephew alone. "For?"

"Thank you for not listening to a stubborn man who wanted to make arrangements to send them to an orphanage. After a long hard ride, I came to the realization that those are Stella's babies. My kin. My responsibility."

"My responsibility." She crossed her arms and was met with a horrendous smell, causing her nose to curl. She dropped her arms to her sides. "However, they are your kin.

The corners of his mouth curved into a heart-stopping grin, and the words she'd read so often by the starry-eyed journalist who wrote about Graham

Staddler came alive. She gulped. His eyes twinkled. *Twinkled like a thousand stars glittering in the midnight sky.* Oh, Fanny was all too familiar with that view. She'd often lie in the bed of the buckboard in the evenings, look up at the sky and wonder how a man's eyes could mimic the stars. Now she knew. Gracious, her weakened state from lack of food and sleep had her woolgathering, and Fanny Ellis should not gather wool. Not where Graham Staddler was concerned, especially now that he was no longer a myth she'd read about in the paper, but real life, flesh and blood.

"At Mr. Taylor's suggestion, I visited Mrs. Wheelwright for advice on feeding the babies." When Fanny's eyes grew wide, he said, "No need to worry. I didn't mention your name to the older woman."

The tension in her neck released. If Mrs. Wheelwright heard of the twins, she might not allow Fanny to move into her respectable boarding house. Fanny would find herself a burden on her brothers. She'd keep them from finding wives and be purposeless. "Thank you."

He sighed. "That's not to say she didn't already know. She ushered me in like a lost son and handed me a written recipe on how to prepare milk for the infants, told me right away to bring this to Miss Fanny Ellis." He handed her a piece of paper and a basket of bottles.

Fanny sank back onto the kitchen chair. Dora had already shown her how to heat the milk and feed the babies with a spoon and without expecting something in return, which Mrs. Wheelwright no doubt would. It was the nature of almost everyone Fanny had encountered. "Did she mention how much her advice would cost?"

"Not a thing as far as I can tell. She said it was her Christian duty to help the helper of orphans. She even said something about the kingdom of Heaven belonging to the children. Not certain what she meant by that, though, since I thought Heaven belonged to good folks."

"*Suffer little children, and forbid them not, to come unto me, for of such is the kingdom of Heaven,*" Fanny said. "It's from Mark 19:14."

"Yeah," he said and shrugged, but shadows clouded the sparkle in his eyes. "Something like that."

The scripture pressed into her mind, pounded with the force of the prayers she'd wept while on her knees. For years, she'd obsessively quoted that scripture during her longing to become a mother. It was a prayer God never deemed fit to answer, and she'd given up. Slowly, over time, she'd given up praying, too. At least when it came to anything for herself. Fanny had believed it was because God thought she was unsuitable and unworthy of good things since she'd hidden while her parents were murdered.

She'd once believed God gave folks things when they proved themselves capable, however, Hiram often spoke of God's plan being much greater than anything folks on earth could imagine. Now, she couldn't help but wonder if he was right. After all, if she'd married and had a family of her own, she might not be here to see these babies were properly cared for.

Graham took two steps past the table and peered down at the infants. "They look as if they've settled nicely."

She snorted, and Graham turned toward her.

"Settled from exhaustion, Mr. Staddler." She sank farther into the spindled chair. "I must confess my fear of failure is beginning to invade my determination to see these babies have a proper home."

He reached out and lifted her chin with the tip of his finger. The touch warm and alarming, sent an unfamiliar spark from the center of her chest clear to her toes. He searched her eyes, and she tucked her feet beneath the chair and she prayed he did not find her weak and lacking in some way, even though she'd just boldly admitted her fears.

This man was larger than life. Every word she'd read about him, every tale she'd heard lived and breathed before her in the flesh. He had purpose and drive, a goal worth chasing. He hunted wanted criminals or was hired on to protect folks from thieves. He was a hero to many. She wanted that, not to be a hero or to have her good deeds overexaggerated by an enthusiastic journalist. No, she wanted a purpose in her life, and she couldn't really find that if she remained under her brothers' care.

They needed families of their own. Her presence interfered with them getting wives. How would they even realize they needed wives when she tended the house and helped with the chores? They would not be open to moving on with their lives until she left them.

Graham dropped his hand from her chin, removing the warmth of his flesh from hers. "You're exhausted. Caring for one is enough, but two... I cannot fathom. You eat that plate Mrs. Wheelwright fixed up for you while I finish unloading the wagon and see Turnip to rights. Then I will take my watch while you find some rest."

Rest? Rest sounded wonderful. Her mattress called to her even now. However, she was certain she wouldn't be able to find a wink of sleep until she washed. After her morning debacle at the creek, she feared going for more water. She hated asking for help, but she was ready to raise a flag of surrender. He was about to disappear out the door when she called out to him. "Mr. Staddler, would you mind hauling some water in from the creek?"

"I'd be happy to oblige," he said as he shut the door behind him.

She gaped. Obliged! What did he mean by obliged? And why had he spoken it with so much...enthusiasm? Did he consider her in dire need of a washing? Had he commented on her disheveled, smelly state without saying she looked a downright mess or carried a stench? Or was he being polite and was pleased to offer her help because she needed it? Fanny was so accustomed to bartering services when she needed something that his politeness threw her. If that was it, he hadn't asked for a thing in return.

The door swung back open, and Graham poked

his head inside. "Oh, Miss Ellis, I know you need to relax after your long day, but would you mind rustling me up some grub. There's fixings in the crate since I wasn't certain what you might have on hand."

Oh, botheration. She was half tempted to let him have her chicken and roasted vegetables.

"Nothing fancy, mind you. Maybe some biscuits and eggs," he said as he quickly shut the door.

Fanny stared at the door, her mouth wide open. Graham had asked her to do the one thing she did not know how to do. Why, she could still smell a hint of the crispy blackened eggs from the morning. He could have asked her to mend his shirt or his socks. She would have been pleased to *oblige* him on that, but make him something to eat? How was she to do that without burning her brothers' home down as she'd almost done this morning?

Her stomach rumbled, and she knew she'd try to make him something to eat because he was not getting her chicken.

Chapter Five

The only path to a man's heart lay in appeasing his stomach. That's what Fanny's brothers always told her whenever she failed to provide them an edible meal. Then they'd go right on and tell her how perfect Miss Gilbert's pies were. She hated the comparison. They were always pitting her against the sought-after lady, which made Fanny declare Eunice her sworn enemy. Who cared if Eunice's pies were perfect and every strand of hair was in place? Fanny's cooking might cause a man to work his jaw a little more or even chip a tooth, but at least the man would be fed.

"Guess that doesn't make the food edible or satisfying, but they weren't starving," she said to the plump calico keeping watch over the babies with a soothing purr. Food was meant to sustain a body, not be pleasant to the taste. "At least you're perfectly content."

The calico's right ear twitched in a way that Fanny had come to learn was a show of annoyance, and then the cat sneezed. "I know, Marigold. I did it again."

Fanny glared at the blackened biscuits. Their crisp flesh smoldered, leaving little wisps of gray smoke that tickled her throat. "I don't suppose Eunice has ever burnt a biscuit."

What did it matter? It wasn't as if Eunice was here showing Fanny up with her perfect pies. Fanny inhaled a frustrated breath. A sputtering cough erupted from her chest, and she covered her mouth with the back of her hand. Grasping the handle of the pan with her folded dish cloth, she tossed Graham's nothing-fancy grub into the fire and watched them disintegrate into ash. Graham was due back any minute and would expect something edible to eat.

She turned on her heel, thankful the babies slept beneath the cloud of haze filling the house. She popped the last bit of roasted chicken Mrs. Wheelwright had sent along into her mouth, savored the last bite as juices filled her cheeks, and then flapped her towel in the air. "Maybe it'd be better if the good Miss Gilbert were here."

It didn't seem to matter that she could shoot better than most men and protect the home. A man wanted to be fed, not protected. If she were the weeping sort of gal, she might cry, but she was an Ellis, and Ellises didn't cry. Not even over burnt biscuits. Not even when the man she was attempting to cook for was a legend around these parts, not to mention the babies' uncle.

"How will I care for these babes if I cannot cook?" Her question fell on deaf ears. The calico did not understand Fanny's ache, just as her brothers never had and wouldn't upon their return. Hiram, Nathan and Seth were completely content. One chore or another continuously beckoned them, giving them a purpose to put their boots on in the morning.

Even Marigold had a purpose. The feline had a basket of kittens nestled in a crate in Fanny's room. Nature had seen fit to provide the mama cat with babies, eight to be exact.

Graham had asked her to fix him some *grub*. He obviously expected she could cook. He was sure to be disappointed when he discovered how wrong he was in his assumptions.

"You're such a good, attentive mama, Marigold."

Fanny, on the other hand, couldn't cook, and her brothers were prone to telling stories of her faux pas with a great deal of exaggeration and colorful details to entertain their neighbors. They wouldn't have to tell Graham. He'd find out on his own when he returned from chores and caught a whiff of the burnt dough.

She huffed, almost wishing they were here to tease her, even if their tall tales about her inabilities stung, pricking her like bare feet caught in a cock-lebur patch. At least she'd laugh a little or pretend to be frustrated instead of being eaten up by anxiety.

Graham was the first man she'd cooked for besides her brothers. His opinion mattered. A great deal. If he was pleased with her efforts, it meant she had a chance of finding a husband, even if she was nearing thirty and one. Of course, she thought gazing down at the twins, if Graham allowed her to keep them for her own, she wouldn't need a husband. She'd have all her heart desired, except for a way to support them. Mr. Taylor would extend credit only so far, not enough to cover the years it would take for the young ones to go to school. Still, if she couldn't impress Graham, he was likely to remove the infants from her care.

She plopped the empty cast iron onto the thick block serving as a countertop. Maybe she should have saved the biscuits and made up an excuse as to why they'd burnt so he didn't think less of her. She needed to prove she was capable.

Swiping at the tear threatening to escape, Fanny cracked a few eggs, added a bit of cream and a few pepper flakes before mixing them together. She scooped a bit of grease into the skillet and settled it over the fire to soften. She took up the rest of the dough, kneaded it a few times and thought to add some salt, cinnamon and sugar. She divided the dough into round cakes and nestled them in the skillet before covering them with the lid.

While she waited, she unhinged the latch on the window and pushed it open. The chilly early May evening pressed against her cheeks. The fragrance of life softened the proof of her inability to be a good wife. The stench of burnt dough no longer made her want to gag, and she leaned toward the window and allowed her lashes to fall against her cheeks as she drew in a gentle breath of fresh air. The songs of spring waltzed into her ears, tantalizing her heart with hope. An allusive hope, especially for a woman of her age.

She turned toward the babies, thankful that she could care for them, even if it was only for a short time. Their moments together would serve to fill her heart for a lifetime.

A soft meow beckoned her. Fanny crouched and scratched the cat between the soft ears. "You are doing a wonderful job, Marigold."

The plump calico's purr vibrated against Fanny's fingers. The cat sniffed the air, sneezed and then lumbered to the back door. "The breeze from the window isn't enough, is it?"

Fanny opened the door, and the cat plopped herself on the threshold, not quite in and not out, which was exactly how Fanny felt internally. She offered the feline a wry smile when she didn't even twitch an ear or give a look of thanks. "At least I don't lack for conversation."

"Talking to yourself, Fanny?" Graham asked from the kitchen doorway with a teasing smile as he sat two buckets of water on the floor.

"Just being polite to Marigold," she said, pointing to the cat.

Graham lifted his nose into the air and sniffed. "You burn the biscuits?"

"Oh, no!"

Using her apron, she yanked the lid from the pan and was quite surprised to discover they weren't burnt. They weren't sticky and uncooked, either. She poked one with the tip of her finger. It felt done. She wrapped her apron around the handle and carried the skillet to the counter. "If you give me a moment, I'll get your eggs. They're already scrambled."

"Here, allow me." Graham snagged the bowl of beaten eggs from the counter and dumped them into another pan. "You relax a bit. You've had a long day."

She scowled. Not because she wasn't grateful. She was, but she had a feeling he was offering because he didn't trust her to cook the eggs properly. Instead of beginning an argument and risk offending the babies' uncle, she quietly said, "Thank you."

"I noticed fresh hoof marks in the yard. Different shoes than the horses in the barn."

Fanny flinched, looking out the windows in search of anyone that shouldn't be lurking. She'd forgotten the possible danger. Was Cal out there watching? Waiting to steal the babies back?

"I heard you have brothers. Could be theirs."

"Yes, I'm sure they are. Nathan recently made a trip to Junction City. I suppose he could have gone to a farrier there."

Satisfied with Graham's suggestion and the fact that he hadn't remarked on anything else out of place, she relaxed and decided to sit. She'd barely sat down at the table and allowed her head to rest on the wooden top before there was a knock at the door. She reached for the pistol buried in her pocket and began to rise.

Graham eyed her and then motioned for her to remain seated.

"I nearly forgot," he said, smiling as he opened

the door. "I didn't think it right and proper for me to be here without a chaperone."

Fanny gulped. "Right and proper?"

"Hello, Fanny," Eunice sang in her perfect sing-song voice as she swept into the house.

"Mrs. Wheelwright suggested Miss Gilbert," Graham said. "Said she's well trained in the art of being a nanny."

Was there nothing Eunice Gilbert wasn't well trained at?

Eunice's father stepped behind Eunice with a carpetbag, and Fanny's stomach rolled around like a swollen creek after heavy rains. She pressed the tips of her fingers to her pounding head. Eunice Gilbert was everything she was not. Tall, thin, poised. She had lily-white skin, perfect manners and she knew how to cook. Oh, and she obviously knew how to care for little ones.

Fanny narrowed her eyes, and she felt her mouth pucker. Of all the women in Oak Grove to choose from, why had Mrs. Wheelwright chosen Eunice? And what was with the carpetbag in Mr. Gilbert's hand?

"Eunice," she said and then turned a questioning glance on Graham. "What exactly has Mrs. Wheelwright suggested her for?"

"Given her experience with babies, Miss Gilbert will be staying here until I find Stella, or until your brothers return." A sheepish grin took over the curve of his lips, and he twisted his hat in his hands. "To make sure nothing untoward should happen between the two of us."

Fanny's brow dipped. What would happen between them? He had been here a very short time. It wasn't like he would be staying here at the farm. "You think that is a possibility, that I would allow that sort of thing to happen?"

"That is not what I am saying, Fanny," Graham said.

"Oh, Fanny, you know how folks talk. One moment you're having an innocent conversation, the next thing the town gossip has you kissing the man, and before you know it, you are ushered down the altar, married to a man who is far from suited to you."

Eunice sounded like she had experience with the matter, which was not likely given she still carried her father's name. But Fanny did not want to ignore Graham' highhandedness, so she held his gaze and refused to become distracted by Eunice's little tidbit. "You thought you would take it upon yourself to invite Eunice to my home, without asking my thoughts on the matter?"

He'd taken it upon himself to invite her sworn enemy to be a guest in *her* home! She clenched her fists to keep from ringing his neck. She nearly imagined Oak Grove's next headline.

BELOVED GUNSLINGER MURDERED BY SPINSTER.

"My brothers will return in no time."

Although she was fairly certain they didn't know one end of a baby from the other, so they wouldn't be much help. Still, if she were given a choice of having her brothers or Eunice Gilbert, she'd rather send her on her way. Her brothers would be back soon enough, two weeks, three at the most. She could hold down the fort and protect the twins until then.

"Yes, Mr. Taylor said they'd be gone a few weeks. He said it isn't right you staying so far from town on your own, even more so now that you have two babies."

Of course, Mr. Taylor would poke his nose into her business and tell Graham she wasn't safe on her own. She clenched her fists against the table. "And he thought Eunice Gilbert was the answer."

It wasn't a question. It was a statement. Eunice couldn't shoot. She'd probably never even held a gun. How was that woman supposed to help keep the babies safe? Would she beat a man with her frying pan? Gracious, Eunice could probably do that efficiently enough, and with grace, as she did everything else. How many times in the last year had she heard one brother or another say, "Eunice this" or "Eunice that." And here the light of Oak Grove stood. In Fanny's kitchen. Right along with the greatest gunslinger in Kansas.

Eunice was as different from Fanny as night was from day. They'd rarely conversed outside of polite conversation during Oak Grove's social gatherings. Fanny didn't like her. Eunice was too perfect, and everything Fanny was not.

"Mr. Staddler was only thinking of your reputation," Eunice declared. Defended him was more like it. Fanny drew in a patient breath. Gracious, all she needed was Eunice Gilbert beneath her roof defending a deemed hero like a true dime-novel heroine. Fanny kept her scream of frustration locked inside her chest.

"And what exactly is wrong with my reputation?" Outside the fact she was quite possibly Oak Grove's only spinster.

"I cannot stay here without a chaperone for you, which is why Miss Gilbert has agreed to stay," Graham stated as if it was a done deal.

Fanny felt her eyebrows shoot upward. "You're staying, too?"

His highhandedness had gone too far. Eunice was one thing. Inviting himself was quite another. She was going to throttle him, like she'd seen her brothers do to each other whenever they got into a row.

"Where shall I lay Eunice's bag?" Mr. Gilbert asked.

Fanny ignored the question and shot off one of her own. "Did anyone consider asking me if I need guests? If I want guests?"

"I've a lot of experience caring for my nieces and nephews," Eunice said. "I can help."

Wonderful. Fanny popped up from her seat with her fists balled at her sides. Was there nothing Miss Perfect Eunice could not do? Did Fanny need to be reminded at every turn how much of a failure she was at being a woman? She blinked back tears of frustration.

"It's only right, Fanny." Graham crossed his arms. "The babies are my kin, and I ain't leaving them until I know all is set to rights. Until I find Stella."

She ground her teeth together, and anger flared her nostrils. An unladylike thing to do, but she couldn't help herself. "I am an Ellis, and we don't take charity."

"Well." Eunice glided toward her as she tugged her pure white gloves from the tips of her fingers. She reached for Fanny's hand. "Don't consider it charity, Fanny. Not at all. When Mrs. Wheelwright and Mr. Staddler approached me, I just knew I couldn't say no. While I'm here, would you mind teaching me a thing or two about sewing? I have forever tried and failed with every attempt."

Disbelief mingled with a good dose of pleasure. Was there actually something Eunice could not do, or was she funning Fanny? "Of course, I'll teach you to sew, but there is no need for you to remain here."

"Fanny," Graham interrupted, "I'll be sleeping in the barn, but I won't risk folks talking about you, about us. And I won't have one of your hotheaded brothers ushering me to the altar if they think I did you wrong."

"Hotheaded brothers! Who do you think you are?"

"Now, Fanny," Mr. Gilbert said. "Your brothers are not always cool-minded."

"Besides, Graham's only repeating what he heard from Mrs. Wheelwright," Eunice added.

Why must everyone converse about other folks' business? She realized it didn't matter, though. What was done was done, and she was tired. Too tired to rationally argue with Graham.

"I gather this is more about your reputation than

mine. Very well, then. I assure you, you have nothing to worry about over my brothers, Mr. Staddler. However, given your sensibilities, I concur it will be better for Miss Gilbert to stay. Eunice, you may take my room. Now, if you'll excuse me, I'm going to get some sleep."

"Well, that went rather well," Graham stated after Fanny disappeared up the stairs. He'd thought she would want the help. He sure did. Taking care of two babies would not be easy. He thought back to that scripture she'd quoted. The one Mrs. Wheelwright had said about Heaven belonging to the little children. He'd failed keeping one safe, which is why he'd brought in reinforcements. Of course, once Stella returned for the babies, he'd go on about his business of keeping to himself.

"We did warn you, Mr. Staddler," Mr. Gilbert said. He placed Eunice's bag onto one of the chairs just as one of the babies began to fuss. "The Ellises are a proud lot."

Graham was taken aback by that comment. It was one thing for it to be true, quite another for it to be spoken about aloud.

"Papa, that's not a kind thing to say. You know they were practically orphaned. Hiram had to raise his siblings," Eunice said and turned to Graham. "Their parents were murdered when they were young."

Graham swallowed his surprise. Was that why Fanny was so against sending the babies to an orphanage? Why she was as prickly as a porcupine?

Eunice rushed to the mewling infant and took it in her arms. "Do they have names?"

"Not that we know of." Graham scratched his jaw. "I suppose that is up to Fanny now. Given they are in her care and all. One's a boy. One's a girl."

Eunice nodded. "I'll set them to rights while you finish cooking, Mr. Staddler."

"I'll head out and see what chores need completing," Mr. Gilbert said. "If you don't mind, I think I'll bunk down in the barn with you . Someone needs to make sure that gal up there doesn't take it in her head to shoot you if you keep managing her the way you're doing."

Managing. Was that what he'd done? He supposed so. He had made decisions on her behalf without considering her wishes. Such as inviting Miss Gilbert to stay with Fanny, like a nanny. He supposed Fanny didn't see the young lady as a nanny for the babies, but a nanny for her. All he'd done was try to help. He guessed she thought there was a better way of helping.

Having experience with a baby, he knew how much work one was. He couldn't speak for two infants, but he figured the more people on hand to help, the better. He'd thought Fanny would be mighty grateful for it, too.

"I'd be obliged, Mr. Gilbert. I didn't realize how big a spread this place was. Can't quite believe the Ellis brothers left Fanny to tend the place on her own for so long."

Mr. Gilbert shook his head. "Don't underestimate

that gal. She's on the small side, but she carries her weight. A shame she hasn't married yet. I'm guessing those brothers of hers have chased every decent opportunity back to where they came."

"Papa!" Eunice's voice rose to a high pitch. "We're here to help. Not gossip."

Graham nodded. "As much as I appreciate the insight into the family who will care for my kin until Stella returns, your daughter is correct. We shouldn't tell tales."

"My daughter's a wise one. You are correct." He shuffled his feet. "I'll feed the animals and be back before the wind has a chance to shift the dust off my boots."

Graham was about to take up the bowl of scrambled eggs when he noticed the two buckets of water where he'd left them. He was certain Fanny had wanted to clean up a little and would rest better once she'd scrubbed the prairie dust from her neck.

"I'm going to take some water up to Fanny." At Eunice's nod, he picked up the buckets and headed for the stairs. He ducked beneath the low doorjamb and caught movement in the shadows. "Fanny?" he whispered.

She stilled, and he marked the courage it took for her to not run from him while she was caught eavesdropping. He liked that about her. She was straightforward, and she didn't run. Should he act like she hadn't heard their conversation or meet the issue head-on. Fanny would meet it head-on. So would he.

"I'm sorry about what you overheard," he said as he topped the step that kept him at eye level with her.

She shrugged as if it didn't matter, but he could see the pale streaks her tears had left behind. "No matter. It's nothing new. Folks always have something to say, even when there's no cause. Some good. Some bad. I've come accustomed to it."

"That doesn't make it right, especially in your own home."

She shrugged again. "I suppose I owe Eunice my gratitude for politely asking her father to close his mouth."

A spot near his heart warmed. He held his laughter in check but one corner of his mouth lifted. "That might be the kind thing to do."

Fanny seemed interested in a spot on the wall and nodded.

"As for me, I owe you an apology. I should have asked your permission before bringing folks to your home. I wasn't thinking about anything except trying to help. Babies are a handful."

"You say that as if you have experience."

Graham clenched his jaw. He wasn't ready to confront his past. Admitting he had experience would be admitting to his failure as a father. He knew the sickness that had taken his family was no fault of his own. The pastor who'd married him and Clea had called it God's will, but Graham couldn't accept it as fact. How could God's will, or rather plan, include the death of those he loved? Graham had promised to love and protect Clea and their son, and he'd failed. "I brought you some water."

"Thank you," she said. Her words were no more than a whisper, and he regretted not talking about his son. He wasn't ready, and he didn't know if he would ever be ready. He sensed letting Fanny into his past would free him from the guilt he'd carried for so long. He sensed that if anyone could help heal his hurts it was her, and he was undeserving of that gift. "Where can I sit it?"

"I'll take it," she said and reached for the handle. He couldn't help noticing the callouses marring the palm brushing against his hand. Those callouses were badges of her hard work. Fanny Ellis was a rare gem, and he had a desire to ease her burdens, even if only for a short time.

Once he was sure she had the bucket secure, he looked at the plank covering the stair and focused on a knot hole in the wood to force his thoughts away from the brief touch between them. "I know Eunice being here seems like a mighty inconvenience, Fanny, but you'll be grateful for the help. After all, it hasn't been a full day, and the twins have already plum worn you out." At her raised brow, he continued, "Not that I'm saying you look tired, but—well, I guess I am saying you look tired. Why, you nearly fell asleep sitting at the kitchen table."

"If you don't mind, I'd like to discuss the arrangements once I'm refreshed."

"Yes, of course." He turned to leave and halted. "Once the babies are settled, I'll bunk down in the barn with Mr. Gilbert. Eunice will keep an eye on the twins. Oh, by the by, have you names for them? We can't keep calling them the babies."

"I will think on the matter."

"Very well. Until the morning, then."

A loud wail filtered from below, and Fanny flinched as if she was about to race down the stairs. Graham held his hand up to stop her. "Good night, Miss Ellis. Get some rest. You're going to need it."

Chapter Six

Fanny snuggled deeper into the mattress and buried her chin in the thick comforter. Strange noises filtered into her consciousness. And smells. Like bacon. Who was cooking bacon? Mama? Was she dreaming? The house sure smelled like it had when she'd wake to her mother's cooking. A soft, lilting lullaby reached her ears and pulled her out of bed more efficiently than a crack of lightning. Her eyes flew open, and she glanced around the room. Why was she in Seth and Nathan's room?

Tossing the covers off, she slid her feet to the floor as she heard a baby's cry. That wasn't a dream. She was currently in charge of two babies, babies left in her care for a short time. Babies belonging to Graham Staddler's sister. She drew in a deep breath laden with bacon. Her stomach grumbled. If she had her guess, Eunice was making breakfast while soothing a cranky infant with her bird-song voice.

Fanny threw on her dress, tied her apron-string

gun belt around her waist and slipped her pistol into
the holster. She made her way down the stairs, careful to hit each of the creaking floorboards to alert
her guests to her presence. It wouldn't do for her to
overhear any more gossip that would send her mind
reeling and her heart hurting.

She'd been shocked and taken aback by what Mr.
Gilbert had said about her brothers chasing every
possible and suitable potential husband away. Hearing Mr. Gilbert speak of her brothers' actions had
made her wonder if she wasn't as ill-suited to be a
wife as she'd believed. Were her brothers being over-
protective and keeping all suitors from her because
the men weren't good enough?

When her brothers returned, she'd be sure to box
their ears until they told her the truth. How dare they
make her believe she would not make a suitable wife.
However, the nagging question that kept her mind
from finding sleep much of the night was why they
would do such a thing? Why would they make her
feel incompetent? She wouldn't receive an answer
until their return.

She opened the door and stopped dead in her
tracks. Eunice sat in a chair feeding one of the babies. Every strand of her blond hair was perfectly
captured into a coif. Her ironed curls graced her
long slender neck. Fanny gasped at her beauty and
understood how the lady appealed to her brothers.
She dug into the pocket of her apron, pulled out a
wide faded and worn ribbon and quickly tied back
her waist-length hair.

Eunice smiled up at her. "Good morning, Fanny."

Even her smile was flawless. Her full, delicate lips didn't dominate her face like Fanny's did. Whenever Fanny chanced to catch her reflection in the mirror, all she saw was wide lips and front teeth big enough to rival Bellflower's at feeding time.

Mr. Gilbert glanced at her from his chair across from his daughter where he fed the other baby. "Morning."

Fanny flinched at his gruff voice.

"Good morning. I hope my oversleeping didn't impose."

"Not at all," Mr. Gilbert said. "It's been a while since I've had the chance to hold one so tiny."

The gravely timbre of Mr. Gilbert's voice was a stark reminder he believed she was difficult and prideful. Like her brothers. However, as he beamed down at the baby in his arms, she could almost forgive him his indiscretion. She supposed she could be prideful. She didn't like to accept gifts without bartering her services. However, she'd never considered herself difficult unless it was warranted. Still, it was not easy to unhear his words from the night before.

She neared the table, intent on relieving Mr. Gilbert of the baby and caught sight of Graham crouched in front of the fire, turning over bacon. He swiveled on his heel. He perused her from head to toe, halting on the makeshift belt slung over her hips, and then back up until he caught hold of her gaze. Her pulse sped, and she had the urge to still the thundering in her chest with the palm of her hand. She settled for swiping at the wayward curls spiraling around her jaw, and then she fanned her heated cheeks.

"You look rested. I hope you're hungry," he said.

"I am." Although she'd shoved every last bite of Mrs. Wheelwright's chicken into her mouth last night, but she was hungry, and her stomach attested to that fact with a loud rumble. What she could really use was a cup of coffee, thick with fresh cream.

"Mrs. Wheelwright sent out some fixings this morning for a grand breakfast." He rose, took the kettle off its hook and poured dark brown liquid into a cup. He walked toward her and held it out to her. "There's milk and cream on the table."

"Thank you," she said, surprised and unsure how to receive the kindness offered by so many folks. Graham was only here due to his kin. There was no cause for Eunice and her father to be nice, and certainly no reason for Mrs. Wheelwright to send supplies. The biggest surprise was finding Graham in the house cooking while Eunice and her father cared for the twins. "I'll just drink this up and see to the chores," she said.

"Already done 'em," Mr. Gilbert said.

"Yep," Graham said, his timbre smoothed over the raw nerves left by Mr. Gilbert like a layer of honey meant to cover a gash left by a rusty axe. "I fear I had a bit of trouble finding sleep. Mr. Gilbert and I wrestled the chores. You've a rascally goat."

"Sunflower?" Fanny sank into one of the empty chairs, imagining the mischief her pet had gotten into. "Tell me she didn't break out of her pen and chase the chickens around the yard?"

Eunice giggled. "What sort of name is Sunflower for a goat?"

Fanny sipped the hot coffee, wrinkled her nose and reached for the cream. "All my pets are named after flowers. Marigold, the calico. Violet the pig, Daisy and Bellflower, the horses."

"What about the milk cow?" Graham asked. "I'd like to know how to address her whilst telling my story."

Fanny waved her hand. "Oh, her name is Pansy."

"Pansy?" Mr. Gilbert asked.

"She likes Pansies." The sip of coffee she pulled between her lips drew her eyelids closed. "She belongs to the family. The rest of them are… Well, I've come by them by other means."

"I heard how you threatened one of your neighbors with a stick over Daisy."

Fanny blushed, but she wasn't certain if she was embarrassed over her actions or angry to hear about more tongue wagging behind her back.

"Mr. Townsend kept Daisy the horse tied to a post without water and food for days. She was no more than skin and bone. I might have had a stick in my hand—" she paused, deciding not to tell him she'd had a pistol, too "—but I paid the scoundrel handsomely for her. She's right as rain now. What'd Sunflower do this time? I hope you didn't find her in the Fowlers' field again. Mr. Fowler about had a conniption last time."

"No, nothing on that grand scale, but she did chew her lead." Graham chuckled as he laid plates out on the table.

"Twice," Mr. Gilbert said with a grin. "Sure as my name's Gilbert, that curmudgeon ate my hat right off my head while I was sleeping."

Fanny and Eunice giggled. Fanny glanced at the lady and warmed to the idea they had found something they could laugh about.

"Then," Graham said as he dished out eggs and bacon, "once we completed the chores and realized she'd disappeared, we looked high and low for your goat. Found her in with the cow, nursing like she was a kid."

Mr. Gilbert guffawed. Eunice giggled and Graham's eyes twinkled with mischief. Fanny gave a blank stare, unable to discern if they were funning her or not. She decided they were teasing and played along. "I suppose Violet the pig was in there, too," she teased back as she broke off a piece of bacon and popped it into her mouth.

"No," Mr. Gilbert said. "Just that goat of yours."

Fanny gasped and swallowed at the same time. She coughed and sputtered. The skillet clattered against the table as Graham swept her out of the chair and pounded on her back. Eunice thrust a glass of water toward them. The pressure against Fanny's eyes made her feel as if they were about to explode. Graham thumped her hard on the back, dislodging the piece of bacon from the back of her throat. She gasped and tried to draw in a breath but met resistance.

"Slow and easy," Graham whispered near her ear.

Fanny looked into his eyes. Hers were filled with forced tears from her choking. His with compassion and concern.

"Are you all right?" he asked.

She did as he told her to, took slow, shallow breaths and then nodded.

He handed her the glass of water. "Small sips as you go."

"Thank you," her voice croaked against the words.

"My word," Mr. Gilbert said. "You do know how to put a man into an early grave."

"Oh, Papa, hush," Eunice said. "Fanny nearly choked to death right before our very eyes. It'd be a shame for these babies to become orphans twice over."

"The babies." Fanny melted into chair as emotion took over her knees. What if she'd died chewing a piece of bacon? What if she'd been alone, and the babies had been left to fend for themselves? They weren't quite old enough to move around much, but they did move. The realization of everything that could have happened took her mind on a ride, like one on an unbroken horse. "What would have happened to them if you hadn't been here?"

Eunice slipped her hand over Fanny's, and gave her a friendly comforting smile. For the first time since her mama died, she felt the touch of another lady that had nothing to do with fittings and pins and needles. She felt as if she might have a real friend for the first time in her life and not the sort of friend she'd thought Clea, no Stella had been.

"Thank God, we were here," Mr. Gilbert said.

Graham clasped her shoulders with trembling fingers. He squeezed as if to steady his hands. "Amen."

That single word uttered between clenched teeth drew her gaze toward his. Gone was the laughter and the compassion. In their place was sheer terror that left Fanny wondering why?

Angry with himself, with Mr. Gilbert and with God, Graham excused himself and stalked out of the farmhouse. Graham hadn't prayed consciously for years. He'd avoided churches at all costs, even when required by the ranch bosses. He stood in the background when blessings were offered over meals to keep from nodding his head in agreement. Asking for blessings upon food meant he acknowledged God cared what happened on earth, and that was something Graham couldn't bring himself to believe, not after all he'd seen, all he'd lost.

Clea and his son had been innocent. They hadn't deserved to suffer the way they had. If Graham accepted God cared for what happened on earth, he had to accept the fact that He'd turned His back on Clea and Jacob when they needed Him, that God had turned His back on Graham.

Gilbert's words had torn at the scabs he'd worked hard to keep in place. He'd worked hard to keep his faith buried with Clea.

All this talk of God, quoting scriptures and praying was suffocating him. It made him feel as if he were trapped in a freshly dug well with dirt crumbling down on him, like he wouldn't get out before the light closed off. He couldn't breathe. The pain in his chest crushed against his heart.

Before he knew what he was about, he was in the barn saddling up Turnip. As he led Turnip from the barn, he caught Fanny standing on the porch with her hands twisted in front of her. A gun belt made of what looked to be apron strings was slung over her hips. She'd attempted to tame her wild red locks with a ribbon.

Gone was her confident, straightforward manner. The sight of her made him stop in his tracks. She looked tired and fraught with worry. He'd been running so long and hard that he rarely took the time to notice other folks' emotions. He was exhausted. The worry he'd carried over his sister these past weeks had taken its toll on his emotions. Laughing with Mr. Gilbert, Eunice and Fanny had made him momentarily forget his purpose here in Oak Grove. Worse, he'd forgotten the fragility of human life.

Fanny hadn't choked to death, but she could have. In his arms. The look in her eyes as she pleaded with him for help, pleaded with him to save her, had been much like the one he'd seen in Clea's before she'd succumbed to the weakness overtaking her body and mind. The effort to breathe had become too exhausting, and she'd done nothing but lie listlessly upon their bed.

The pain of losing those he loved had lessened over the years. His anger had not. Neither had the cold hard facts of reality. Life was tenuous. People died. He couldn't lose another person he cared for, which meant he needed to keep his distance from Fanny and the little ones. He needed to lock his armor back into place, forget he had kin. Forget the green eyes above a pert nose and a wide serious mouth.

He would not allow his heart to fall prey to the delicate emotion of caring. He'd learned the hard lesson that any amount of caring led to other emotions, and those emotions would destroy him if he allowed them to.

It was just as well he did not care what happened to Fanny, outside the fact that she currently cared for his niece and nephew. He knew it wouldn't take much to succumb to Fanny's big pleading green eyes and the selfless, giving heart he'd seen since he met her. He needed to get his business done and leave town. He swung into the saddle and turned Turnip toward the road.

"Graham," she called, her voice still hoarse from coughing.

All his muscles tightened, including those around the reins. She'd said his name, nothing more than that, but she'd called to a part of him that wanted to live, a part of him that he'd buried deep in the dark recesses of grief.

"Thank you," she said.

He shoved his hat low on his brow and tipped his

chin in acknowledgment. He didn't need to hear her words to know she was grateful for pounding on her back. There was no way of knowing if it was his efforts that had saved her or her coughing. Whatever the case, he was thankful to God, even if the admission of that thanks was like pulling a thorny splinter out of his hand.

"I'm heading into to town see if the marshal is back. I'll return before dinner. The Gilberts will stay a spell."

"If you wait a bit, I'll ready the wagon and go along," she said. "I need to gather some things from the sewing shop."

His jaw worked out the tension while a knot formed in his throat. "What about the twins?"

"Eunice and Mr. Gilbert have agreed to keep watch over them."

A tentative smile curved one corner of her full lips. The movement drew his attention and curiosity. Would they be soft and smooth, or dried from the sun?

"I have it on good authority she is capable of caring for the babies."

Clearing his throat, he considered the consequences of escorting her to town. "Miss Gilbert is here to help you and teach you, not take your place."

Surprise and hurt registered in her gaze, leaving him wondering what had caused her reaction. He almost asked her but was worried about opening dangerous doors. Doors he was unprepared to peek through. Best to leave all questions about Fanny Ellis unasked. "If you make a list, I can gather what you need."

"Thank you, kindly, Graham, but I am afraid after the chaos of yesterday, my shop was left in disarray. Even with a list, I'm not sure you would find what I need. If you'd rather not have the company, I can go on my own, and if you're worried over the safety of the babies, Mr. Gilbert is a seasoned soldier."

"Very well." He would much rather go alone. His own company was preferrable. Well, except when his thoughts rambled astray and started thinking about Fanny, as they had last night after he'd bedded down in the barn. He'd never been more thankful for the antics of a goat before. Or any animal for that matter.

Having her traveling beside him at the snail's pace of the buckboard would be folly. He couldn't fathom having the object of his continuous thoughts within sight for the long ride to and from town. And yet the thought of her traveling alone knotted his innards, especially since she carried her weapon on her hip like a man. The pistol in her holster was certain to invite trouble but saying something to her would only invite her wrath.

"I could use the company," he heard himself saying. The leather of the saddle creaked as he swung off Turnip.

"Very well. Just give me a moment," she said as she disappeared inside the farmhouse.

Turnip snickered as if he were laughing at the predicament Graham found himself in. "You think this is funny, do you? Certain as the sky is blue, you won't be laughing when I put you back into the stall. You were itching for a ride as much as I was, and you cannot deny it, old friend."

As soon as Graham stepped into the cool shadow of the barn, Daisy and Bellflower whinnied. Turnip yanked his head back and used his long legs to dig into the hard-packed dirt. His horse yanked and pulled all while neighing. Graham patted his neck and attempted to soothe the wildness from Turnip's eyes, but the horse swung his backside around and knocked Graham off his feet.

Graham jumped up and dusted off his jeans. Turnip liked their rides, but he'd never seen the horse behave this badly. Turnip seemed to get along fine with the other horses, so Graham didn't understand what had him spooked.

Graham grabbed the reins, dug in the heels of his boots and tugged. Turnip bared his teeth and drew up on his hind legs as a small shadow appeared in his peripheral vision. He was about to tell Fanny to get back when she yanked her pistol from the holster faster than any man he'd seen.

Gunfire exploded, filling his nostrils with gunpowder. He scanned the area, looking for the threat, but he didn't see anyone. He released Turnip's reins and dove toward Fanny. He knocked them both to the ground and sheltered her with his body.

Fanny squirmed and shoved at his weight. When no more gunfire sounded, he lifted himself slightly off her and peered around them before looking down into her sun-kissed heart-shaped face. Big green eyes glared up at him beneath the rim of her bonnet. Her wide lips flattened.

"You all right?" he asked.

"I would be if you'd get off me, you oaf," she said, struggling to scoot from beneath him.

Not even four feet in front of him lay a rattler.

"Oh, my!" Eunice gasped. "Fanny just saved your life, Mr. Staddler."

Mr. Gilbert chuckled. "Sure did."

"You did that?" Graham rolled from Fanny and jumped to his feet. She'd shot the rattler dead-on. He saw the pistol lying in the dirt beside her and swung his gaze to hers. He offered her a hand to help her up. The snake, nearly five feet long, could have done some real harm. How had he not seen it? How had he not heard it? He knew the reason. His thoughts had been tangled up with a petite redhead who knew how to shoot. No wonder Mr. Taylor had suggested taking Fanny out to the railroad camp for protection. If she could snuff out a snake from that distance, she could lay a man low with a single shot.

"You know how to shoot?" At her silence, he said, "You shot the rattler?"

"Don't sound so surprised. It sure wasn't the goat who shot the viper." She tugged her hand from his and dusted her skirts after he'd pulled her up. "I'll have you know, Mr. Staddler, there are some things I am good at. Cooking may not be one of them, but I can shoot, maybe even better than you."

His brow shot up beneath the rim of his hat at the venom behind her words. She was back to calling him Mr. Staddler. Had he struck a nerve? He thought back over their conversation and couldn't recall mentioning anything she could not do. He supposed offering the Gilberts' help had been tantamount to suggesting she couldn't take care of the farm and the babies. He certainly was not going to step in that pile of mud, so he settled for safer ground. "Like shooting snakes?"

Mr. Gilbert stepped between them and emitted a low whistle. "She sure shot it dead."

Fanny bent at the waist to pick up her pistol, reloaded it and slipped it back into her holster. "My brothers have taught me well. I am an Ellis, after all."

He'd encountered an Ellis down south who could shoot a button off a shirt, but he looked nothing like Fanny. They couldn't possibly be related, could they? He hadn't heard her mention her brothers' names, which was just as well, given he didn't want to know much about Fanny. Knowing too much would only pique his curiosity and tempt him to stick around longer than he should.

"It's not wise for anyone, man or woman, to be without a pistol, just in case of situations like this," she said. "Why, the warmer it gets, the more we'll see them coming out of their holes. A body should be prepared. Isn't that right, Graham? A few more steps, and he would have gotten you."

"I'll retrieve your horse, Graham." Mr. Gilbert motioned to Turnip nibbling on the green grass near the road. "Eunice, don't forget about the babies."

"Of course, Papa." Eunice took her father's hint and slipped inside the house to give them privacy.

Graham crossed his arms and nudged the toe of his boot into the dirt. A handful of dust kicked up and swirled on a breeze. "My boots would have protected me just fine, Fanny."

She arched an eyebrow, attesting to her doubt of his statement. He'd encountered a few snakes in his time and knew the folly of his words. He knew strikes occurred above the cuff. Still, he hadn't needed rescuing by a woman, even if she was an excellent shot.

"Good thing we'll never know," Fanny said, piercing him with a look.

"That must be why Turnip was having such a fit," he muttered.

Fanny stepped inside the barn and brought out a pitchfork. She scooped the snake onto a prong like it was an everyday thing around here and tossed it into an empty bucket near the pig's pen. "Guess you should learn to listen to your animals, Graham. They're smart when it comes to things like this."

So was Fanny, carrying a pistol on her hip as she did. He was half embarrassed to have thought she invited danger wearing a gun belt. It was practical. Just like she was. "I agree. I'm afraid my thoughts were somewhere else. I was thinking about the babies and my sister."

Fanny's shoulders inched downward, and her lashes fell against her cheek. "I'm sorry. I shouldn't be giving you a difficult time. I guess we're all a little out of sorts. It's not every day a double blessing is deposited at your door, and with the added worry of your sister." She reached out and touched his arm. "We'll find her."

Her last words didn't carry the confidence he wished they did. He felt her worry like a punch in the gut, but he didn't blame her. He had his doubts they'd find Stella, too. He breathed in the spring air. "I hope you're right, Fanny, but I think you and I both know the kind of man Stella's husband is."

"At least he had the decency to give the babies over."

Graham stilled. All he'd learned about his brother-in-law as he hunted his sister told him decency was not in Cal's character. "How much do you know about Cal?"

Fanny shielded her eyes from the morning sun as she considered him. Her mouth twisted. A breeze swirled around them and caught the scent of lavender. Was that her? He scanned the yard and didn't see any flowers close by. He leaned forward and sniffed. It was her.

"Your sister worked for me for a few months. I know enough about her husband to know he's as bad as they come." She dropped her hand. "You don't think he would give the babies over freely?"

"Not unless he's dead," Graham said.

Chapter Seven

Fanny considered herself a practical sort of woman. Riding with Graham to town in the buckboard instead of going on her own was practical, especially since she wasn't certain if Cal might be looking for her. Whenever she'd finish reading about Graham Staddler's feats in the weekly paper, she'd spent entirely too much time with her head in the clouds, gathering too much wool, wondering what it would be like to stand beside such a man and experience his greatness. That was the only explanation for the tingling sensation wreaking havoc on her senses each time his thigh bumped against hers.

She needed to think of something other than his entirely delightful warmth before she suffered a fit of vapors. Tall grasses waved at them as they passed by, but nothing caught her attention enough to remove Graham from her thoughts. Perhaps a bit of conversation would distract her from thinking about the man sitting next to her. They hadn't said anything to one another since he had so gentlemanly offered her his hand and helped her into the buckboard. Gracious, even recalling that sent a thrill of excitement through her. She'd been clambering into the buckboard without the assistance of anyone, not even her brothers, since she could remember.

Fanny tucked the hand Graham had held into the folds of her skirts and rubbed the texture of the fabric in between her fingers to remove his touch. What had they been talking about before they left the farm? Cal Anderson. No, Cal James, she reminded herself. Graham thought he might be dead.

"Dead?" Fanny blurted out.

Was it possible? Dare she hope the dire warnings given to her by Mr. Davies held no threat at all? She'd thought about very little else since she'd spoken to Mr. Davies and Dora. She was always watching, wondering where Cal was and if he'd come back for the twins. If he was dead, she could let her guard down and not worry about him anymore. However, even the thought he might be dead didn't purge Mr. Davies and Dora's warning. It was as if they knew more than they'd told her.

The buckboard slowed, tugging Fanny from her internal conversation. The placard declaring Oak Grove stood high and proud above the grass. On the other side was nothing but dust. The little town kept the area clear of vegetation to protect it from fire. It was a hard lesson the settlers who'd come before the town founders had learned.

Graham glanced at her from beneath the rim of

his hat. Sunlight played with the lines of his jaw, giving his beard a red glint. Fanny smiled, one of those smiles that took over her entire face. It wasn't often she came across anyone who wasn't an Ellis with red hair, and as blond as Graham was, she was surprised to see the sparks of fire in his beard.

His hands slid over the reins as he slowed Daisy, and she grabbed a mouthful of the grass poking through the worn tracks. "Dead?" he asked.

"Cal. Do you really think he might be dead?" She tore her gaze away from his hands and the recollection of how nice his larger one fit around hers as he'd helped her into the buckboard.

Adjusting his hat, he leaned against the back of the hard seat. "Seems logical."

"Yet Mr. Davies said Cal's the one who dumped the babies with him."

"True enough." He clucked to Daisy, urging her forward. "Think he'd lie about something like that?"

"Honestly? I don't know. Mr. Davies is rascally. He skirts the edge of morality on every level, but I've never heard about him crossing the line. However, he was fond of Cl—Stella, and very protective of her."

In fact, Mr. Davies had brought Clea—Stella—to Fanny on more than one occasion to sew up a cut left behind by Cal's cruelty. It wasn't the sort of thing Fanny liked doing, but she understood why Stella hadn't wanted to involve the town doctor, who'd more than likely confide in the marshal. Fanny had kept her mouth shut, not because Cal had scared her, but because she'd known Stella would reap the fruits of Fanny's gossip if Cal caught wind of anyone saying anything. Besides, Fanny knew what it was like to be spoken about. Folks needed to get their own opinions of newcomers, not be persuaded with what others believed to be true.

"Are you thinking it's worth going out to the camp and questioning them again?"

Fanny ran her gaze over him. "If Mr. Davies didn't mention who you are, they'll take you for a lawman with one look."

"I'm the furthest thing from a lawman, Fanny." His beard rippled. "I've done things a man can never be proud of. Don't get me wrong, I've worked for whom I thought were honest men, to protect their homes and properties... Well, let's just say I have blood on my hands."

"No different than a lawman wrestling up a horse thief, in my mind." She notched her nose a little higher. If the last article she'd read about him was true, Graham had shot a gun clean out of a man's hand after the man kidnapped a farmer's daughter. Graham might have blood on his hands, but he'd done all he could to keep that from happening. "Still, folks out at the camps don't trust strangers, unless you're deemed one of their sort."

"What sort is that?"

"Oh, you know, a vagabond looking to earn a coin for his next drink until he decides it's time to move to the next town. Not a one of them know a thing about roots and settling down."

"I should fit in right nicely, then."

Whatever did he mean by that? "Surely, you have family settled somewhere."

He flinched. "Nope."

That's all he said. *Nope*. One thing for certain, conversation with Graham Staddler left a lot to be desired. How was she to get to know him if he was less than forthcoming about his past? "I'd like to know what sort of people the twins come from. When they get older, they're going to have questions about who they are. Seems all I know about their mama is a lie, and everything I know about their father is best left unsaid."

"There's not much to tell, Fanny." He pulled the buckboard down the lane behind Main Street. "Stella's two years younger than me. Our parents died in a fire when we were barely out of the schoolroom. We've been on our own ever since. Like I said, Stella and the babies are all the kin I have left. I believed she was happily married. Turns out, I was wrong. Now, don't you think the babies need names?"

"I suppose you're right. I was thinking—"

He cleared his throat. "Might I suggest no more flower names."

She laughed. "Flowers make me happy. They also represent a lot of what is good in the world, right along with my menagerie of animals. They go hand in hand."

She'd had enough death surrounding her. Besides, many of the girls in the orphanage were named Mary, Catherine or Elizabeth. None of them had been nice. Not that she could recall.

"I'll grant you that, but aren't there any other names you can think of?"

"My mother's name was Lily. Will that work?"

Graham smiled. "Lily, I like it. My mother's name was Rose."

Fanny's eyes crinkled with mischief. "A flower, huh?"

"I suppose. Lily Rose sounds right fine."

"It does. I'm afraid my father's name isn't quite suitable. Darrow."

"Darrel?" he asked.

"No. D-A-R-R-O-W. I'd say it was misspelled, but it's an old family name carried over from Scotland. It means oak tree."

Graham's burst of laughter rolled right through her, shaking the buckboard. "Another plant?"

"My mother's maiden name was Jacob."

The muscles beneath his beard rolled like a ripple in the creek. His eyes turned dark, the blue going nearly black. His Adam's apple bobbed, and Fanny thought he might be holding back tears. He pulled the brake, jumped to the ground, walked around to the other side and offered her a hand. She stared at it, eagerly wanting to feel his warmth again, yet hesitant to do so since she didn't know what she'd said to upset him. His avoidance of her gaze cut straight to her heart. What had she said that angered him?

"I'll be at the marshal's if you need anything. I should be back in half an hour."

And just like that, Graham dismissed her and left her standing in the cool shadows of her sewing shop. She searched through their conversation. One moment they were laughing, the next his face was as stony as the Flint Hills, his shoulders rigid and unmoving. Fanny's gaze settled on his back as he walked away, and tears filled her eyes. She hadn't meant to hurt him, but somehow, something she'd said had done just that.

The last thing she'd offered was the mention of her mother's maiden name. Had that caused him pain? Fanny wasn't sure, but she did know one thing, she would unbury Graham's secrets and soothe his wounds if she could. For the good of the babies. They needed an uncle who didn't brood like a grumpy old man. The babies needed him. Lily Rose and… Sam. Sam? Where had that come from? She liked the name. She liked it so much that she nearly chased Graham down to see if he had any objections. However, given his mood, she decided not to stir the embers.

Fanny skirted the buckboard and found the door to her sewing shop had been replaced with new wood. What really caught her eye was the placard neatly crafted and designed with the word *FANNY'S* intricately whittled into the wood in large letters. Below them in smaller script were the words *Sewing Shop*. Little flowers on vines bordered the edges. She drew in a breath and held it, amazed that someone had taken the time to consider her. Not just the necessity of a new door, but a sign declaring this spot as hers.

She climbed the stairs and ran her index finger over the letters. The wood was smooth as glass. It wasn't anything fancy, but this close she could see the fine workmanship. There were smaller bits of ivy carved into the letters of her name.

She'd been renting from Mr. Taylor for nearly six months and hadn't talked her brothers into making a sign for her. She knew if they had, it would have been nothing more than a piece of sawed wood with her name crudely painted on the surface. There was something about this sign that made her heart smile.

Since she didn't know who'd made it, she couldn't say it had been done out of admiration for her, but she could see that the craftsman not only had talent, but he also appreciated his art. She wondered again who'd done it. She half fancied herself in love with the crafter, but that was a silly notion. Why, given her advanced age, she did not believe in love at first sight. At least she'd never encountered it or heard about it. She'd only read about it.

Of course, the warm feelings she had toward Graham upon realizing he was *the* gunslinging Graham Staddler she'd so often read about in the paper didn't count. She felt as if she already knew him, as if he were a longtime friend. The fact the journalist seemed to depict Graham's true goodness so well helped solidify her connection to him. It was as if they were cut from the same cloth. Well, mostly. Fanny was still trying to find her purpose, her reason for being on this earth.

She could probably fall in love with whoever had made this placard for her. Unless it was old Mr. Henry. He'd buried four wives already. Still, it would be nice to know who'd made it so she could thank him properly. It certainly wasn't Mr. Taylor's doing. He had balked at the idea of even having her door fixed. Then she thought about the expense. Certainly, she couldn't allow such a kindness to go unpaid. She had to discover who the craftsman was, and the only way to do that was to ask Mr. Taylor.

She fished out her key from her reticule and tested the lock. It gave, and her door sprung open, welcoming her into the small space she'd carved out as her own. It was a place she could be herself without fear of being judged for her lack of skills. It was a place where she owned her craft. Excelled. She took pride in her simple yet elegant designs and her tight stitches. Here she had a sense of accomplishment, a place where she didn't feel like a failure.

She stepped into the cool, dimly lit room and breathed in the freshly cut wood before opening the curtains to allow the sunlight an entrance. She was surprised fear did not follow her like a shadow. Even knowing it had only been Mr. Davies who'd broken into her shop, and for a good reason, she'd still expected fear to attack her. She was grateful it had not.

She spun in a circle, inspecting the area to see if all was as she'd left it. There was almost a tinge of disappointment when she discovered everything was where it had been yesterday. For a moment, she imagined her little shop had been transformed into the sketches she'd created while daydreaming about the ideal shop to serve the ladies of Oak Grove. She blamed her hopeful expectations on the new door and sign. The scent of cut wood had obviously given her hope that such a gift, such as new shelves to hold her fabrics and a larger cutting surface, had been handed to her. "Guess it was not meant to be."

Laying her reticule on her worktable, she gathered several pieces of cut calico she'd begun for the McMillan sisters and the rich silk fabric she'd need to complete Mrs. Daniel's social gown. She placed them into a basket. She took up another bit of uncut fabric, folded it neatly into the basket and double covered it with a dust cloth to prevent the prairie dust from staining the material on their way back home.

As soon as her supplies were ready on the worktable, she slipped into the mercantile and found Mr. Taylor dipping his quill into the inkwell. The sound of a hammer striking a nail drew her attention, and she noticed Mr. Thomas fixing the front door.

"Mr. Taylor," she said, "I wanted to thank you for having my door fixed. I'd be willing to trade sewing for the expense." She bit the inside of her cheek and prayed the proprietor didn't demand immediate payment.

Mr. Taylor looked up from his ledger, his brow furrowing beneath the rim of his spectacles. "No need to thank me, Fanny. Mr. Staddler spent the better part of yesterday afternoon fixing that door. He was even able to repair the old lock."

Her jaw dropped and then snapped shut. Her heart galloped against her chest. Thundering wildly. Out of all the men she'd imagined who might have made the sign, she hadn't thought of him. She might have secretly wished it to add to the kind deeds piling in his favor, but she hadn't dared give in to that hope.

Mr. Staddler might be the sort of man a gal fancied herself in love with, but that was purely due to the fascinating tales surrounding him. Graham wasn't the sort of man a woman should love. He wasn't the type to settle down. He was too much like her brother Seth. Their boots were always itching for the next town. The next adventure. To find Graham had made the sign surprised her and gave her pause. She twisted her fingers together. "He—he did?"

"Sure enough," Mr. Taylor said.

Why? He'd done this yesterday, after he'd been fiery mad when she'd told him his sister had been using another name, a name of someone long deceased. At first, she'd thought Clea might be another sister or their mother, but now she wondered if Clea had meant something more to him. If she'd been someone who'd held his heart. Is that why he was always moving from town to town?

Each article written about him had been set in a different place. Different town. Could it be he was running from a woman who'd broken his heart? Fanny had wanted to ask him last night, but she'd been overly grateful for his presence at first. Then the Gilberts had arrived at the homestead, and she'd been too irritated and too exhausted to trust her words wouldn't cause offense. Was his thoughtfulness with fixing her door an apology for running off the way he had? What about the sign, the one someone had put so much care into making.

"I haven't seen the sign for myself, yet, but several of the ladies heard about what happened and stopped to check on you. They even brought some things for the babies." Mr. Taylor jerked his thumb over his shoulder to a pile of items in the corner behind him.

Fanny stared speechless at the gifts and wondered how she would repay the ladies of Oak Grove for their kindness, because she was an Ellis and Ellis's didn't take handouts. Not even for the good cause of caring for orphans. Guilt gnawed at her a little at having judged the ladies of Oak Grove as nothing more than interfering gossipers.

"If you'd like, I'll have Les load them up for you."

The gangly stock boy settled the broom handle into a corner. "I'd be happy to do that, Fanny."

"Thank you." She nodded as she swallowed the emotion clogging her throat. Outside of the appreciation her clients showed for her dressmaking skills, Fanny thought the folks of Oak Grove didn't like her much. After all, she'd practically been an orphan. She'd been raised by her three brothers, men who didn't know a thing about raising a young girl to be a lady.

Fanny knew she was rough around the edges. Her manners were coarse, like that of a seasoned cowboy. She wore a gun like a man, and no matter how hard she tried to soften her speech and speak as a lady should, her words always came out wrong. For the ladies of Oak Grove to offer her help, it made her feel as if she wasn't such a pariah as she'd believed. She began to leave and then stopped.

"I will be working from home for the next few days. I will send letters to my customers to let them know so as not to bother you."

"It's no bother, Fanny." Mr. Taylor waved. "Yesterday's little mishap has increased business today, all thanks to you and those young'uns. Guess there is something to say for gossip."

Fanny snorted. She'd never known anything good about gossip. All of it caused trouble as far as she could see. "If you say so. However, I'd appreciate it if I wasn't the topic of such gossip."

He smiled and pushed a black-and-white folded paper toward her. "This came in this morning. I know you like looking at the latest fashions and fabrics."

A thrill of excitement rolled over her. She always enjoyed looking at the paper, and not just for the fashions. The paper was where she'd first read about Graham. He'd gone after several horse thieves on his own. He apprehended all but one, and that one, according to the journalist, had been caught in the crossfire and shot by one of his comrades, not Graham.

With all that had happened in the last day, she'd forgotten the paper was due in. She perused the front page for news of Graham and then poked around the other pages for any news of Stella and Cal before flipping to the section she really wanted. Leaning over, she peered closer at the finely drawn details of the dress patterns. Oh, how she wished the authorities on women's fashion would do away with tight corsets. They were not practical. Especially for life out west.

Her gaze followed along the images, taking note of the hemlines, ruffles, and waterfall drapes until she settled on an advertisement for a sewing machine. A machine would shorten the time it would take her to complete a dress. However, she couldn't afford it, especially not since she intended on moving out of her brothers' home.

Wait, what about the babies? Sam and Lily Rose. She sighed. How would she make her own way apart from her brothers with the responsibility of the twins in the event Stella was never found? And certainly, Graham couldn't care for them moving from town to town as he did. Fanny couldn't stay with her brothers. It would be only a matter of time before her brothers married. They would not need her to help care for the house while they tended the fields. Their marriages would bring children. The twins and Fanny would be extra mouths her brothers would have to feed, and she could not be a burden.

There was very little room at the shop to care for the twins while she sewed, and the ladies of Oak Grove would likely protest driving out to the family farm. After paying rent to Mr. Taylor and a boarding fee to Mrs. Wheelwright, there would not be anything left over to hire a nanny.

If she purchased a sewing machine, she could complete sewing orders quicker and possibly earn more to provide for the babies. Still, spending a great deal on a machine seemed irresponsible and would prolong her stay at the farm. She twisted her mouth. Would Mrs. Wheelwright have a room large enough for her and the twins?

"Lord," she prayed beneath her breath. "What am I to do?"

Graham walked away from the jail, frustrated and with no answers. He hadn't been able to find the marshal at the jail or at his home, and the deputy he'd run into hadn't seen Cal for months. Graham dug his fingers into his beard and scratched, perplexed by Cal's behavior.

If there was one thing Graham had discovered from the months chasing down his sister, it was that if Cal had been in town to give up the babies, he wouldn't have passed up the saloon and a game of cards. Graham had questioned the proprietor of the saloon, who'd told him his brother-in-law had been chased out of town months before. The more questions Graham asked, the more confused he became. He was beginning to think he needed to revisit the railroad camp and talk to Mr. Davies. Something was amiss. Were the twins even his sister's?

He turned the corner and strode down the back alley that led straight to Fanny's establishment. He saw a weedy young man he recognized as Mr. Taylor's stock boy deposit a crate in the back of the buckboard. He tipped his hat toward the young man. "Howdy."

"Hiya. Miss Fanny might be a while."

"That's fine. I'm in no hurry." He was itching to

ride out to Mr. Davies and scare the truth out of him, but he wouldn't rush her. He didn't relish the thought of her forgetting an item and needing to return to town.

"She's perusing the paper. Looking over dresses and whatnot." The boy laughed. "If I were to guess, she'll be there until after dinnertime if you're in no hurry."

At the widening of Graham's eyes, the boy bent over at the waist with laughter. Graham patted the kid on the shoulder as he passed by him and took the stairs in one step. "Guess I should fetch her, then."

The new door and placard gave him pause. Had Fanny seen the sign he'd made? He couldn't help wonder what she thought of it and if it had made her happy. The thought of her smiling and him being the cause made him want to do it more.

Graham stepped into the mercantile and saw Fanny leaning over the counter with the tip of her index finger tapping against her lips. The scent of sweet candies, tobacco and ink warred against each other. He moved closer to look over her shoulder and followed the line of her perusal. A sewing machine? Didn't she already have one?

He sifted through the images stored in his mind from when he'd inspected the shop for the intruder yesterday. He recalled bolts of fabric, a worktable and a smaller table along with boxes storing supplies for the mercantile, but he couldn't remember seeing a sewing machine. He knew from speaking with Mrs. Wheelwright yesterday that Fanny was an accomplished seamstress. Had she been doing it all by hand?

He leaned forward for a closer inspection and caught a whiff of sunshine and…a field of wildflowers. He'd been swallowed up by her scent while they traveled over the rutted path from her home to Oak Grove. The perfume, uniquely belonging to her, warmed him and made him want to linger.

He sensed her movement and shifted his gaze. Soft green eyes, a color between moss nestled against the base of a tree and delightful blades of grass after a drought-breaking soaker, stared up at him.

"Hello," she said, smiling up at him.

She'd seemed freer and more relaxed once he suggested Cal might be dead, and he wondered why. Did she fear Cal confronting her and taking the twins from her? If Cal was still alive, did he pose a threat? He didn't like the idea of Fanny anywhere near Cal James.

"Hello." Had his voice deepened in the moments since he'd spoken to Mr. Taylor's stock boy? Sure sounded like it to him.

"Hello," she said again, turning toward him with her wide smile. "I'm looking over the latest fashions."

An eyebrow shot upward, questioning her statement.

"See?" She pointed. "Straight from Chicago. I hope to incorporate the drape of this gown for Mrs. Daniel. I think she'll really like it, and it will suit her nicely."

"I see." His gaze shifted from the image she'd

pointed out to the sewing machine in the lower right-hand corner. A bold number sprung from the paper. Sixty dollars? Burnt beans! That was more than four months' wages. He poked his finger at the thick black image. "Will this make it easier to sew such a garment?"

"Most certainly, but it's an expense I cannot afford."

"Says here it makes over three hundred stitches a minute and can out sew seven people. Seems to me it's an expense worth its salt." He fished out some bills and laid them out on the counter. "Mr. Taylor, would you mind ordering this here machine for Fanny?"

Mr. Taylor looked between them and then at the stack of bills before scooping the money into his hand. "Of course."

"Graham, no." Small fingers dug into his upper arm. "I cannot possibly accept such a gift. Not from a mere acquaintance, especially when you've done so much already. Folks might get the wrong idea and start talking."

He arched his brow. "What do you mean? I haven't done anything."

"The supplies, taking care of the farm while I see to the babies. Bringing Eunice and Mr. Gilbert out to help. The beautiful sign. Thank you for that. It's thoughtful and more than I could have asked for."

He was surprised she'd thanked him for inviting Eunice and her father out to the farm.

"You're welcome." He'd done nothing more than whittle her name into a piece of scrap wood left from making her door. He'd figured it would help folks in need of her sewing find her, and after speaking with Mr. Taylor, he'd known it was something she'd wanted for a while. According to the proprietor of the mercantile, Fanny wasn't a nagging sort of woman. She hated bothering folks and never asked for favors unless she could barter; that endeared her to Graham all the more.

She would make a wonderful mother to the twins, until his sister served her time. and if he didn't find Stella? Fanny would raise them with her same morals and fortitude and instill in them her practical nature, too. He couldn't have chosen a better woman to keep his niece and nephew. He knew when he left Oak Grove, they would be well taken care of.

Purchasing the sewing machine might be inappropriate, but the more time he spent with Fanny, the more he wanted to give her everything she wanted. Besides, the machine would help care for his kin. It was a good thing he'd had very little cause to spend his wages over the years and that most of his jobs included room and board. He'd tell her that if it would persuade her to accept the gift, but he suspected his financial means wouldn't budge her pride, not even a mite. He touched the tips of her fingers with his and held her green gaze. Brown and gold flecks vibrated to life. His breath caught in his throat at the sight. "We're more than mere acquaintances, Fanny."

She released his arm and smacked the thick part of his upper arm with the ball of her fist.

"Ow! What was that for?" he asked, rubbing the spot she'd punched with her small hand.

"How dare you say such thing," she spoke through clenched teeth so only he could hear her. "And in public. The whole town already thinks I'm a wild ruffian because I wear a gun belt. You'll have them believing I'm less than virtuous."

He burst into laughter. "I can see how my words might be misconstrued, Fanny, and for that, I apologize." It seemed like he was always apologizing to her for one reason or another. "However, we are more than mere acquaintances, as I am certain Mr. Taylor will agree." He stole a glance at the proprietor and hardened his gaze to procure the man's agreement. He hadn't meant for his words to sound improper in any way, and he was doing what he could to remedy the situation. "After all, you are the guardian of my niece and nephew."

Mr. Taylor nodded. "That is true, Fanny. You're practically family."

"We are family," Graham readily agreed. "And if my sister cannot be found, we will remain family. Since I'll be moving on once we discover the truth about my sister's whereabouts, I cannot take an active role in the twins' lives, which means your livelihood is of utmost importance if you are to care for them properly. I trust you will do so with this." He emphasized his words with another poke of his finger at the picture.

The sewing machine was a gift he sensed she deserved whether she kept the babies or not. There was something in his words that pulled at his insides and reached toward the ground Oak Grove was plotted on. That something, whatever it was, made him want to shuck off his boots and grow roots. "I won't always be around to help support their needs financially. The least I can do is provide you with a better means of doing so."

"Oh," she said, her brow furrowed. He assumed she was considering all the options and the consequences. He could tell by the glint in her sparkling emerald eyes when she concluded it would be all right if she accepted the machine.

"He has the right of it," Mr. Taylor said. "I won't mention a thing to your brothers."

"It's not like they won't discover it sooner or later," Fanny responded.

"Will they object to the gift, Fanny?"

She tugged her lower lip in between her teeth and shook her head. "They might question your intentions."

Mr. Taylor burst into laughter. "There won't be any questioning."

Fanny glared at the proprietor. "I'm certain they'll question, and then they'll shoo Mr. Staddler away like a lost dog. Of course, you'll be gone before the machine arrives, so there will be nothing to it."

Graham considered Mr. Taylor. From all he'd heard, the Ellis brothers were protective of their sister when it came to courting. He wondered why. She was beyond the age of marriage. Maybe they hadn't found a man worthy of her attentions. The more he came to know her, the more he understood how rare and special she was. At least he didn't have to worry about her brothers forcing him into matrimony. As long as he kept reminding himself that any spark he sensed between them was due to the twins, he'd ride away from Oak Grove unscathed.

Fanny smacked the flat of her hand onto the counter and then held it out to him. "All right then, I accept your bargain. You can purchase the sewing machine in exchange for me taking on Sam and Lily Rose."

He arched a brow. "Sam?"

"Yep. Hope you like it, because I've become accustomed to it. I have settled on Sam in mind."

He struck out his hand and shook it. "Agreed. Now, how about we take another ride out to see Mr. Davies."

Chapter Eight

Fanny could hardly contain her excitement. In a little under two months, she'd have a fancy machine to sew fancy dresses for the fancy ladies of Oak Grove. She only hoped the machine wouldn't be too difficult to work. Oh, and where would she put it? At her shop? At the farm? Disappointment snuffed out the excitement quicker than a cold bucket of water on a blazing fire. There was little room for the machine in her shop. The room she intended renting from Mrs. Wheelwright was barely big enough for a single bed and a small dresser. There would be little room for the babies. Keeping it at the farm meant she would have to accept the inevitable and never leave her brothers' home. She'd be living with them for the rest of her life.

"Is everything all right?"

Graham's timbre interrupted her thoughts. She blinked back the ennui. The buckboard hit a rut and rocked from side to side. His firm, muscular forearm, bare beneath the rolled sleeve, brushed against her calico sleeve. The heat of his skin warmed hers through the fabric of her dress. She drew in a breath and glanced up at him. His gaze was on the road, but his Adam's apple bobbed. Had he felt the heat between their arms, the spark from their touch?

They'd knocked into each other on the way to town, but she hadn't been nearly aware of his presence as she was in the current moment. Had his kindness and consideration bamboozled her into finding his inquisitive dark blue eyes, blond curls and muscular form even more attractive? She thought about all the heroics she'd read about him and wondered if she was enamored with the man written about in the papers or if she was beginning to fall for the man himself. He inched the rim of his hat upward with his finger and stole a glance at her before returning his eyes back to the rutted path.

As if she hadn't heard his question the first time, he asked again, "Is everything all right?"

"Yes, of course. Why do you ask?"

"I thought you'd be happier about the sewing machine." He shifted in his seat, seemingly to move farther from her. "I hope you're not regretting the decision."

"Oh, not at all. I am thrilled, more than thrilled. The machine will increase my ability to sew faster. It's just… Well, I don't know where I'm going to put it."

"Your shop?"

Her shoulders fell. "There will not be enough room

for it and Lily Rose and Sam. I'm afraid I haven't come up with a grand solution to continue my business and care for the twins all on my own. It seems as if one will keep me from the other."

"I see," he said, letting the reins draw through his large hands. "What of Eunice?"

"Eunice might be helping at the moment, but she is young and has many prospects for marriage." Fanny come to believe would be one of her brothers. "She'll marry and have her own children soon enough. Besides, most of my clients offer barters, not cash, which will make it difficult to pay for a nanny.

While living with her brothers, accepting bartered items and services often worked. Now that she had a family to support, she'd have to rethink acceptable methods of payment.

"Would one of the local women exchange your services for watching the babies?"

Fanny bit on the inside of her cheek. The ones who could afford to pay weren't the type to care for their own children. They hired nannies. She recalled the dirty cheeks of the shoeless children running freely around the railroad camps. The women in the camps often bartered with chickens, pies or family heirlooms, but most of them had too many children of their own to keep a dutiful eye on the twins. "I fear not."

Graham slowed the wagon as the tops of the canvas tents came into view. Preoccupied as she had been with the various scenarios of her future, she'd forgotten he'd said they were going to visit the rail-road camp.

"My sister worked for you."

In the two days she'd known this man, she'd come to learn he was a man of few words, so she understood his statement as a question. Perhaps it was due to being raised by men.

Clea—Stella," she corrected at his flinch, "did sort of work for me. I gave her jobs she was confident she could complete, and I gave her what the client paid. She rightly earned it. It wasn't money out of my pocket." She wouldn't tell him about the times she'd worried over Stella's well-being when she didn't show to complete a job, or how his sister had stolen from her. No one knew Stella had taken Fanny's hard-earned money except her brothers, and they only knew because Stella had gone to the farmhouse and taken from them, too. Knowing Stella's difficult situation, they'd all agreed to keep the theft to themselves.

Fanny didn't know how much Graham had discovered about his sister's marriage, but she didn't want to tell him how bad it had been. If she did, he might lose hope they'd find Stella alive. After seeing the abuse Stella had endured at the hands of her husband, Fanny was finding it difficult to not think the worst.

After the first time Stella hadn't shown for work, Fanny had searched for her, and Stella's black eyes were enough to let Fanny know the situation. It might have been a bad business practice to finish jobs Stella had begun and keep her on, but her heart had gone out to the young woman.

Fanny believed Stella and the other ladies living among the railroad workers deserved kindness. She liked to think her kindness was being rewarded now with the opportunity to care for not one but two babies. Even if it was for only until they found Stella. At least she'd know what it was like to be a mother.

"I appreciate your kindness to my sister."

Fanny nodded. "Anyone would have done the same."

"I don't think so, Fanny." He adjusted his hat and rested his elbows on his knees. "I haven't encountered one person who had a nice thing to say about Stella or Cal James." He turned his head toward her, and she could see the way his gaze searched hers beneath the shadow of his hat. "You're a rare gem, Fanny. A real rare gem."

His somber expression and compliment cracked a door open in his hard reserve, and she nearly asked him who Clea had been to him and why he seemed to grow angry at the mention of the gal's name, but she thought better of it. He'd tell her when he was ready. And if he left before he was ready, she'd let it sleep.

"What are we doing here?" she asked, changing the subject. Excitement and worry had consumed her thoughts since he'd helped her into the buckboard, and she'd forgotten they were heading to the camp and not the farmhouse.

"Seems my brother-in-law hasn't shown his face in Oak Grove for months. If he'd been here to give

Lily Rose and Sam up, he would have no doubt stirred up some sort of trouble while he was here. He wouldn't have passed up the saloon."

Fanny nodded, knowing what he said was true. She'd been at ease ever sense Graham mentioned Cal might be dead. Now she was back to worrying, and Dora and Mr. Davies's dire warning was running in her head. She knotted her fingers together, wondering if the twins were fine. Her only consolation was the fact Mr. Gilbert was there, protecting them. "Except Cal was run out of town for cheating at cards. He may not dare show his face."

Graham focused on the camp ahead of them, and Fanny followed his gaze.

"If I understand correctly, he was caught cheating the men he worked beside, not the men in town."

She disliked repeating tales she'd heard among her patrons, but this seemed important. "That is my understanding."

"It's my belief that Mr. Davies didn't speak all the truth. If he spoke any truth at all."

"And you expect him to tell it to you now?" She couldn't keep the surprise from her voice.

Graham nodded. His short, clipped nod spoke of confidence and assurance that he could persuade the man to loosen his tongue. Fanny had her doubts. "Folks out here are tight-lipped. Unless you threaten to shoot him, I'm afraid he won't say a thing."

"We've got to find my sister." His mouth pressed into a firm line.

So he could move on to the next town? A small

ache formed in her chest at the thought of Graham leaving Oak Grove, but there was nothing she could do to make him stay, not even for the sake of the twins.

"I understand you wanting to protect her and find her before a zealous bounty hunter does, but, Graham, you might have to let this one sleep."

His nose twitched as if to hold back emotion. He swallowed and then said, "I must know if she is dead or alive."

The tension knotting in her gut eased at his words. If he knew Stella's demise was a possibility, she didn't need to keep her own suspicions from him. However, she would proceed with caution. She didn't want to be the one to snuff out his hope, especially since he voiced the words she'd refused to speak.

"I won't rest until I get my answers, Fanny. Even if it means I need to threaten Mr. Davies with a gun."

Fanny pressed against the back of the buckboard and fidgeted with the folds of her skirt. "Is that your intention, to shoot Mr. Davies?"

He cast another glance her way. The sun beat down on them, and a rivulet of perspiration slid down his brow and disappeared into his beard. "No, Fanny. I will only threaten him if I have to."

"Seems to me, if you're making a threat, you should be prepared to follow through."

Graham burst into laughter. "Seems to me, you might be right, Miss Ellis. Do you have any other suggestions?"

She worried her bottom lip, uncertain why her

words made him laugh when she spoke the truth. They were words she'd heard her father say to the ruffians right before they killed him and her mother.

"Mr. Davies worries I'll shoot him. He doesn't care about facing a man. Says he can hold his salt against the best of them, but when it comes to me, he doesn't think a lady should carry the burden of such actions."

Graham scratched his beard. "In that case, would you like to borrow my gun."

"Or you could borrow one of my dresses," she said matter of factly.

Another burst of laughter came from Graham before he leaned back and flicked the reins, propelling Daisy into motion. The buckboard swayed back and forth, and the rocking motion forced the right side of his body to brush against the left side of hers. Their arms met and parted with the movement, as if waltzing from one end of the barn to the other. A longing she'd kept in her heart as she'd watched ladies dance with their partners at the barn dances threaded through her. A quick drop of her lids and she could almost imagine herself being held in Graham's arms as their feet glided across the floor.

"I'll say it again, you're a real gem. Can't believe some man hasn't snatched you up already."

Her mouth gaped. She searched for a response, but her forthright nature abandoned her in one fell swoop, like a hawk diving toward an unsuspecting critter hiding in the tall grasses.

Gone.

Snatched away. Could a man like Graham Staddler believe she was worth hitching to for life?

She closed her mouth and pondered an appropriate response, but she didn't rightly know what to say. How did a gal take a compliment? Thank you didn't seem quite appropriate, especially since he hadn't given her a compliment, but rather insulted her for remaining single at her grand age of thirty. Saying thank you could very well show her a fool when it came to dealing with men. She'd never been good at discerning their intentions, except when on the wrong side of her pistol.

She bit down on the inside of her cheek, hard enough to taste her own blood. All the thoughts trampling through her mind revolved around the idea that no man had ever considered her worth courting. No man had even tried. Unless what Mr. Gilbert had said was true, and her brothers had chased off those who'd come courting.

She drew her gaze along Graham's profile. He was the most handsome man she'd encountered. She couldn't recall ever seeing another as fine as him. If no other man had paid her compliments, why was he? Why would this man pay her attention and stir the long-dormant desire in her heart to be married? A desire she'd given up on.

Ever since the signs of womanhood had transformed her body and she'd exchanged Nathan's hand-me-down britches in for skirts and bonnets, all the boys at school had begun treating her as if she had leprosy.

What made her so different from the rest of the girls was that she would never know the touch of a beau's hand on hers. Most women of her age were married with a passel of children. She had never even been asked to dance at any of the town socials. Did her straightforward tendencies make a man's stomach turn? Was it the fact she didn't know the top side of a skillet from the bottom? She knew the latter to be true, as her brothers had said as much. Still, if she'd been graced with Eunice's beauty, her lack of domestic skills might have been overlooked. But the truth was, she had about as much prettiness as Violet the pig after a good shake in the mud, which is probably why no man had ever paid her a compliment.

Graham's full mouth drew her gaze, and she bit the inside of her cheek again. If his bare arm brushing against the fabric of her sleeve had caused a spark, what would it be like if their lips touched? Would the touch consume her? Cause her to disintegrate into ash? The thought frightened her. Maybe her brothers had preserved her life by chasing any would-be suitors away.

Did her response to Graham's compliment have something to do with her curiosity about kissing him, or was it all about the heroics she'd read about in the paper? Still, nobody had ever called her a gem before. As far as she knew, a gem was shiny and beautiful, something to treasure and keep safe. She sighed. She wasn't even certain what Graham meant by that, and just like she was too yellow-bellied to ask him about Clea, she was too yellow-bellied to ask him what he meant by calling her a gem. Given he was a man of few words, she doubted he would be forthcoming on his own accord. So she'd let it sleep, just like she'd let her question about Clea sleep. Some issues were best left alone, and she had a feeling both these things fell into that wagon.

Graham sensed Fanny had something to say, but he'd let her keep silent. It wasn't like he was looking to court or hitch up to any woman. If he were, Fanny Ellis would sure be at the top of the list. Petite and as generous with her curves as she was with her kindness, the woman was full of fire and beauty and practicality. And she could shoot, too. Not to mention her straightforward nature. That was a rare find, and it attracted him more than it should. If he weren't careful, he'd be like a moth to a flame and scorch his delicate wings. He'd do well enough to leave all compliments to be spoken by another man.

Burnt beans, what was he thinking saying such things to an unmarried woman. Especially since he had no intentions of courting her. Marriage to Clea cost him a great deal. Allowing his heart to be won over by a sweet and genteel lady had nearly killed him when she'd died. Deeming Fanny a gem was one of the worst things he could have said, until he'd gone and pointed out the fact that she remained free of the bounds of matrimony. Worst of all, he said he couldn't believe it, indicating she was a dame worth catching.

Riding alone with an unattached woman, even

if she was considered the town's spinster, was dangerous to preserving his single status. When he was alone with her, he was focused on her. Only on her. The way she tried to tame a curl dancing with the curve of her jaw. How she smoothed her palms over her skirts as if to iron out the wrinkles left by their travel to and from town. How the scent of wildflowers clung to her like they were a part of her. The pull of her confident words, and even when she wasn't feeling so confident. The way excitement took hold of her eyes and brightened them to a vibrant green with ribbons of gold.

In the short time he'd spent with her, he knew entirely too much about her. He liked what he saw, and he had no business doing so. He'd have to put on a pair of blinders and plug his ears if they continued in each other's presence too much longer. He hoped Mr. Davies would loosen his tongue so he could find Stella and depart Oak Grove faster than a twister tearing through town. If he didn't discover anything about his sister here... Well, he'd have to make sure he spent as little time with the spinster as possible.

He'd heard Fanny called a spinster by Mrs. Wheelwright and the Gilberts. He knew the term wasn't considered a compliment, and although he didn't get a sense of her discontentment, he knew most women longed to marry. Why hadn't Fanny married?

There went his thoughts again, turning right back to the gal sitting beside him when she was the last subject he should be pondering. Still, as far as he could tell, there wasn't a thing wrong with her. So why hadn't an eligible man scooped her up and ridden away with her yet? His mind went back to what Mr. Gilbert had said about her brothers chasing away all her suitors. Her brothers must care for her a great deal to keep the wolves from devouring her. Having a sister, he could understand their need to protect her, especially a gem like Fanny. He sure wished he would have done the same for Stella, then maybe he wouldn't be hunting her down because she was wanted for bank robbery.

Thankful his thoughts had rolled back to his sister, he pushed the idea of paying Fanny more compliments to the back of his mind. "You think Mr. Davies is at camp?"

"I don't rightly know." She slid her palms over her skirts. The movement brought a curve to his mouth. He flicked his gaze to her eyes but found them shielded by the rim of her bonnet. "It is the middle of the day, not quite lunch yet, I suppose. If it isn't washing day, Dora will know where to find him. Still, Mr. Davies won't tell you a thing even if he is here. No one out here will."

"Not even with you at my side?" He pulled in a hot breath through his nostrils at the tendril of excitement swirling around in his chest. The thought of Fanny at his side brought to mind everything that was good and right in this world. The reins pressed into his palms, and he scowled. He'd have to pay more attention to his words before they trotted out of his mouth.

Is that what scripture meant by taking every

thought captive? He pulled on his memory to recall the rest of the verse and came up blank. He thought it might be something along the lines of taking those thoughts and lining them up with the word of God. He knew scripture also said it wasn't good for man to be alone, which is why the good Lord created Eve for Adam, but that bit didn't hold true for Graham Staddler. He'd said wedding vows, until death do us part, and then God saw fit to rip his heart from his chest.

Graham had been alone for years, and he intended to stay that way. That feeling of watching someone he loved die while he remained helpless to do anything about it was enough to fell a man to his knees and keep him there. Graham pushed all his armor back in place, where it should be. He wouldn't allow himself to be taken in by Fanny's forthright nature and her beauty. He wouldn't allow himself to be taken in by her at all.

"Mr. Davies said he told me the truth. I did have to pull it from him like Doc yanking a bad tooth." She drew a slender finger over her ear and pushed a tendril of hair from her eyes. "He isn't likely to change his story."

"You sure know how to dampen a man's hope," he said as he pulled the buckboard between the main row of tents billowing in the prairie breeze. He needed the real truth, the one as God saw it, not Mr. Davies's version, and he would get it.

Chapter Nine

Fanny sank her hands into the dough just as Eunice instructed her and squeezed. She rolled the dough over and punched her fist into it. She continued with the movements, taking her frustration out on the unsuspecting flour.

They'd left the camp disappointed. Mr. Davies and Dora had gone to Junction City and weren't due back for days. And as she'd warned Graham, not a soul spoke one word about Cal or Stella James. Fanny knew they feared the consequences if they spoke out of turn. Folks needed the wages Mr. Davies paid them and would heed his direction when it came to divulging information to outsiders. Even if the outsider claimed kinship to one of their own.

Much to her surprise, Graham hadn't threatened to shoot anyone. He hadn't even grabbed them up by the collar and shaken them as she'd been tempted to do, especially since she needed to know if Cal James was alive.

Graham had kept silent the entire ride home, even when she'd commented on the scenery or pointed out a doe off in the distance near the back of the Neosho. She'd like to think it was because he was irritated with the circumstances. However, his silence had assaulted her emotions, and it had taken everything in her to not cry.

It was a good thing Fanny had had practice dealing with her brothers' cantankerous moods. She'd come to discover their frustration toward her really had nothing to do with her and everything to do with circumstances she had no control over. Over the years, they had learned to soften their reactions toward her, but she still kept her distance from them when she knew they were in a fit. At least Graham hadn't snapped at her. Although she might have preferred that to him keeping his lips clamped tight.

She scooped up the dough and slammed it onto the block. Men! She'd lived with three of them her entire life, and she still didn't understand much about them. Like why they couldn't say exactly what was on their minds. *Like, yes, Fanny, I'm mad Mr. Davies wasn't there, or I should have strangled the truth out of one or two of them. Or, Fanny, not now, I'm frustrated and overly worried about my sister, and I don't want to talk.*

She sighed. She supposed his lack of response was communication enough. It'd been obvious he did not want to talk. Not to her, anyway. He'd just shut her out. She wished she knew he didn't blame her. Of course, he was a smart man, capable of understanding that she had nothing to do with Mr. Davies's absence from the camp. It wasn't like she'd scheduled his appointment in Junction City with his bosses. Still, Graham's silence had unnerved her more than she'd expected. She suspected it had a great deal to do with him claiming they were more than mere acquaintances. *Practically family*, Mr. Taylor had said. If that were the truth, wouldn't Graham have spoken to her and told her what was on his mind?

She supposed not. It wasn't like she was his wife, only the guardian of his niece and nephew.

After another punch into the dough, Fanny paused with her fist deep in the soft mound. Given that she couldn't imagine the angst Graham felt at not knowing where his sister was and whether she still walked the earth, Fanny should offer him grace and let her mind rest. When her parents took their last breaths, Fanny had known they were dead. She'd known as she peered through the crack in the chifforobe that she'd never sit beside her mama watching her poke a needle through fabric again, and she'd never ride in front of Papa as they checked the fields. At seven, she'd known they were gone. But if she hadn't seen their deaths with her own eyes, would she have accepted the fact?

How could she convince Graham that Stella was most likely gone from this world without causing a greater rift of silence between them? Fanny's gut told her it was a high possibility, because what mother would willingly leave her children?

Fanny placed herself in Stella's shoes for a moment and cringed. Cal would have met his maker the first time he gave her a black eye, and her brothers would have beaten him thrice over for causing her bodily harm. Why hadn't Graham known the sort of marriage his sister had? Had she run off without Graham's knowing, or had Graham simply not cared enough about his sister? Those were questions she wasn't certain she had the right to ask. Not yet. However, if Stella couldn't be found and Fanny ended up with the twins, it would be her responsibility to ask the man who claimed kinship to them about his past.

"You don't need to kill the dough, Fanny."

Startled, she jumped. "Oh, Eunice. You scared me."

She'd been so deep in thought about Stella that she'd forgotten she was learning how to make biscuits.

"I see that." Eunice adjusted Lily Rose in the crook of her arm, sparking a wave of envy in Fanny's heart. She longed for the day when holding Lily Rose and Sam was as natural to her as the way Eunice made it look.

"Here," Eunice said as she gripped the dough with her free hand and rolled it forward, clasping it and dropping it back to where it began. "It's called kneading. Firm, smooth motions to make sure all the flour mixes in. If it gets too tough, you can add a little cream and start your kneading all over again. It's not an animal to wrestle to the ground."

Fanny giggled along with Eunice. "I'm sorry. I guess I don't know any other way than aggression.

Most of my prey fights back. Even when I'm gathering eggs, the hens are usually pecking at my hands."

"Yep, they do peck." Eunice giggled as she pulled her hand from the dough and held it up. Small bits clung to Eunice's long slender fingers. "See."

Fanny scanned Eunice's white hands and was surprised at the marred skin. There were telltale signs of beak wounds. "Oh, my. I thought it was only gals like me whose hands were beaten by the animals." Fanny dropped her gaze to their feet, wondering if the tops of Eunice's toes were bruised by her milk cow, too.

As if reading her mind, Eunice said, "Being much younger than my siblings, I'm the only one there to help Pa around the farm. Ma and I both have bruises on our feet. Now, roll the dough into several little balls."

Eunice handed Fanny a cloth. When she began to wipe the dough from her hands, Eunice touched her arm. "That is to cover the dough. It's like a blanket to keep it soft and warm as it rises."

"Thank you." Fanny nodded. She'd seen cloth-covered lumps on Mrs. Wheelwright's table. She'd never thought to ask what they were when she'd seen them. Fanny dipped her hands into the water bucket Graham had fetched earlier and scrubbed her fingers. Seeing the water grow cloudy from the dough, she made a mental note to retrieve another bucket from the creek. "I thought you were ladies."

"Oh, Fanny, we are ladies. Caring for our homes does not remove that from us."

Sam began to fuss, and Fanny scooped him out of

the drawer Eunice had fashioned as a bed for him. She settled on one of the kitchen chairs and bounced him in her arms. "As you have heard, I never had much of a woman's influence. My mama died when I was young, and I'm afraid my brothers don't know much about raising a lady."

Eunice sat next to her and placed her hand on top of Fanny's. Fanny was shocked by the gesture but steeled herself to keep from jerking her hand back.

"Your brothers have done right by you. I know I'm younger, but I have a mama and several older sisters. Being a lady is more than appearance. If you'd like, I could share some of the things I've learned."

Fanny's head bobbed. "I would like that very much." She surprised herself by readily accepting the offer, but she was tired of holding her shoulders back and her spine straight while she tried to fend off the world. And she did want to know what it was like to be a lady, a real lady, one as graceful as Eunice Gilbert. Fanny might have lost her chance to be a wife, but now that she had Lily Rose and Sam to consider, it'd be a good idea to know how to be a lady so she could teach Lily Rose how to be one. Not to mention she'd need to guide Sam into finding a lady when he was ready to take a wife.

"Very well, the first thing you should know, Fanny, is that not all ladies are ladies."

Fanny's brow dipped in confusion, and she averted her gaze from Eunice. She felt as she did whenever she spoke to another woman, as if they saw right through her and found her lacking. As if she didn't measure up to the standards set by society of how a gal should comport herself.

"Fanny." Eunice's soft voice cut through the self-doubt driving her back into her shell like a turtle when Calico pawed at it. "The second thing you should know is that most ladies could take lessons from you."

Fanny snapped her head up, her eyes wide and mouth open. "They…they could? But I thought… I mean…" She searched for the correct thing to say, but everything that came to mind might offend Eunice.

"You're kind and giving. You don't judge those less fortunate than you. And you're honest. There is no better example of a lady than that in my book." Eunice drew her hand back and tapped her fingers on the table. "I envy you. You don't allow men to bully you."

"I suppose that comes from having brothers," Fanny said with a smile.

"I find your stubborn tenacity admirable."

Fanny's eyes grew wide as heat fired her cheeks. She didn't know if that was a compliment or criticism. Given the course of their conversation, she took it as a compliment. She hadn't liked Eunice yesterday, and yet the woman had stepped up and offered help when Fanny needed it, and she'd called Fanny kind. She'd even claimed to envy her.

Shame threatened to hunch Fanny's shoulders, but she knew she had to own her mistake. "I judged you, Eunice. Yesterday, I didn't like you. You're perfect.

You do not have a hair out of place. You dress in the finest fabrics and latest fashions. You're genteel and soft spoken. And you know how to cook."

Laughter tore through the kitchen. When she was done, Eunice swiped at her eyes. "I am far from perfect, Fanny. Would it offend you if I told you I do away with my petticoats when the summer heat hits? It's too hot and difficult to move as a lady should with so many layers sticking to her legs."

"Of course not." Fanny smiled. "I wear britches when I do chores, except when we have company."

"Oh, how I admire your freedom." Eunice tucked a bottle of milk between Lily's rose-petal lips. "I think I shall do the same especially since the marshal's wife was seen about in a pair. They are rather practical, aren't they?"

"They are." Fanny nodded in agreement."

"I think those who dictate women's propriety and fashion have never lived on the prairie."

Fanny couldn't agree more.

"We should make a pact that from now on we'll wear britches while completing chores." Eunice held out her hand to Fanny.

She eyed it like a rattler about to strike. "What of the men?"

She couldn't care what her brothers thought, but would Graham think less of her if he saw her in britches? Would she shock him and Mr. Gilbert? She considered those questions a moment and wondered if she even cared.

Eunice leaned against the chair. "I'd like to see them wear all these layers while milking the cow."

"Or traipsing through the pig pen to feed Violet," Fanny laughed. "I've had a time figuring out how to keep my hem from becoming muddied."

"See," Eunice giggled. "We women on the prairie need to consider the practicality of our clothing. Long skirts and chores do not mix."

This time, Eunice reached out and gripped her hand. "We're going to make fine friends, Fanny. Just you wait and see."

Friends? Fanny hadn't had a friend in a long time. Outside of her brothers, she hadn't had a companion since she'd left school at the age of twelve. Her pets often set her mind and heart at ease, but they didn't communicate, not in ways she could understand, and they'd never once offered her sound advice on how to go about finding a husband. Now it was too late. She was beyond the age for marrying.

Sam cooed, and she gazed down into his wide eyes. She didn't need a husband. She had all she needed and more with Lily Rose and Sam. They filled her heart. At least for the time being. She drew in a ragged breath. She didn't wish ill-will on their mama. She prayed God would see Stella restored to her babies, but a part of her wanted to be Lily Rose and Sam's mother. Of course, for that to happen Stella couldn't be found, and Fanny did not wish that at all, especially for Graham's sake. He needed a resolution where his sister was concerned. That way he could move on to the next town and be the man he was meant to be, a man who hunted criminals and helped innocent people retrieve their property. If Graham didn't find Stella, would he stay in Oak Grove? Most likely he wouldn't, but oh, how she wished he would.

Fanny pressed her lips into a fine line. How could her two prayers be at odds with each other? One prayer being answered would cause heartbreak for someone else. That would make her selfish, which did not sit well in her heart. She resolved to set aside the longing to be the babies' mama and pray for Stella's return and absolution from her crime.

The twins needed their mother, and Graham needed closure. And Fanny, well, she just needed a purpose, something to help her make her way in the world. If she had a friend once she moved into Mrs. Wheelwright's boarding house, perhaps it would ease the pain of losing the twins to their mother upon her return. Perhaps having a friend would ease the pain of watching Graham ride off into the sunset, too. She squeezed Eunice's hand back. "I'd like that, Eunice. It's been a long while since I've had a friend."

Graham pierced a pile of hay with the pitchfork and tossed it into the empty stall. A firm hand settled on his shoulder, and he spun on his heel, the pitchfork ready to attack.

"Whoa, son!" Mr. Gilbert held one hand out in front of him and a ladle of water in the other hand. "I thought you could use a drink of water. You've been torturing this poor pile of hay for the better part of an hour."

Graham leaned the pitchfork against the pole dividing the two stalls and took the ladle offered to him. "My thanks. Just trying to get chores done."

"Looks to me like you're trying to work out a great deal of frustration."

"I'm not one much for words."

"Most men aren't." Mr. Gilbert sank onto a stool and wove his thumbs beneath his suspenders. "We're not filled with words, but I think I know a bit about what you're going through."

Graham leaned against the post next to the pitchfork and crossed his arms. "No disrespect, Mr. Gilbert, but I highly doubt you could know."

"Not something I like to speak on," Mr. Gilbert continued as if he hadn't heard Graham. "Don't like to be judged for my past shortcomings, but rather for the man I am today." Mr. Gilbert pulled a cigar from his front pocket and stuck an end in his mouth. He rolled it around on his lips a little and then tucked it back in his pocket. "The wife doesn't like it when I smoke, but every now and then, I get an urge, especially when I'm about to say what I'm about to say."

"Sounds serious," Graham said, removing his hat from his head and resting it against his thigh. There'd been plenty of times he sat around a campfire with comrades and listened to their stories of woe. Some were worse than his, some not so much. He'd never once shared his story for fear of grief catching up with him.

"I guess that depends on what side of the story you sit." Mr. Gilbert retrieved the cigar and shoved it back into his mouth. "I haven't always been the best sort of man. Years ago, before Eunice came along, I was married to my third wife. The first two died in childbirth."

Graham shifted uncomfortably. At least he didn't have the guilt of causing Clea's death, only the guilt of not being able to save her.

"The third, well, let's say her demise was a result of my grief. I loved my second wife. Loved her afore my first, but her father wouldn't accept me. She was too good for the likes of me, and looking back, I now agree." He dipped the cigar back into his shirt, and Graham could almost smell the scent as if he'd snuffed it out on his boot. "She died birthing my Caroline. I married Levester, but there weren't no love betwixt us. I needed a mother for my small children, and she wanted a husband. I'm guessing she wanted a husband to love her, but I'd given all my love to my first wives and put the rest of me into my whiskey."

Graham felt those words knot deep in his chest. He believed he'd given all his love to Clea and wondered if he could ever love another woman. If he did, was he being unfaithful to the vows he'd spoken to Clea? *Til death do us part.* The words came unbidden. He'd said them at Clea's grave. He knew he was no longer bound to her by the laws of marriage, but his heart still felt the ties, and he would not offer any woman a cold heart that was buried with his wife.

"I'm sorry for your losses, Mr. Gilbert." Graham settled his hat onto his head, ready to dismiss the older man and get back to the more pleasant deed of chores. He didn't want to think about how his actions had forced Stella's hand to a life of crime, or how his inability to read Cal James might have led to her death. He did not want to think about Clea or what it might mean if he opened his heart to another. To Fanny.

"I know you care a great deal for your sister, and I understand the need to find the truth, but don't let it consume you, son. My grief consumed me. I did things I wouldn't likely have done if I'd been sober. I've being paying for my shortcomings ever since."

Graham wanted to rail at Mr. Gilbert and tell him he was wrong. There wasn't another man on earth who knew the pain and the guilt of what he'd done. He'd helplessly watched Clea and Jacob die, and his grief had caused him to be blinded to Cal's deception. He swallowed the knot of emotion and nearly choked on the thickness of it.

"I don't rightly know what to say, Mr. Gilbert. Thank you for sharing your past, and know that I don't judge you. I see the sort of man you are and how much your daughter loves you. You're obviously at peace with your past."

"Some days I am. Others I find myself thinking I don't deserve the life God has allowed me to live in my old age. I have a good wife and wonderful children. I can't complain. I made a promise to God that whenever I see a young man like yourself, I'd share my story. I know it's hard not knowing where your sister is, and you probably blame yourself a great deal, but there are folks around to help, like myself and my daughter."

"My thanks," Graham said as he shoved his hands into his front pockets. "Not sure how I'll ever repay you. I know you have your own home to see to."

"No thanks needed. I have sons and sons-in-law to see to my home." He rose from the stool and adjusted his suspenders. "I couldn't help noticing the tension between you and Fanny. Don't forget she is helping, too. She is not your enemy. And if you're thinking of using your tongue on her like you used that pitchfork on that pile of hay, I might have something to say about it."

Graham pulled in a breath. "Yes, sir. I've taken care to keep my words from spilling."

"I gather that, but you should know that silence can be as loud as any words you might speak."

That surprised Graham. He'd never considered his silence might be as damaging as speaking.

"Guess a man don't like being wrong. She gave me advice on the folks at the camp, and I ignored her. I should have listened and saved us both the time it took to ride out there and back."

"Well, no need holding a grudge against a woman when she's right on the occasion."

Graham laughed. "I suppose you're right. Guess I better apologize. Again. Seems like that's all I do."

"Son—" Mr. Gilbert clamped his hand on Graham's shoulder "—one thing you'll get to know about womenfolk is that we men are always apologizing for one thing or another."

Graham wasn't so certain about that. He'd been married before for a little over a year, and he couldn't recall apologizing to Clea before she'd gotten sick. Then it seemed like he'd apologized every time he bathed her brow until he had no more apologies left. The only thing he was grateful for was the fact she hadn't witnessed the death of their son. That was an agony he wouldn't wish on his worst enemy. Not even Cal James, with all he'd put his sister through.

"If you and Fanny are going to get along, you're going to have to talk to each other. Be honest with each other about what your concerns are. What you're feeling, and if you're hiding anything, son, I suggest you get it out in the open. Best to tell her up front what she's dealing with rather than her discovering it on her own. After all, whether you like it or not, she might be the mother to your kin, and that will keep you connected a long while. Might as well learn how to get along."

"Thank you again, Mr. Gilbert. I guess if Miss Ellis and I are going to be kin by way of my niece and nephew, we're going to have to communicate some. However, it sounds like you're giving advice to a newly married man, and I have no intentions of marrying." Not ever again. "If we're to get along for the babies, I just believe some things are better left unsaid." And some things are better left buried in the past.

Chapter Ten

Fanny sat on the quilt next to the babies while Eunice worked on making dinner. She was ever so grateful to have the pressure of cooking off her shoulders. She cooed and made funny noises as they kicked their tiny legs. She'd been thinking about her life for much of the day. The idea of having a sewing machine made her happy, and she was certain she'd figure out a way to keep her business and properly care for Lily Rose and Sam if she needed to. Graham's continued silence and disappearance into the barn bothered her, and she wasn't even certain as to why.

She didn't like discord between herself and anyone, but she usually shrugged off other people's displeasure of her. Mostly because she'd believed she could never measure up to the expectations society held for women. After talking with Eunice, she was beginning to believe otherwise.

However, for some reason, it mattered what Graham thought of her. She wanted his approval, maybe

even his admiration. He was a man with a reputation
of being the best shot. He went the extra mile to apprehend wanted criminals and keep them alive. He
didn't want blood on his hands and wanted them to
meet justice. How had Cal James ended up marrying such a man's sister?

Fanny had thought about Cal throughout the day.
She'd never wished death on any man, but his death
would ease her mind a great deal. She'd experienced
a roll of emotions since yesterday after Mr. Davies
and Dora's warning. It was like watching an impending storm blow north, knowing it would leave destruction in its wake. As long as Graham was around,
she didn't worry over much. He believed Cal might
be dead, and given what they knew about Cal James,
she was inclined to agree. However, she just couldn't
shake the idea he might be alive and coming for the
twins.

If Cal was dead, why would Mr. Davies lie about
him giving him the babies? Fanny assumed Stella
had died, which is why Cal had given them up to
Mr. Davies, but if Graham was correct about the
scoundrel's character, which she suspected he was,
Cal wouldn't have done that. Not when he could have
sold them or raised them and worked them out for
gambling money.

Of course, raising Sam and Lily might be more effort than Cal wanted to put in. Still, he wouldn't have
just given them away. Mr. Davies wouldn't have paid
a hunk of dirt for them, even if Dora had pleaded
with him to do so. If Cal had been intent on giving

the twins away, he could have left them on any doorstep or dropped them at an orphanage, not leave them with Mr. Davies with the intention of giving them to her, especially since Cal James despised her.

Fanny gasped. Her spine straightened as firm as a broomstick handle. Why hadn't that thought crossed her mind? Cal James never would have given her his children. He hated her, had threatened to kill her once when she pointed her pistol at him when he came to retrieve Stella from the shop. Fanny had tried to protect Stella from Cal's meanness, and he knew she would do everything in her might to protect the babies. If Cal hadn't given Lily Rose and Sam to Mr. Davies, who had and why? Or was Cal intending on using the babies to somehow seek his revenge on Fanny for trying to protect Stella from him? Would he use the babies to manipulate her to do his bidding?

"Hi." Graham's deep voice cut through her last thought like a hot knife through lard.

She jumped and glanced up at him. Should she tell Graham about her concerns? No, if she told him, he might not leave once he found Stella. "Hello."

"What has you so lost in thought?"

She looked toward the kitchen at Eunice's back and noticed she was busy placing the fried chicken onto a serving dish. "I was thinking about Cal." The words came out on their own accord. She rushed on to continue as if her worries hadn't been centered on Cal. "And Clea. I mean Stella." At the slight tensing of his shoulders, she rushed on to say, "I'm sorry. It's hard for me to think of her as anything other than Clea. That's who she was to me for months."

He knelt beside her and touched his index finger to Sam's little palm. "Have you come up with any answers?"

She bit the inside of her cheek and shook her head. However, realizing this was an opportunity to voice her thoughts, she said, "I am not certain, but I believe you are right about Cal. He wouldn't have easily given up the babies without getting something in return. He would have demanded payment." Cal had once arrived at the sewing shop and threatened to kill Stella if Fanny didn't give him a few dollars. Thankfully, her brothers had arrived before she could fish a few dollars from her reticule. "I am certain Mr. Davies would not have given him a thing." She tilted her chin a little. "Come to think of it, I believe Mr. Davies disliked him enough to have apprehended him and taken him to the marshal if he showed his face around the railroad workers. Cal didn't have a friend among them."

"Then why wouldn't they speak to me?"

"As much as they dislike Cal, they don't trust outsiders." She drew her legs to her chest and hugged them. "I've thought about little else today, Graham. I tried to place myself in Stella's shoes, and in Cal's and Mr. Davies's, and nothing makes sense. If—if something happened to Stella to keep her from giving the babies up herself, Cal wouldn't have given them up to me. And I don't believe Stella would have given them up unless she felt it was necessary."

"You think my sister is alive?"

She drew in a breath and dropped her gaze to Lily Rose when she let out a coo. She didn't want to give Graham false hope, but she didn't want to consider Cal was out there somewhere waiting to wreak havoc on her and the twins. "For their sakes, I hope so. But, Graham, I honestly don't know. I fear she isn't, and if she is, something is keeping her from her children. No mother would abandon her children willingly, of that, I am certain."

Had Stella known she was wanted for bank robbery? Fanny guessed so since she'd used an alias. A name that seemed to set Graham's jaw to stone and his back rigid whenever it was mentioned.

"Dinner is about ready," Eunice said. "Mr. Staddler, would you mind fetching my pa?"

"Yes, of course, Miss Gilbert." Graham held Fanny's gaze for a moment and then rose to his feet. "Thank you, Fanny, for your honesty. You've given me some things to ponder."

Fanny swallowed the knot in her throat. She hadn't been completely honest. She wasn't sure how Graham would react if she told him about Mr. Davies's warning. She just needed to keep her eyes and ears open until her brothers returned. They would help her reason out her suspicions about Cal. Fanny changed the babies' nappies and tucked them into their makeshift cribs. She made her way toward the dining table. "What can I do to help?"

"If you would set the plates. The bread turned out wonderful."

"Thank you," Fanny said. "I suppose the proof will be in how it tastes. If it's good, I owe it to your instruction."

Eunice laughed. "I'm certain it's the beating the dough took."

Heat filled Fanny's cheeks. "I'll remember that the next time."

"My I ask you a question?" Eunice asked.

"I suppose it depends on what you ask," Fanny responded.

Eunice twisted her hands into her apron and stared at the floor. "Well, I was wondering if you'd teach me how to shoot."

Out of all the things Fanny thought Eunice was going to ask, that was not it. Usually, people wanted to know why she hadn't married yet.

"I saw you save Mr. Staddler the way you did this morning, and I think learning to shoot is a practical skill for a woman on the prairie to know. I'd like that."

Before Fanny could respond, Graham and Mr. Gilbert stepped through the door. Eunice busied herself with laying out the food as if she hadn't asked Fanny to teach her a practical skill. The men took off their hats and hung them on the hooks. Graham's had left an impression in his blond curls, and Fanny's fingers itched to fluff them back into place, but then her mind went to Clea, and she wondered if she'd been a lady who did such things for Graham at one time after he came in from a hard day of chores. The more she pondered the thought, the more the question burned on her tongue, but the four of them were about to sit down and eat at the table. It seemed that was an idea foreign to Graham, given that he stared at the spread like it was a rabid dog out to get him. One arm crossed his chest, while the other propped his chin.

"I think Eunice cooked it well enough. It isn't going to bite you," Fanny teased as she set the gravy bowl in the center of the table.

Graham's blue eyes flicked to hers. His long lashes kissed his tanned cheekbones. He dropped his arms to his sides, pulled out a chair for her. Fanny scooted into the seat and inhaled. The scent of creamy gravy and the distinct smell of crispy fried chicken had her closing her eyes. "Smells right fine, too. Better than Moore's, I think."

"Now, Miss Ellis, don't you be starting rumors to get my gal in trouble," Mr. Gilbert laughed. "Although, Eunice's chicken is a mite better than Moore's, if I say so myself. She has taken my mother's recipes and perfected them."

"Oh, Papa, do hush. Thank you, Fanny." Hands covered in thick quilted pads, Eunice settled a platter piled with chicken next to the gravy and then sat in the chair Graham held out for her. "The recipe is my grandmother's. That's where I learned to cook. Before I followed Papa to Kansas."

Graham went to check on the babies and then hovered near the table. He'd seemed right as rain only moments before he retrieved Mr. Gilbert. Now, his face looked as if an alarming storm approached and he didn't know where to put himself.

"Graham," Fanny said, capturing his distracted attention. "It's been a long day, and I believe we could all use the sustenance to carry us through the evening. Would you mind sitting a spell?"

Graham's knuckles whitened when he clasped the chair.

"Fanny made the bread rolls," Eunice said.

The legs scratched against the floor and the chair groaned in tandem with Graham's sigh as he sat. Before Graham was able to scoot his chair forward, Mr. Gilbert dropped his head to pray. Fanny caught the unsettled look in Graham's eyes. She reached out and touched his hand.

"Amen," Eunice said after her father, breaking the awkwardness of Fanny's fingers upon Graham's warm sun-soaked hand.

Mr. Gilbert poked a piece of chicken with a fork from the top and handed it to Graham. "Go on, try it. Meat so tender it'll melt in your mouth."

Graham took the crunchy thigh and dropped it on his plate. Fanny snagged a drumstick and then added potatoes and gravy to her plate, but it was the golden, flaky slice of bread she sank her teeth into first. "Mmm," Fanny said as she savored the flavors in her mouth. "You wouldn't happen to be looking for a husband, would you? I mean, I know I made the bread and all, but it wasn't without your guidance."

The dishes clattered at the flinch of Graham's knee against the table. Fanny laughed. "You have a fear of matrimony, Graham. I've seen it a thousand times whenever the topic of marriage enters my brothers' hearing. No need to worry. I wasn't thinking about you anyhow."

"I appreciate that, Fanny." His shoulders relaxed, and he leaned forward to bite into his chicken.

Fanny smiled at Eunice, who broke off a dainty piece of white meat and popped it into her mouth. The turn of conversation removed Cal from her inner thoughts, which suited her just fine.

"I have three wifeless brothers. Eunice can have her pick. They're handsome enough, I suppose, and they have a strong appreciation for good cooking."

Besides, they'd always praised Eunice for one thing or another. Her beauty, her genteel, graceful glide as she moved across the dance floor. Her smile. Her scent. The way her brothers spoke, Eunice Gilbert came straight from Heaven.

Eunice continued to take small bites. Fanny sank her teeth into the soft bread, chewed and swallowed it down with a glass of lemonade. She wasn't about to give up. If Eunice took it in her head to marry one of her brothers, Fanny would be pleased as punch. She hadn't liked Eunice overly much before yesterday, the gal was too perfect by halves, but she could now see any of her brothers would be blessed to have her. Not to mention she felt they were becoming good friends. "Hiram's the oldest."

"Fanny, if you don't mind," Eunice interrupted her, "I'm not looking to get married."

"Much to my displeasure," Mr. Gilbert said around a mouthful of potatoes.

"I've seen what the state of matrimony has done to my sisters. They've become shells of themselves. Nothing more than unpaid servants shackled to the whims of their husbands. No thank you."

Fanny blinked back her surprise. She'd never heard of a genteel lady not wanting to procure a husband. She thought all women wanted to get married, become wives and dutifully serve their husbands. Even Fanny had had dreams of marrying, until she met her thirtieth summer and realized that dream had long disappeared beneath the prairie dust. "I don't understand. Every woman I've crossed paths with talks about marrying. It's the thing to do, their only aspiration in life."

A quick look at Mr. Gilbert and Graham told her they agreed. So why did Eunice feel differently? Especially since she cooked so well and knew how to care for both babies while Fanny fumbled around.

"Not mine. I would never marry without love, and I'm sad to say most unions are not fashioned in love, but rather out of convenience. Why, my oldest sister married her husband before she'd ever met him. You cannot tell me they loved each other," Eunice said matter-of-factly.

"Now, Eunice," Mr. Gilbert said. "To be fair, they've come to love each other."

"The fact remains, they didn't before they took their vows and made promises to love each other. That is a risk not worth taking." Eunice drew in a breath. "I want to open my own restaurant. I want to be a business owner and run my own life without a man telling me what to do and when to do it."

"Marriage can't be all that bad," Fanny said. "I'm certain there are marriages formed out of love."

Eunice shook her head. "I have no doubt that if you ask any lady of Oak Grove, she'll tell you otherwise. Fashionably, love has nothing to do with marriage. It's for a woman's survival as there aren't many options available for a viable life for her without marriage. I do not want to feel as if I'm dependent on a man. You, Fanny, have inspired me. You are your own woman and have made your own way."

Fanny blinked. She hadn't made her own way. Certainly, she was not married and didn't have a husband to please, but she did have brothers, and they were the ultimate authority in this house, which was why she wanted to move into the boarding house. "As a man, how do you feel about the idea of marriage, Graham?"

"Can we talk about something else," Graham's gruff tone broke through the sound of silverware scraping against the dishes.

"You're that scared of marriage, you can't even talk about it?" Fanny asked.

He scooted from his chair and stomped out the door without his hat. Fanny's fork full of mashed potatoes bathed in gravy hovered outside her mouth. "What did I say?"

Mr. Gilbert shrugged as he continued to shovel heaping spoonfuls of food into his mouth.

"Do I need to argue my case further?" Eunice asked. "Men need wives to support them in their efforts at making a living, in exchange women marry men to enjoy the fruits of their labor. For some, it is a win-win. For me, I might as well be suffocating in a jail cell."

"Even as a woman of thirty who has not had the opportunity to marry or have children, it saddens me a great deal to think that you feel as you do. Every eligible man in the vicinity speaks highly of you, Eunice. I am certain one of them would make you a decent marriage."

"That is the thing, Fanny. I don't want decent. I want to be loved and to love."

"Can't blame my daughter for that," Mr. Gilbert said. "I've had both sorts of marriage, and the one based on love is preferable."

"I supposed there is merit to having love. Given I've had neither, I assumed all marriages were based on love with the added benefit of convenience." Fanny wiped her mouth. "Now, if you'll excuse me, I think I should apologize to Graham for pushing the conversation when it obviously made him uncomfortable."

She found Graham in the barn, running his fingers down the length of Turnip's nose. "Graham, does this have anything to do with Clea?"

His shoulders tensed.

"She was your wife, wasn't she?" She wasn't certain how she'd arrived at that conclusion. Perhaps it was the way he was an easygoing sort of man until

Clea's name was mentioned or the topic of marriage was brought up. Then he ran like a chicken from a fox. Fanny sensed his displeasure, but she pressed on.

"You have everyone walking on eggshells." Mainly her, but she wasn't going to let him know that. Eunice and Mr. Gilbert seemed to keep their mouths closed when it came to irritating Graham Staddler. "We can't rightly know what is going to upset you if you don't tell us. Your sister was known in town as Clea Anderson, not Stella James. So I guess I'm saying you're going to hear Clea's name, because that's how Oak Grove knows your sister. And you can't run off every time you hear the name." By the time she had her words out, her fists were clenched at her sides.

He swung around and stabbed his fingers through his lush golden curls. "My sister's name is Stella."

"And your wife's name was Clea. Clea Anderson, at least before she married you. Then it was Clea Staddler." His silence told her all she needed to know. She drew in a breath and continued to trudge toward deeper, darker waters. She prayed the good Lord would help her out here, because she didn't know how to swim, and she sensed the question burning the tip of her tongue was as important to Graham as it was to her.

"Graham," she whispered as she shook her head. "I am sorry. I know those words don't offer much balm, and I've never loved another, but they are all I have."

A tear escaped the rim of his lashes and slid down

his cheek. His jaw flexed. He had the look of a man who'd kept all his emotion in a bottle and put a cork in it. She'd seen it with Hiram after their parents had been murdered and he took on the responsibility of their family. She'd only been seven, but she'd understood the change in him, the change in all of them after their parents' deaths. "I may not have lost a spouse, but I know grief."

He remained stiff as a large oak tree rooted to withstand a squall. He stared at a spot over her shoulder. She shifted, and her skirts danced around her legs, then she took a step forward and touched his forearm. "Graham, it's all right to mourn the woman you loved."

Stormy blue eyes flicked toward her, but it felt like he was looking through her, not at her. "I didn't know your wife, but I imagine she—I imagine Clea wouldn't want you to run each time someone said her name. In fact, I'm near certain that if I were her and I had loved a man as fine as you, I'd want him to smile every time he heard my name in remembrance of the time we'd spent together. I'm sure Clea would feel the same."

His lids slid closed. He drew in a ragged breath and several tears streamed down his cheeks. They sparkled like diamonds in his beard.

"Three years," he choked out.

Fanny nodded as she took another step toward him so she could comfortably weave her fingers through his calloused ones. She waited.

"Clea—and our son," he murmured.

A sharp breath of air hit the back of Fanny's throat. Graham had a son? No wonder he was so good with the twins.

"They got real sick. Nothing I could do."

"Oh, Graham," she cried, wrapping her arms around his waist. She squeezed, pressing her head against his side so her own tears would dry on his shirt. "I am so sorry. I didn't know."

"I tried. The doctor couldn't help. No one could, not even God."

She pulled away and glanced up at his tear-stained cheeks. "Graham—"

"No, darling, I don't blame God. I blame myself. I should have been a better man, a better husband."

Before she knew what she was about, her fingers reached up and captured a liquid diamond. "I can't imagine you weren't good enough, Graham. Sometimes there just isn't a reason. When we go looking for excuses why God didn't help us in our time of need, we start rewriting God's story and that's not our job." His furrowed brow creased further, and she continued to explain. "If you blame yourself, it's because you see shortcomings where none exist. You're doubting God's love for you. What Jesus did on the cross no longer becomes about His love for a fallen world, but about our efforts to earn our way into His grace."

Turnip neighed as if in agreement. She felt her thoughts resonant deeply in her. It had taken years for her to understand these truths, but once she had, she clung to them.

Graham slid down the wall of the horse stall and brought Fanny down beside him. His arm was secured around her shoulder, but more importantly, her ear was nestled against the beat of his heart. "You mind if we sit here a spell while I ponder your words?"

She wouldn't leave if a twister were barreling toward them. All she knew at the moment was that she wanted to be by Graham for as long as he would allow her. It just felt right. However, she wouldn't allow herself to be lured into opening her heart to him. She cared for him, and they had the twins to consider, but love wasn't an option. She'd missed that mark now that she was thirty, nearly thirty-one, and Graham had loved already. Now she understood why he was right scared of the word *marriage*. He'd suffered enough with the loss of his son and wife, and she wanted more than anything to protect him from such a loss again, which meant helping him find his sister alive.

"I gave up on God a long time ago, and I'm not certain how I can come to terms with Him," he whispered.

"Believe it or not, I understand, Graham." She shuddered on her sigh. "I watched my parents' murder. I was only seven, but I blamed myself for hiding instead of stopping it."

Graham stilled the circles he drew on her hand. "That is ridiculous, Fanny. You know that, right?"

"Just as ridiculous as it is for you to think you could have saved your wife and son?" she asked.

"Graham, you are known for your heroic deeds and your uncommon chivalry. There is no doubt in my mind that you did everything you possibly knew how to do to make them well."

He didn't say a word, but when he resumed drawing circles on her hand, she thought he might be considering her words a little. She hoped he was. She thought about asking, but she was fully content listening to his heartbeat against her ear.

Graham startled awake and realized his arm was weighed down. His side was warm, hot even. He eased his eyes open and peered into the inky dark. The shuffle of a hoof along with the sweet scent of hay revealed his location. He must have fallen asleep in the barn.

He glanced at his chest and made out Fanny's fiery red curls nestled against him. The soft cadence of her breath and her long slender palm pale against his shirt lured him into a false sense of security. He could remain here holding her until the morning light spread over the eastern sky. He listened to the air move around them, felt the rise and fall of her breaths and basked in the scent of a field of wildflowers with her beside him.

But this temptation came with consequences. Consequences that would break an oath he'd made to himself, out of spite, to God. His heart lay buried with his wife, and he could not allow it to surface. Not even for a woman like Fanny, who was straightforward, kind and selfless. She was precious. As he'd told her earlier, she was a rare gem. She was so precious and needed someone to care for her the way she deserved, and he was not the man for the job. Proof of his inability to protect a family resided deep in the ground.

He shifted his hand to shake Fanny awake and immediately recalled their conversation about loss and grief. He could not remember falling asleep, a sleep more sound than he'd had in years. She rubbed the sleep from her eyes, and Graham sensed her gaze upon him. He sensed her smile. He drew in a breath but didn't say a word. Thankfully, she didn't, either.

He hoped they would both forget about this little incident and move on as if nothing had happened. However, he knew he'd never forget the feel of her against his chest, or the way she seemed to fit so perfectly against him. Or how nice it was to wake up with her at his side.

Low voices mumbled, and Turnip echoed a neigh from Daisy. A lantern floated toward them, growing larger as it drew closer. Graham reached up to shield his eyes from the brightness, not knowing if Mr. Gilbert had come looking for them or if danger lurked.

The height of the lantern seemed much higher than Mr. Gilbert. Graham shifted, readying himself to lurch at the intruders. Fanny pushed away from him, her long red curls untangled against his arm. She rolled to her feet and crouched. A pistol flashed in her hand, and Graham marveled at her swift actions. She'd readied and drawn her pistol faster than any man he'd known, maybe even faster than himself. The fact that he had yet to move only proved he was becoming too comfortable with his surroundings. Time on the Ellis farm was softening his reflexes.

"Francis Elanor Ellis," a man's voice rumbled through the barn, causing Fanny to flinch. The pistol in her hand trembled. Graham scrambled to his feet and pushed Fanny behind him.

The lamp light illuminated a man tall enough to look him in the eye. Thunderclouds creased the man's brow, and his eyebrows were knit together. The burnished curls cutting against the man's collar told Graham all he needed to know. This man was one of the infamous Ellis brothers. A brother who fiercely protected his sister's spinsterhood.

Fanny swatted Graham's arm and moved in front of him. She slipped her pistol into her pocket and thrust her hands on her hips. "What are you two doing back so early?"

Two? Graham shifted his gaze to the other man in the shadows near the barn door. Head bent, arms crossed, Graham knew the man was contemplating his actions, and he hoped they didn't include murder.

"The question is what are you doing out here with a strange man? In the dark, no less?" Lantern light caught the silver end of a gun in the man's right hand. Graham swallowed.

"It's not what it looks like, Nathan," Fanny said, and then she looked around her brother's shoulder to catch the other man's attention. "Hiram, tell him."

The man called Hiram shrugged.

Nathan moved a step closer. "Tell me, little sister, what is it you think it looks like, then? We've been in Oak Grove nearly two hours and heard all sorts of tales about you having a strange man living up here."

"A strange man who happens to be helping me with two infants who were left in my care."

"You're playing house?" Nathan seethed, his knuckles white around the butt of his gun. Graham was thankful his finger wasn't on the trigger.

"To be fair," Graham interjected, "I recruited the help of the Gilberts, who were nice enough to act as chaperones until my sister can be found."

"And where might they be? Out here in the barn in the dark with the two of you?" Graham sensed the man's cheeks were probably crimson enough to match the color of his hair. It was difficult to tell with the added glow of the lantern. "What exactly was it the two of you were doing?"

"Sleeping!" Fanny belted out at the top of her lungs.

Graham felt the world grow dark as her single word thrust into his heart. Both brothers rocked back on their heels as if they'd been knocked over by a gust of wind.

"Fanny," the quieter brother, Hiram, said. "I think it's time you run up to the house and help Miss Gilbert while we speak to Mr. Staddler."

"Mr. Staddler, is it?" she questioned as she leaned forward. "I don't recall giving you his name, which means you know good and well why he is here."

"He's not here to sleep with *my* sister in a dark barn," Nathan growled and reached for her arm.

Graham pushed himself between them, not knowing if her brother was the sort of man to abuse a lady. He turned to Fanny. "It's all right. I'm sure Miss Gilbert has her hands full with the twins."

Fanny narrowed her eyes, and he thought she would argue, but they softened, and she nodded her agreement. She stepped around him and poked a finger into her brother's chest. "If you hurt him, so help me, Nathan Ellis, I'll hang you up by your toes."

The shorter brother stepped into the light, and Graham could see the loving expression in his eyes. "You have my word he won't be harmed. We just need to talk to him."

"Thank you, Hiram." She looked between each of them. Shoulders pulled back as if she were about to face an army, she swept out of the barn, and Graham immediately felt a chill fall on him.

Graham crossed his arms but forced his legs to relax as he assessed the brothers until he heard the door to the farmhouse close. "All right, I know what it looks like, but I'll do right by her for the good of Sam and Lily Rose."

They'd have a difficult time growing up as it was since their mother would spend most of her life behind bars somewhere. He'd do right by Fanny to stop any rumors that might cause harm to the twins. Didn't mean he would stay in Oak Grove, though. Holding her next to him had been too much of a delight, one he could get used to over time if he ever forgot his failures as a husband and father.

"We'll discuss our sister later. First, we come bearing news you may not want to hear," Hiram said.

"I don't want to hear I'm going to be married. What could you have to say that would be worse?"

Nathan leaned forward. "My sister is a fine catch. Any man would be honored to have her."

"Not saying they wouldn't. I just wasn't planning on taking a wife. Ever." Graham thrust his fingers through his hair.

Hiram's gaze flicked toward his brother. "We're not married ourselves, so we understand. But as I said, we'll discuss Fanny at another time. Right now, you need to ride to town with us."

"In the dark?"

"Didn't stop you from holding our sister in your arms," Nathan shot off.

Heat rushed into his cheeks. How could he have been so foolish? How could he have let his guard down? Because Fanny had ambushed him with her straightforward questions and her compassion. Years of grief had been released in a few tears, and for the first time in a long time, he felt unhindered by guilt.

"Nate, shut it," Hiram said. "We found your sister out on the cattle drive. Of course, we didn't know it was her until we brought her back to town. She's at Doc's."

"Thank the Lord," Graham said, relief nearly taking him to his knees. "Wait… Doc's? Is she all right?"

The brothers remained silent.

Fear clenched his heart. "She's alive?"

Hiram nodded.

Nathan said, "Don't know for how long, though. She was beaten badly. Left for dead."

Graham scrubbed his hand over his jaw. If he weren't experiencing such a great deal of guilt over Stella's circumstances, he'd chase Cal down and make him pay for his crimes. "Fanny will want to see her, and Stella will want to see her babies."

Stella would want to see the good she was leaving behind in the world. She needed to see the good she was leaving behind so she could go in peace. He needed her to see the good. He needed to assure her he and Fanny would take care of her babies.

"We thought as much, too." Hiram clamped his shoulder. "I'm sorry we brought you bad news."

"Don't be sorry," Graham said. "I am thankful you brought her back to me."

Chapter Eleven

Fanny twined her fingers together as they approached Doctor Harden's office. Welcoming candles lit the front windows, and the warm glow belied what Fanny feared they were walking into. She hadn't liked riding to town in the dark, especially with Lily Rose and Sam, but she understood they didn't have much time to see Stella, or for her to see her babies. The fact two of her brothers and Graham rode with them had set her at ease. After hearing about some of Stella's wounds from her brothers, Fanny knew Cal had gotten hold of her and left her for dead. She didn't voice her suspicions to her brothers or Graham for fear they'd make her stay home with the twins. That instinct, unfounded by anything other than her gut, had her scanning the dark for moving shadows, listening for noises other than the horses and the buckboard, and her pistol at the ready.

Hiram pulled back on the reins. The buckboard rolled to a stop, and before she could maneuver little

Sam so she could climb to the ground, Graham was there holding out his hands.

"I'll take him," he said. Fanny handed him the baby and then took his offered hand. She turned to Eunice and noticed Hiram helping her with Lily Rose. Feet on the ground, she motioned for Graham to hand Sam back to her. Since he'd have his attention on his sister and Doctor Harden, he didn't need a fussy infant distracting him.

Eunice sidled next to Fanny and shook out her skirts. "Can't say I've ever traveled in the dark before."

"Thank you for coming, Eunice," Fanny said. "I wasn't certain how I'd manage both babies."

"Not to mention your brothers and Graham," she responded. "The ride was silent, but you couldn't hack the tension away with an axe."

"I'm sure the condition of Stella has a great deal to do with that." Fanny had noticed the tension and tried to ignore it, hoping the atmosphere had nothing to do with her brothers finding her asleep in the barn. In Graham's arms. She didn't recall going to sleep, only holding him as he shed the tears he'd kept shackled for way too long.

The door to Doctor Harden's office swung open. The doctor wiped his hands on a cloth. His lack of greeting sent a chill of dread down her spine. Had they arrived too late? Was Stella gone?

"I suppose you two should go on in," Hiram said.

"Not without an escort," Nathan snapped as he tied the reins of his horse to the hitching post near Doc's front porch.

Fanny glared. "I don't need an escort. Graham is a gentleman. Unlike someone else I know."

"The fact you call him by his Christian name says you need a chaperon."

"Gravy, Nathan! We're here to see his dying sister, will you beg off a moment?"

"Let her be, Nathan" Eunice said, giving him a narrowed gaze. Nathan's mouth opened and closed until he finally clamped his lips shut, much to Fanny's surprise. She'd never seen anyone make Nathan speechless. Eunice took Sam from her arms. "Go on now. We'll bring the twins in when you're ready for them to see their mama."

"Thank you," Fanny whispered.

Fanny touched the back of Graham's arm as he paused at the base of Doctor Harden's stairs. She didn't expect him to turn around or even acknowledge her gesture of comfort. When he reached back and squeezed her fingers, a spark leaped in her heart. She told herself it was only a reaction to the fact that it looked like he was about to experience more loss after he'd suffered so much grief in the last few years. Another loss he seemed to blame himself for. He carried too many burdens on his shoulders. She'd like to tell him he wasn't God, but she feared he'd jump on Turnip and ride off into the inky night.

He swept his hat off his head and settled it against his thigh. "Shall we?"

Fanny nodded and stepped beside him. They twined their fingers and climbed the stairs together.

"Mr. Staddler," Doctor Harden greeted him with

an outstretched hand. "I wish we were meeting under better circumstances. Your sister, she's hanging in there, but I fear it won't be much longer. She's mighty anxious about something, though."

Graham shifted his weight, forcing Fanny's fingers to loosen from his. He looked Doctor Harden in the eye. "She was beaten that badly?"

Doctor Harden looked between them until he settled back on Graham. "The Ellis brothers didn't tell you?"

"No, sir. Just that she was beaten and left for dead," Graham said, his Adam's apple bobbing, "and not long for this world."

"She was beaten. Never seen anything like it, though." Doc's hand settled on the door. "There's more and you should prepare yourself, Mr. Staddler. I've had the occasion to see your sister when she was in town, and, well, she isn't anything like she was. In fact, Fanny, if I were you, I'd stay out here. It's not a sight for a lady."

Fanny stiffened, but before she could open her mouth to speak, Graham did. "I'm quite certain Miss Ellis's delicate nature can handle what is on the other side of this door, Doctor Harden. And if she can't, well then she can lean on me until she's ready to leave."

She had her own thoughts and her own voice, and she sure knew how to use them, but she was mighty grateful to Graham at the moment. Odd, though, since she disliked when her brothers got all heavy-handed and spoke for her.

Doctor Harden opened the door. Graham's boots stayed rooted to the floor. Fanny's gasp clung to her throat as if her life depended on it. She didn't want either man to shove her out the room because of what they considered a weak constitution. However, if she didn't gather herself, she was going to lose what little dinner she had eaten. Drawing in a breath, she rushed to Stella's side and smoothed strands of hair caked with blood from her friend's face. "Oh, Clea!" Fanny whispered and then corrected herself. "Stella. I am sorry. I should have—"

"Fanny?" Stella croaked as her discolored hand floated toward Fanny's cheek.

Stella made a slight movement of her head, and Fanny was certain Stella knew Graham stood near the door.

"Graham, you came. Didn't think you would after all I'd done to you."

Stella's garbled and slurred words passed broken teeth and deformed lips. There was a large slice cut from the top of her mouth and across her chin. There was another gaping hole in the side of her cheek. If Fanny had any doubts about Cal James being dead, seeing Stella's condition told her he was alive and out for blood. Mr. Davies' warning rang an alarm in her heart. Fanny swallowed the bile burning the back of her throat. She wanted to run from the room. Not because she thought she would be ill, but because she believed Cal would come for the twins, and he wasn't going to be nice about it. But if she ran out of here, Graham might follow her, and Stella had something she wanted to say. She could wait a few moments more, and once they were home and safe, she'd tell her brothers and Graham she believed Cal would come for the babies.

Cal was the worst sort, but even this was beyond what Fanny thought him capable of doing. A gag worked up Fanny's throat, but she choked it back down and continued to stroke Stella's head.

Graham's boots sounded against the hardwood floors. His fingers hovered over Stella's hand as if he was afraid to touch her. "You haven't done a thing wrong to me."

"Ishouldhavecometoyou." Herdarklashestwitched, and the tip of her tongue darted out to moisten her disfigured lips. "So you'd know, I wouldn't have done what they say I did if I'd had a choice."

Kneeling beside the bed, Graham folded her hand between his. He rested his head on their folded hands. "I know, Stella. I know."

"Fanny, I'm sorry. I shouldn't have stolen from you."

"Shh," Fanny said. "You did not cause me any hardship."

"You have the babies?"

"I do." Fanny didn't like the rattled breathing coming from Stella's chest and imagined the noise unsettled Graham, too, so she kept talking to drown out the noise. "Wasn't sure about their names, so we've been calling them Lily Rose and Sam."

If Stella's mouth weren't so swollen, Fanny was certain she'd smile. "I like that. A lot. Davies, he's a good. Hid me, the babies. Dug a grave to show Cal if he came. Davies said he'd give them to you. She moistened her lips and glanced at Graham. "I was turning myself in—but Cal," she mumbled and lift her hand. "He found me."

"Would you like to see them?" Fanny asked, ready to run from the small room for a breath of fresh air, one that wasn't tainted with death.

Stella shook her head. "I know…they're y-oung. I can't. Not. Like. This. Tried my best. They need a good mother."

Fanny's head bobbed up and down. "They'll know what a wonderful mother you were, Stella."

"You." Stella breathed out, pointing her finger toward Fanny. "I. Know. You'll love 'em. Like your own. Protect them from him."

"I will." With everything she had in her. She'd keep Cal James from destroying two innocents like he had their mother.

"Graham." Stella paused and took several shallow breaths. "You didn't ask for this. Sorry, brother. I shamed you."

"Don't." Graham's one word cut through the room as if he could keep Stella from saying all she had to say. As if he could turn time backward and undo all that had been done.

"You are, good man, Graham." Stella reached her hand up and touched his jaw. "Don't deserve the pain you've suffered."

His Adam's apple worked in his throat. A muscle ticked beneath his beard, making the curly thickness tick, too. A tear slipped over the rim of his eyelid and disappeared into the beard.

"Protect them, too?"

He flinched at his sister's question as if he'd been on the receiving end of a horsewhip, and Fanny wondered if he would deny her an answer. She knew he blamed himself for the death of his wife and son. She was fairly certain he blamed himself for Stella's situation, too.

Graham was a man bent on shouldering the evils of this world. If only Fanny could make him see that wasn't his responsibility, make him see all he was coming to mean to her. But it was useless. He'd be leaving soon. Now that he'd found Stella, he'd leave quicker than a duster blowing across the prairie, leaving a trail of destruction in its wake.

Just like grasses regrew and trees renewed their limbs in the spring, she would be fine. She'd need to do nothing more than dust off her knees. She didn't need him. She'd care for the babies without his help,

"I will." Graham spoke in a low whisper. "That's a promise."

Fanny was taken aback by the spoken words. Even more by the promise. However, she knew he needed to move on, to keep one foot ahead of his grief. She'd release him from the vow made to a dying woman. Release him from any responsibility he might feel toward the twins. They were hers now.

Stella squeezed her eyes shut and dipped her chin toward her chest in thanks.

"They're my kin, Stella. I love them like I love you. I'll love them as I loved Jacob."

Fanny turned fully toward him. That's why he'd been fiery mad earlier after she'd mentioned her mother's surname. No wonder he'd barked at her when she suggested they name Stella's boy Jacob. She should have known he wouldn't get angry without cause, without pain, like an injured dog cornered. She might as well have poured salt in his wounds.

"Thank you." A tear tainted pink with the wounds marring her eyes slid down the side of her cheek. Fanny wiped it dry, leaving her own tears to stream at will. "Hear me, Graham. He's coming. For. Them. For. Fanny."

Fanny stroked Stella's brow and waited for her to say more. She assumed Stella meant Cal. Just let him show his cowardly face in her presence. Let him try to take her babies.

Air struggled its way into Stella's lungs. Her chest rose and then rumbled as she breathed out. For several long seconds, Fanny stared at Stella's chest, waiting for another rise. Fanny held her own breath until she thought Doc would have to fetch the smelling salts, then another force of air rattled through Stella. Her chest expanded and deflated again. Graham climbed to his feet, and Fanny heard his boots clatter across the floor, the front door open and click shut. Fanny continued to wait, counting seconds between breaths, but no more came.

She pulled herself off the floor and shook out her skirts. She gazed down at the lifeless woman for a second, trying to recall how she'd looked before Cal's brutal hand had destroyed her. That's when she saw the locket draped around Stella's neck. Fanny lifted it in her fingers and opened it. Inside were pictures of a younger Stella and Graham. It must have belonged to their mother, the babies' grandmother. Fanny unhooked the clasp and dropped it into her pocket. She branded an image of the once-beautiful woman into her memory so she could recall picture for the children left behind as they grew older.

"Go in peace, Stella. Don't you worry. I'll do right by your babies." *And your brother, too.* The thought came unbidden, and Fanny tucked it away in the back of her mind. Once Graham left Oak Grove, he'd be gone for good.

Graham smashed his hat onto his head. Tears burned, threatening to spill. He had every right to mourn the loss of his sister. However, he did not have the time. If Cal was coming after Fanny and the babies, Graham couldn't be idle. He wouldn't risk Fanny or the twins. Which meant he had to hunt Cal down before the scent grew cold.

He caught movement in his peripheral vision. His hand flashed to the hilt resting on his hip, and he snapped his six shooter out in front of him as he scanned the darkness. Was Cal lurking there?

"Whoa!" Nathan held his hands up in front of him and positioned himself in front of Hiram and Eunice, who held his niece and nephew. There were three sets of eyes on him. Eunice, Hiram and Nathan stood near enough to the front porch for him to see the varied expressions on their faces. Eunice's held the paleness of the moon. The men were wary, cautious. They'd known the state of his sister. Hiram dropped his gaze to the baby in his arms. Nathan cleared his throat and then twisted his mouth. "Mind holstering your gun?"

Graham glanced to his hand. He gulped and dropped the barrel into the holster. He shook off the need for revenge. He'd never been a man out for blood and had always taken precautions to do the best he could to keep from taking a life. He needed to gather himself before he set off to formulate a plan of action, one that should not include killing Cal James, no matter how much he wanted to. Even though the scoundrel deserved it and worse. "Guess I'm a little jittery."

"As expected," Hiram said.

"Don't know what I'd do if Fanny were the one beat up in there," Nathan said. "I imagine I'd be looking for a fight and seeking revenge."

Revenge wasn't his way, which is why the last ranch boss had hired him. Graham had a reputation for calmness and an even temper. "Not my way."

"Are you ready for Lily Rose and Sam to go?" Eunice asked hopefully as she glided toward him with her arms outstretched. "I daresay I've done all I could not to intrude. Such sweet things should see their mama."

Graham's teeth locked together. Tears attacked his eyes. He stepped off the porch and strode toward

Turnip. He grabbed the reins and shoved a boot into the stirrup. Before he climbed into the saddle, a hand clamped on his shoulder, one offering comfort.

"I am so sorry, Graham," Nathan said, surprising Graham.

The young man had shown him nothing but discord since they'd arrived back in Oak Grove, and rightly so. If he'd been a better brother, one as good as Nathan Ellis was to his sister, maybe Stella wouldn't be ready for the grave.

"I'll do right by your sister and give her my name when I return." Graham shrugged off Nathan's hand and climbed into the saddle. "I'm going after the scoundrel. Where'd you find Stella?"

The black of night threatened to swallow him as he listened to Hiram's detailed directions. "Don't you think you should wait until Stella's in the ground?"

Part of him beckoned the nothingness to swallow him, but the other part fought to find a flicker of light to keep him from drowning in his failure and grief. The soft click of the door drew his attention to the doctor's home. Fanny was silhouetted by the flickering lights, her small frame and fiery red locks glinting in the light. Everything in him shouted at him to protect her, and the only way he knew how to do that was to hunt down the man threatening her and the twins. To snuff out the threat. "No time. Can't let the trail grow cold."

Stella's words had pierced him like the sharp end of a penknife to the throat. He'd seen the life seeping from his sister, heard the death rattle quaking her body as she slipped from this world to the next. When he'd seen her lying there almost unrecognizable, battered and beaten, all he could think of was revenge, but that wasn't his way. Never had been.

Papa had always told him to turn the other cheek, and he did. Most of the time. But there hadn't been an exposed area of flesh that wasn't colored by Cal's abuse. Stella's skin had been nothing more than a slab of meat for his knife. Graham knew the marks etched in his sister's flesh would haunt him for months to come. How could he turn the other cheek to that? Especially since the same man who'd caused his sister that sort of pain threatened to come after Fanny?

Stella's garbled plea, the dire warning, would remain with him until he knew Fanny and the babies were safe. Free from Cal's threats.

"Graham," Fanny's soft voice cut through the fog. "Are you leaving?"

Yes! He wanted to shout, but to be honest he had no idea where he was going beyond hunting down a rabid dog who needed to be put down. He shook his head and then realized Fanny probably couldn't see his response. "I need to find him before he makes good on his threats. Will you see to Stella? Have the marshal wire Fort Scott of her death?"

There was no need to look for a bank robber when she was dead.

"Your—your sister is gone?" Eunice asked. At his nod, she bowed her head and mumbled a small prayer. A prayer that was far too late for Stella.

"Graham," Fanny said as she placed her hand on

his leg. Somehow, she'd moved across the yard with the swiftness of a hound on a trail. "You're not going after Cal, are you?"

He ground his teeth together and pulled a harsh breath into his lungs.

"It'll wait, Graham. We'll get the marshal. My brothers will go."

"And leave you unprotected?" Turnip danced beneath him. Dust shot up from under his hooves, reminding Graham of the long days on the trail. Cal could be anywhere, but if he rode out to where the Ellis brothers had found Stella, he could hope for a lead. "I can't wait. The trail is growing cold as it is."

Her hand slid from his leg, and her eyes narrowed to mere slits. "You think he's going to keep moving west? Then go ahead and follow your trail. I'll stay right here and fight the scoundrel when he comes for the babies, because that is what he is going to do. He's going to come for me, and he knows where to find me."

She had a point. Maybe he shouldn't leave. Not yet. Although his instincts told him it was best if he did, to head Cal off before he arrived at the Ellis farm. But what if he missed him? What if he followed a lead that led nowhere, like when he'd wasted time taking Fanny out to the railroad camp to question Mr. Davies only to discover the man wasn't there?

Turnip cranked his head and nipped at Graham's leg. Graham drew in a sigh of resignation. His best course of action for Fanny and the twins—for him—was to stick to their side until Cal was apprehended.

A few chunks of the armor guarding his heart tumbled to the ground. He was falling for Fanny, falling for the woman who would soon be his wife whether she knew it or not, which was why he couldn't stay in Oak Grove once their vows were spoken. He gazed down into her beautiful face, but images of his sister's battered one mingled in his vision. If anything happened to Fanny, he wasn't sure what he would do.

The truth was, he was scared to death. Scared that he wouldn't be able to protect Fanny from Cal James.

He couldn't live with himself if he failed another woman he loved.

"Cal James might be a coward, but I've never heard of him not making good on a threat. So you just go right ahead. Do what you think is best, run if you need to, but as you're running away from your grief in the name of hunting down a murderer, the rest of us will be here living, Graham Staddler. We won't be running. If Cal James wants to come after me, he knows where to find me, and I'll be ready."

Graham looked to her brothers, hoping they'd offer some common sense and intervene. He found them busying themselves with helping Eunice onto the buckboard and settling the babies on her lap. Once they were done, they curiously looked away and mounted their horses as if they didn't want to get involved. This was their sister. They should be stepping in and demanding she lock herself in a room until Cal was no longer a threat.

He stalked cattle thieves for a living, and knew they preyed on the innocent and unsuspecting. He didn't like waiting on his prey to make the first move, but this was Cal. He was the worst sort of vermin scurrying the prairie, and after seeing what he'd done to Stella, he couldn't allow Cal anywhere near Fanny. He should have known Cal would target whoever he believed had Sam and Lily Rose, but he'd believed Cal was the one who'd given up the babies. He'd believed Cal James might already be dead.

"You're right. If Cal is going to make good on his threat, he'll come to you." The thought frightened him like he'd never been frightened before. He wanted to hog-tie Fanny and hide her away until he knew she was safe. Until she *and* the twins were safe, he corrected his thoughts. But all his efforts at keeping Clea and Jacob safe had failed him. *Trust in the Lord with all thine heart; and lean not unto thine own understanding. In all thy ways acknowledge him, and he shall direct thy paths.* The passage his mother had quoted as she rocked in her chair before the fire while her wooden knitting needles clicked together came unbidden. He'd prayed all through Clea's illness, but he hadn't trusted. He'd leaned on his own understanding. His anger toward God. His grievances. He hadn't acknowledged God as a higher power, a wise authority or an expert navigator of this life. He'd only acknowledged his own efforts and failures. Maybe it was time he stopped that. No matter what tomorrow might bring, maybe it was time that he hit his knees and just ask God for His will to be done. Not Graham's wishes, but God's will.

"It's not often a man tells me I'm right," she said.

He dismounted, drew Fanny into his arms and buried his head into her neck. He pulled the scent of her into his lungs, and it settled him. She offered him hope and light with one glance. For the first time since Clea and Jacob died, he thought he might want to stay in one place, grow some roots. However, he couldn't allow himself the luxury of handing her his heart, not when it was just beginning to piece itself back together.

He pulled away and gazed down into her mossy green eyes. "I'm not leaving."

Fanny turned and suspiciously wiped at her cheek. Stella must have meant so much to her.

"I won't let Cal hurt you, Fanny"

"Don't stay to protect me." She bawled her hands into fists. "I'm not scared of him. I won't let him intimidate me or harm my babies."

"Fanny," he said, reaching out to her. "I'm staying."

Her chin inched up a notch. "I'm glad. For you, Graham. At some point, a horse runs out of steam and collapses to the ground, spent and too tired to get up. I'd hate to see that on any man, especially you, but don't stay on my account."

He didn't know how to respond. She was right. He was tired, bone-tired from trying to outrun Clea's and Jacob's deaths, but even more than that, he wanted to stay. For her.

Chapter Twelve

Fanny allowed the reins to relax in her hands and gave Daisy her lead. She knew the way home better in the dark than Fanny did in the light.

"My condolences on Stella. I know you two were friends."

Friends? Had they been friends? Stella hadn't trusted her enough to come to her when she needed help the most. Instead, she went to Mr. Davies, and that hurt. If Stella had come to her, perhaps she'd still be alive. Fanny tipped her head toward Eunice, but the dark cloaked any hard expression she might have in her eyes. "Can't exactly say we were friends. Then again, I am not sure what friends are anymore. I've only had acquaintances at school and customers, as you know, but I've never had anyone go out of their way to invite me for tea. believe.

Eunice gasped. "Fanny, I didn't mean to offend you."

"Oh, bother," Fanny said, scratching her head.

"You didn't offend. And I should not have voiced my thoughts aloud. Other ladies do not seek me out for companionship, and I only assume it's because I am rough around the edges, lacking a hem, so to speak, but none of that has to do with this."

Stella may have only come to her for work and the ladies of Oak Grove may not trust her with anything beyond a needle and thread, but it was dealings with Graham that had her thoroughly upset her. She manipulated. She'd used her words to undermine his resolve to leave town.

She waved her hand into the night before she sank against the back of the buckboard. "I am frustrated with myself."

"Why ever so? I can understand being upset over Stella's death, and now you have these two precious beings to worry over, but what has occurred for you to be frustrated with yourself?"

How could she tell Eunice about the confusing thoughts and emotions over Graham when she didn't even understand them herself? "You see, Graham intended to move on and continue with his life as he's been doing with no responsibilities outside of himself and the job he's hired to do. That's the way he likes it. That's what he wants."

"And you don't want him to leave?"

"Exactly," she blurted out and then clamped her mouth shut. "No, I don't care if he leaves or stays."

That was the confusing part. It seemed she'd become accustomed to his presence during the last few days. The way he speared his fingers beneath his hat whenever he stalled for time or was deep in thought. The way he smelled like Turnip and hay and outdoors. The way he sung to the babies whenever they began to fuss. How he was considerate and thoughtful.

"I see," Eunice said.

"I don't think you do," Fanny responded, wondering why she was fiery mad that he'd decided to stay when that was what she really wanted. "He should stay because he wants to, not because he thinks I need protecting. And that is why I am mad."

There. She'd said it. She wanted him to stay for the right reasons, not the wrong ones.

"Hmm… Is Cal a threat to you?"

"I'm not scared of him." Her cheeks burned with indignation.

"That is not the question, Fanny. Is he a threat to you?"

Fanny sighed. "I suppose, but I can take care of myself. My brothers taught me to shoot."

"There is no doubt you can." Eunice shifted on the hard seat, the babies sound asleep in her lap. "Have you maybe considered it is no longer just you? You have two little ones to consider. If anything were to happen to you, if Cal somehow got to you, what would happen to the babies?"

Fanny didn't rightly know. The thought of her brothers taking in orphans was nearly laughable. They'd raised her right fine, but she'd been seven. Lily Rose and Sam weren't even a month old. Fanny shrugged. "Suppose I'll leave them to you."

"I am honored, Fanny, and I would care for them as if they were my own, but don't you think you should lay your pride down and allow their uncle to help protect you and them?"

"It's not about pride." Was it? She'd decided to free him from the deathbed promise to his sister, and then, like a simpering female, manipulated him into standing his ground and staying in Oak Grove. Because that's where Cal would come. And why? Because deep down, as much as she didn't want to need him, she wanted him to stay. But she wanted him to stay because he wanted to, not because he felt obligated to.

"Isn't it?" Eunice asked.

Daisy turned down the lane toward the farmhouse and slowed as she neared the barn. Mr. Gilbert appeared from the barn and helped Fanny down, and then Eunice after Fanny took Lily Rose. "All right as rain?"

Fanny shook her head. "I'm afraid not. Stella has died. The man who killed her… Well, I suggest you and Eunice leave at first light. With my brothers home, I don't need the help any longer, and Mr. Staddler will be leaving in the morning."

She would miss Eunice's cooking and her companionship. If she ever had a friend, she imagined she'd be like Eunice.

"What about Lily Rose and Sam?" Eunice asked, hugging Sam to her chest. "Will they be safe?"

Before she could respond, the clop of horses' hooves announced the arrival of her brothers. She looked over her shoulder to say they'd help keep them all safe, but her gaze locked on Graham. A flutter tapped against her chest, and she nearly sighed. Then she remembered she was mad at him. Or was mad at herself for nearly begging him to stay in Oak Grove when she knew all he really wanted was to leave.

The men dismounted, and Mr. Gilbert offered to brush the horses down. Fanny, not wanting to encounter the object of her ire, took one of the twins from Eunice, and said, "Come on, Eunice, suppose we should see to the babies and find sleep ourselves. It's been a long night."

Not that sleep would come tonight. She didn't think it would be welcome anytime soon. Each time her lids blinked, she saw Stella. Battered, beaten, lifeless.

A shiver raced down her back. Stella hadn't been recognizable beyond the color of her hair and the heart-shaped locket she always wore around her neck. She was surprised Cal hadn't sold it or lost it gambling. Fanny dipped her hand into her pocket and felt the etching graze her fingers.

It was difficult to not carry guilt. She'd known of Cal's abuse, but she wasn't certain what she could have done to help Stella Interfering more than she had, would have seen Fanny dead, too—still might if she didn't prepare for the encounter.

The turn of the knob clicked as it released. The scent of Eunice's fried chicken enveloped her, and her tired eyes revived. Her stomach grumbled, and she recalled she'd had nothing more than a biscuit before she'd fallen asleep in Graham's arms. Had that only been a few hours ago? It seemed like an eternity. A lot had happened since that moment, and she'd nearly forgotten how she'd held Graham as he cried for his wife and son.

She prayed those tears had been healing tears, ones that would eventually release him from his guilt. It'd taken her years to even understand she suffered from the pain of guilt after watching her parents die and wondering if she could have saved them. Believing she should have saved them and not been too scared to leave her hiding place.

It wasn't until her brothers had explained that her parents' murders weren't her fault. It had taken some time for the peace to unsettle the guilt, but it had. She didn't want Graham holding on to the guilt for years, wasting away while it ate at the goodness inside him until it disappeared.

"You want me to put the babies to bed while you get some sleep?" Eunice asked.

"I'm not tired right now," Fanny said, knowing she needed to formulate a plan for when Cal did show up. However, she'd wait for Hiram and Nathan so they could plan together. "You go on up. And, Eunice, thank you for all your help."

Eunice hugged Fanny with little Sam sandwiched between them. "Of course, what are friends for?"

Eunice laid Sam on the blanket and disappeared upstairs. The boards above Fanny's head creaked as Eunice readied for bed. It wasn't until silence met her ears that Fanny tended the babies. For the first time since Graham had invaded her home, Fanny was alone with Lily Rose and Sam. It was something she would need to get used to, given she couldn't move Eunice in unless the girl married one of her brothers, but then that would mean Fanny and the babies would need to find a new home.

With the babies asleep, Fanny snagged a biscuit from the cloth-covered bowl and sat at the kitchen table as she contemplated what she would do with the babies when Cal came. The door swung open. Nathan hung his hat on a hook and slipped his boots off. "Smells good. Don't tell me you've learned to cook while we were gone."

His attempt at teasing her warmed her heart. "No, that's all Eunice."

Nathan's eyes grew as round as the teacup saucer nestled with the rest of Mama's chipped dishes.

Perfect Eunice. Pretty Eunice. A real right lady. Fanny smiled to herself. A few days ago, anything her brothers might have said about Eunice would have irritated her. Eunice was a grand prize Fanny could never emulate. Now, however, she was…what? A friend. Yes, Eunice was a friend. One to be cherished and admired. Her new friend may not know how to shoot a pistol or sew a tight seam, but she knew how to cook. More importantly, she was selfless, kind and giving. And she said Fanny was more of a lady than most.

"I don't suppose there's any chicken left?" The chair legs scraped across the floor as he sat.

Fanny looked toward the babies and held her fingers to her lips to hush him. "They're sleeping. Did Seth come home, too?"

"He drew the short straw and stayed with the cattle drive while we brought Stella back."

"Thank you for that." The corner of Nathan's mouth turned slightly upward. He kicked his feet out and slouched against the wooden rungs. When he crossed his arms, Fanny knew she was in for a lecture. Would he burn her ears about Graham staying at the farm or about placing herself in danger by keeping the babies?

Before he could start, she opened her mouth and said the first thing that came to mind, the first thing she'd intended on telling all her brothers before Mr. Davies had deposited the twins in her sewing shop. "I didn't say anything beforehand because I didn't want to give you guys a reason to stay, but even before I knew about Lily Rose and Sam, I intended on moving out when you came back."

Nathan jolted upright, but she held her hand up. "Give me a moment, as I've got a lot on my mind. It's high time you, Hiram and Seth get married and start families of your own. You can't easily bring home a wife when I'm here."

"What gave you a hairbrained idea like that?"

She twisted the biscuit in her fingers. Biscuits she'd made under Eunice's tutelage. "I'm nearing my thirty first birthday, Nathan. I'm beyond the age of marrying, and you, Seth and Hiram… Well, it's time you got yourselves some wives and children. You know, before you're old like Mr. Gene down the way. Why, he can't hardly stand up straight to work his fields. Spent his youth cultivating land to leave to a legacy, and what does he have? That's right, Nate, nothing. He's so desperate to marry and have children, he's come poking his head round here."

Nathan chuckled and then quickly sobered. He reached across the table and took her free hand in his. "Fanny, I can't speak for our brothers, but if I found a lady worth her salt, I'd marry her. Truth is pickings are slim around here. Even our own marshal ordered a bride through the mail."

"Not intentionally, Nathan. He was duped by the judge's wife."

"The fact remains there aren't that many eligible ladies in Oak Grove. When the time is right, we'll hitch up, but until then, we're fine going on as we are."

"Then why are you always comparing me to Eunice Gilbert as if she were the greatest gift to men?" And as if Fanny was a burden.

"Miss Gilbert?" Nathan cocked an eyebrow upward as if he was surprised by her question.

"Yes," she said and then lowered her voice to mock his. "Eunice is the light of Oak Grove. Her pies are near perfection if perfection existed. Oh, Fanny, you should take comportment lessons from Miss Gilbert." She paused for effect. "Maybe you'd find yourself a husband."

"Fanny," he said, running his palm down his thigh. "We never meant—"

"No, I'm certain you didn't, but as I mentioned before, I had made plans. I was going to move to Mrs.

Wheelwright's. However, I see the impropriety of living there with Lily Rose and Sam while Mr. Staddler is staying there. Once Cal James is dealt with and Mr. Staddler moves on, the children and I will move to Mrs. Wheelwright's."

She rose from the chair, brushed the crumbs from her biscuit into her hand and dumped them into a pail hanging on a hook by the door.

"Well," he said. "I'm mighty glad you've at least reasoned out you're best off here until Mr. Staddler leaves, but is that what you want, Fanny?"

Leaning against the counter, she stared out the window into the darkness, wondering where Graham was. Was he settled in for the night or had he gone after Cal?

"What I want is not up to me. I have Lily Rose and Sam to think about." She wanted Graham to stay and be a part of the babies' lives. She wanted him to stay because she couldn't imagine not seeing him. She'd never imagined herself sweet on a man or caught herself daydreaming, but for some reason most of her thoughts led to Graham.

"Why, Fanny? Why take them on when they aren't yours?"

She turned on him. "They are mine, Nathan. They're as much mine as if I'd birthed them."

"Taking babies isn't like bringing Daisy home, or Violet, or Sunflower. They're babies."

"I know what they are, and they're mine." They were probably the only opportunity she'd have to be a mother, but she wasn't about to tell her brother that. He'd only tell her she was being silly and that her time would come. Well, this was her time, and she would thank God every day for the gifts He'd laid in her arms. Every day. "No need to worry, Nathan. I will not ask you or Seth and Hiram to take on the responsibility of these babies, and I will not, under no circumstances send them to an orphanage, so don't even think it. And if anything were to happen to me, Eunice has agreed to take them."

Nathan pushed from his chair and placed his hands on her shoulders. "I think I can speak for Seth and Hiram when I say that you keeping those babies is all right. We'll support you, Fanny, but we won't let you leave this house until you're good and married."

The curve of her nails bit into her palms. She nearly raised her voice, but at the sound of an infant shifting on the blanket, she drew in a calming breath. "I'm a grown woman, Nathan Ellis. I'll move out if I please, and there is nothing you, Seth or Hiram can do about it."

Graham walked the perimeter of the house and barn for the fifth time before sitting against a small tree where he could see the house and barn. He'd tried to go to sleep, but each time he closed his eyes, he was riddled with nightmares. Most of the images morphed from Clea to Stella to Fanny. Each one pleading for him to help them. Sometimes he stood near the graves he'd seen on the hill next to the big old oak tree, pulling up the grass until they were seen and remembered.

Near the break of day, when he knew Mr. Gilbert and the Ellis brothers would be stirring, he strolled to the barn and laid his head down to rest.

He woke to the cold end of a barrel poking the side of his head. He opened his eyes to see the end of a rifle pointing down at him. He followed the line of the steel until he met the mossy green eyes of Nathan Ellis and breathed a sigh of relief.

"Time to get up, we got business to attend." Nathan's gaze narrowed. "I know your reputation for being a good shot, and I don't intend on giving you a chance of running out, not before your vows are spoken."

"I won't run off." Graham knocked the barrel away and rolled to his feet. "I told you I'd do right by your sister. I keep my word."

"Well, we're going to see about that today," Nathan said as he rested the rifle against his shoulder, barrel pointed upward.

"Have you talked to Fanny about this?" He couldn't even bring himself to utter the word *wedding*. He was certain she wouldn't be too happy about being forced down the aisle. He wondered how she'd taken the news she was to be his wife. "I don't want to be shot in my sleep."

"Can't say I blame you. My stubborn sister doesn't always know what's best for her." He shifted his stance. "Look, Fanny has determined to make her own way. Soon as you leave Oak Grove, she intends on taking those babies and moving into a boarding house. I won't have it. It's not safe to be boarding with the various sorts of scamps tramping through Oak Grove. She needs a husband who is willing to—"

"Be bamboozled at every turn?"

"Well, I wouldn't exactly call it that. She does have her antics, and she can be stubborn to boot, but I won't have her living in a boarding house. You're going to do right by her and give her a home before you leave Oak Grove as Fanny believes is your intention"

Graham nodded. "Understood."

"However, me and Hiram don't think you're too keen on leaving, and we guess our sister has something to do with that. Maybe it's because your sister left those babies in her care, or maybe you're just sweet on Fanny and want build a family with her. I don't rightly know, but I can't say I've ever paid a lady attention the way you did my sister last night, even if I was grateful to her."

Graham wasn't sure if he wanted to stay in Oak Grove or not. He knew he wanted Fanny safe and the twins cared for. He was willing to marry her and give her his name to make those things happen. Without the aid of her brother's shotgun. "She'd had a shock," he said to explain away pulling her into his arms last night.

"I see, and what about before, when we found you together in the barn?"

Graham pressed his mouth together in a tight line on that subject. The reminder spurred a long-lost sensation in the depth of his bones. His arms ached to hold Fanny, to feel the warmth of her breath seep through his shirt. To feel the rise and fall of her breathing next to him. "I'd like to see my sister buried first."

"I suppose you'll need a time of mourning, too?"

He considered Nathan's question with a drawn-in breath. He'd spent too much time mourning, too many years. Maybe not for Stella, but it was time he picked up the challenge Fanny had tossed at his feet. It was time for him to live and quit trying to outrun the grief he'd been dodging since he buried Clea and their son.

A great deal of doubt tormented him over whether or not he could live with so much guilt clinging to his shoulders. However, if he was going to marry Fanny out of propriety and for the twins, he'd just as soon get it done now, rather than later. Before… Before what? Anyone else snatched her up? That couldn't possibly be the reason.

He didn't want to get married. He didn't want a wife and he didn't want to grow roots in one place. If someone else took her on, all the better for him. Still, the idea of another man holding her in his arms as he had last night soured his stomach. "No. I'd have the minister marry us right after the burial, but out of respect for Fanny, I think we should at least be married in the church surrounded by her family and friends. And let's not forget Cal James is still out there posing a threat."

"Having the minister come is safest and will give James little opportunity to make his move without being seen," Nathan said.

Graham considered the words. "I suppose you're right."

"Nathan," Fanny called from the open double doors.

Nathan froze. His eyes widened, and he lost all color in his cheeks. The rifle quivered, and Nathan tucked it beneath his arm, barrel pointing toward the ground. Graham guessed Fanny had no idea what her brother was about.

"What are you doing?" Her hair hung loose down around her waist. The morning sun grasped the strands and caught them on fire. Oh, how he remembered the feel of the soft silkiness entangled around his arms, tickling the bare curve of his cheek. He drew in a breath to catch the scent of wildflowers. A scent belonging solely to her.

"I'm discussing plans with your beau here."

Graham was pleased Nathan didn't outright lie to his sister.

"Beau," she snorted. "I don't know what you're doing, Nathan, but it looks like you're up to no good." She stalked toward Nathan and snagged the rifle from him. She poked the pointed end of her finger into his chest. "You best not be making threats you cannot carry out, brother."

Graham grinned like a boy with his fingers sunk deep into a piece of cobbler left on the windowsill to cool. He couldn't help the smile curving his lips. His bride-to-be looked ready for a duel at dusk, and if her brother wasn't careful, he'd end up with a lot more trouble than he bargained for, which is probably why the man was so eager to send his sister down the aisle. But if that was the case, why had they chased near every suitor away from her?

"Where's Hiram? Does he know you're out here accosting Mr. Staddler? He's done nothing to warrant your actions."

Mr. Staddler, was it? What happened to Graham? Did she somehow know they were on the precipice of matrimony and was attempting to place distance between them? Well, he'd see about that. "Good morning, Fanny. I trust you slept well."

The flicker of light in her eyes struck a chord in his gut as she turned on him. Burnt beans, she was more beautiful in a temper than when she was calm.

He should tread with caution. He didn't want to disintegrate into ash. He hadn't slept much between the nightmares pulling him to awareness and thoughts of Fanny tempting him to keep his eyes open so he could contemplate what a future might look like with her. He pulled back his teasing. "Your brother was kindly waking me up. We have to see to my sister and the marshal."

"Oh, well, breakfast is ready." Her skirts billowed around her as she turned to go, and then she stopped. "I don't rightly feel comfortable taking Lily Rose and Sam into town. Eunice and Mr. Gilbert have offered to stay, but if Cal makes his way here while we're gone, I'll never forgive myself."

Nathan shifted, looking between the two. "Hiram is the better shot. Mind if I ride into town? I can talk to the marshal and grab the preacher. We can have your sister buried out on the hill just south of here."

"Seems like the best plan. Cal can't ride up without any of us seeing him," Graham said as he scratched his jaw. "Still, I don't like having the twins and Fanny in the one place Cal expects them to be."

"We'll be fine," Fanny said. "I know this house, the barn, the land. I know the alarms the animals make when they are nervous. This is the safest place for Lily Rose and Sam."

He didn't miss the fact she'd left her name from the list.

"I have to agree. With Hiram here, we're not easy prey."

"All right, if Hiram doesn't mind my sister buried on his land."

"My land," Nathan said. "That piece belongs to me. I've just begun laying logs for my cabin. Our brother will stop at the land office in Junction City to mark his plot."

Graham was beginning to understand Fanny's desperation to leave the farm. With her brothers grabbing land, she must feel as if they were moving on without her. In her way of thinking, her circle was breaking, leaving her confused about her place in their plans.

Graham's gaze fell to the ground. He kicked the toe of his boot into the thirsty soil before looking to Fanny and then to Nathan. "You're all right having a bank robber rest in peace on your land?"

Fanny's mouth pressed together. "Your sister likely had no choice in the matter. She may or may not have done the deed. For all we know, Cal did it himself or coerced another lady into robbing that bank."

"Fanny, witnesses claimed it was her. You saw the wanted poster. You know—"

"What I know is your sister was a good woman. She was kind and considerate. She risked punishment to spare what kindness she could. And now she is dead."

"Don't matter, anyway," Nathan interrupted. "She's gone and can't deny or confess to her actions."

"I suppose you're correct." He shoved his hands into his pockets. "The fact remains, folks will have their opinions. They may not like you harboring a fugitive, even a deceased one."

Nathan pulled back his shoulders. "What I do and who I have buried on my land is no business of anyone, except my own. I hold no judgment against Stella." Nathan cleared his throat. "After what she went through, she deserves to rest in peace, and what better place than on a bluff overlooking some of the most beautiful land created by the hand of God."

Emotion pressed against the wall of Graham's chest, the expansion uncomfortable and almost painful. It welled into his throat like water gushing from a freshly dug well. Fanny moved toward him, her skirts brushing against his legs. She threaded her hand through his arm and squeezed his forearm.

"Graham, Nathan has the right of it, even if Stella had wronged us, she deserves forgiveness. It's God's way, and we have no right to withhold it from her."

His mama's voice entered his head as if she read

straight from the Bible. *For if ye forgive men their trespasses, your heavenly Father will also forgive you. But if ye forgive not men their trespasses, neither will your Father forgive your trespasses.*

He recalled the chapter and verse. He also recalled what had spurred that reading from Matthew chapter six, verses fourteen and fifteen. A neighbor had stolen their milk cow and then set their barn on fire. Graham had been ten at the time, and his father had traveled to town to replenish their supplies. Graham had been left in charge of protecting Mama and Stella. Seemed like his failures went further back than he believed. Before Clea and Jacob. How would he ever find redemption?

He dropped his gaze to the top of the vibrant red curls glinting with gold strands. How would he protect her and the twins when he'd often failed protecting his loved ones?

He wouldn't. He'd marry her. Make right on his word to her brother and keep her virtue safe, but he'd leave Oak Grove at the first opportunity. Once Cal was dealt with. He'd at least see that through. And with Fanny's brothers keeping vigilant, too, there was little chance of losing her to the scoundrel's evil.

"Fanny's right. Doesn't matter if Stella robbed a bank or stole from us. It's not for me to withhold forgiveness. She is welcome here."

The backs of his eyes stung. The morning spring air burned against the sensitive flesh of his nose as he pulled in a breath to dislodge the gratitude threatening to spill forth. He adjusted his hat until it shadowed the upper part of his face. He didn't know what it was about these folks, but they'd sure turned him weepy-eyed. He'd cried, or nearly cried more in the last day than he had since the day he covered his wife and son with dirt. He managed to swallow the knot of emotion and forced his gaze to Fanny's brother, the brother who'd shown him nothing but contempt.

"My thanks. Not sure how I'll repay your gratitude, but I will."

Chapter Thirteen

Fanny left the morning dishes in the steaming tub of water, dried her hands on her apron and strode across the room to a squalling Lily Rose. She scooped the infant into her arms. "What's wrong, sweet girl?"

Sam had been perfectly content lying on his back, looking around the room without a care in the world until his eyes closed. Lily Rose had kept her up through the night, fussing. Fanny imagined the little girl missed her mother. The baby drew her knees into her stomach and wailed. A quick check told Fanny she didn't need changing. She snuggled Lily Rose firmly against her chest, just as Eunice had shown her. She bounced as she paced, and the snugness and movement seemed to settle Lily Rose. Fanny was grateful. She didn't mind the cries or the fussing, but fear sure snaked around Fanny's heart when she couldn't comfort them.

"Suppose you have an upset tummy, just as Eunice suggested." Fanny's gazed at the innocent child in her arms. Fanny cooed and hummed all while pacing and bouncing as a mental list of chores needing done rolled through her mind. It was a good thing Nathan and Hiram were back. They each had their specific duties to tend each day to keep the farm running properly. Fanny's duties were to feed the animals, gather the eggs and keep layers of dust from decorating the interior of the home.

Somehow, she'd have to adjust and find a way to do all that needed to be done and still care for twins. She prayed God would grant her the ability to all that needed done.

Lily Rose released a little hiccup, and Fanny smiled. The twins had won her heart over in only a few days. She couldn't imagine life without them, and she knew she'd do everything she could to protect them from their father. If the coward ever dared to show his face. A part of her believed he was more bark than bite, but after seeing the abuse Stella had suffered, Fanny knew she had to be cautious. Alert.

The door swung open and bounced against the wall. Lily Rose jerked at the sound, and Fanny gave the intruder a glare. However, her glare quickly turned to alarm at the sight of Graham's stern face. "What's wrong?"

"A rider's coming up the road. It's not Nathan, and Hiram is out scouting the land for tracks."

Fear froze her in place. She'd tried to consider what she would do when this moment occurred, but fear stole her wits.

"With the Gilberts gone, it's just us. Is there a safe place for you to hide with the babies?"

Thoughts galloped through her mind as she considered her options. She must have tightened her hold on Lily because the baby let out a wail. Fanny squeezed her eyes closed and cradled the baby closer. She opened her eyes. "Graham, she's been like this all night. Even if I find a place for them, keeping her quiet enough to stay hidden is nearly impossible."

What were they going to do? She should have sent the twins with Eunice, but if Cal found the babies in her care, he'd likely kill her. He'd likely kill all the Gilberts. Panic rose in her chest. She did all she could to tamp it down, but she couldn't. She was scared. Sacred for Lily Rose and Sam. "What are we going to do, Graham?"

He strode toward her and brushed a finger down her cheek, drying the tear she hadn't realized streamed from her eye. "Don't you worry, sweetheart. I've faced worse enemies. I'll handle Cal. You keep the babies. You have your pistol?"

She fished it from her apron pocket. She'd kept it close all through the night, with a watchful eye on the door and the windows, looking for any shadows that the moon might reveal.

He smiled. "That's my girl. Do you have a cellar?"

She nodded, but then said, "Part of the roof caved in."

"Does the door to the stairs lock?"

She nodded.

"It might not do much, but it'll buy you some

time. Take the babies upstairs, lock any doors you go through. And if for some reason Cal makes it past me, I want you to shoot, sweetheart. Don't let him anywhere near you."

Eyes wide, she nodded again. "I'll aim true."

Graham tilted her chin and held her gaze. His thumb stroked the indentation beneath her mouth. "Promise me."

"I promise," she said. Before she could say another word, he was out the door. She peered out the window and watched his purposeful strides. He scanned the yard, and she imagined he was assessing the area.

Fanny dropped two baby bottles into her pocket and gathered Sam next to Lily Rose. She opened the door leading to the upper floor and locked it behind her before racing up the steps. At the top of the stairs, she started for her room but decided to take Seth and Nathan's since it faced the barn and the wide open lane in front of the house. If the unexpected visitor was Cal James, she'd have an unhindered view, giving her the advantage and a clear shot. She laid Sam on the bed and rolled Seth's quilt to form a barrier around him. She snagged one of Seth's shirts from a hook and wrapped Lily in a snug cocoon, hoping to give her the sensation of being held, then she lay her next to Sam.

She inspected her work and then rushed to the window, careful to keep in the shadows so she couldn't be seen from below. A thin column of dust rose from the well-traveled path, telling Fanny a single rider approached. And it was much too soon for Nathan to return. Her stomach clenched into a knot. She slid to the floor and hugged her knees. She rocked and tried to convince herself all was well.

Graham would stop Cal in his tracks, wouldn't he? After all, he was a gunslinger with a reputation. A bead of perspiration slipped down her brow. Her gaze slid around the room and welded to the doorknob. Had she locked it? Easing up to peer over the windowsill, Fanny scanned the yard and found Graham standing with feet shoulder-width apart and his arms crossed. Two horses descended the hill, but there was only one rider. She narrowed her gaze to focus. The horses moved at a slow canter. A shape took form, and colors cleared. She jumped to her feet. The black-and-white paint belonged to Mr. Davies.

What was he doing out here? He'd gone to Junction City on business, which is why they hadn't learned who had given him the twins. He wouldn't have had time to get there and return.

Lily Rose began to fuss, and Fanny, no longer certain a threat existed, picked her up and cradled her next to her heart. Graham pulled his gun from his holster. The rider held a hand up and slid from the horse. The second horse looked an awful lot like her brother Seth's horse. *Buttercup*? She rubbed her fist against the window, but it remained clouded with dust on the outside.

If that was Mr. Davies, why would Graham have a bead on him? Fanny took in their movements with bated breath until Graham slid his gun back into the holster and stuck out his hand. The rider took off his hat and revealed a shock of thick dark hair. Seth? He was her only brother blessed with her mother's coal-black locks instead of the Ellis red.

Seth! She glanced at the riderless horse and knew without a doubt it was Seth's Buttercup. She jumped in excitement. She took up Sam and Lily Rose and carefully descended the stairs as quickly as she could with both babies. She unlocked the door to the stairs. She laid the babies in their makeshift cribs and then strode across the kitchen. She swung the door opened, and that is when she noticed the white bandage wrapped over her brother's shoulder and around his neck, holding his left arm against him. Seth had been hurt. She flew across the yard.

"Seth! What happened to you?" she cried out as he slid out of the saddle. "Why are you riding Mr. Davies's horse?"

"Whoa, little sister." He focused on a spot past her shoulder. "Seems you've some answering to do, too. It isn't very often a man comes home to find his sister holed up with a right fine gunslinger like Mr. Staddler here. Should we talk about why Mr. Staddler is staying at our home first?"

"No," Fanny said, turning toward Graham with a pointed finger. "Don't you start. I'll find out why his arm is in a sling before I offer explanations."

Graham hid his smile with the dip of his chin. "Sorry, Seth. I'm not one to interfere with family matters."

"Smart man," Seth said. "Still, I'd like answers."

"And you'll get them soon enough. Now, how'd you get hurt?"

"Nothing more than a little mishap on the trail."

She didn't like his evasiveness. Something more than a little mishap had happened. The small red stain seeping through his shirt told her that truth, but she wasn't about to argue at the moment, or poke her finger at the spot of blood to prove him wrong. "Buttercup?"

"Is just fine. I thought I would give her a rest from the cattle drive. As far as Mr. Davies, well, I'm afraid he wasn't in any condition to speak."

A sharp inhale stole down her throat. "Dora?"

Seth shook his head. Franny wavered on her feet, and Graham steadied her with his arm around her shoulder.

"I am sorry, Fanny," Graham said.

She lifted her gaze to his and saw compassion. She was stunned, and while she hadn't known Mr. Davies and Dora well, they were nice enough folks she'd seen weekly. One word rung in her mind. "Cal?"

"I wish I knew, sweetheart," Graham said, as his hand massaged her shoulder.

She had no doubt Cal had hunted Mr. Davies and Dora down, and she didn't need to know the details of their deaths to know that fact.

"Cattle boss had some men ride on to Junction City and alert the law there," Seth said. "I'm sorry, little sister.

Lily Rose began to fuss so Fanny took her from

Graham. "You both will come to the house as soon as you've seen to the horses?"

She didn't want to be alone. She wanted to demand they both come but posed it as a question, knowing Seth would more than likely drag his feet if she did not. She loved all her brothers, and although Seth was more reasonable than Hiram and Nathan, he didn't take well to orders, especially from her. He seemed to understand her more and didn't coddle her as much as the other two. She knew him well enough to know he was being vague and not telling her the truth, which was not like Seth at all.

"Yes, little sister, I'll come in as soon as Graham and I discuss a few matters."

Her brow dipped into a *v*. "What could the two of you possibly have to discuss?"

"Go on, Fanny," Graham said. "We'll come in soon, so don't go chewing up the babies' ears with a tirade."

"Babies?" Seth's brow arched, and then he burst into laughter. "You can fill me in when I come in." He turned to Graham and said, "You know my sister well."

She balled her hands into fists. "Arghhh!" She turned, walked back toward the house and kicked the door closed with a satisfied groan.

"Your uncle," she started and then stopped as Graham's words rang in her ears. Oh! The man was impossible. How dare he take a high hand with her and tell her to go onto the house. He wasn't one of her brothers, and he most certainly wasn't her husband. The worst part of it all was that she'd complied without a single objection. She knelt beside the dresser drawers holding the babies. "Don't worry, little ones, I'll keep my thoughts on your uncle to myself." She picked up Lily Rose and laid her on the quilt, and then Sam. She sat between them on the floor. After propping their heads with a bit of cushioning, she fed them while she prayed for patience and grace where Graham was concerned. One minute she had her head in the clouds, thinking a better man had never walked the earth. The next she wanted to throttle him.

"Dear Lord, I need a great deal of patience and grace where Graham Staddler's concerned." She hoped her prayers would be answered with a great deal of haste before she succumbed to prairie madness. It wouldn't do to shoot Lily Rose and Sam's uncle. All she needed was a little time, then he'd leave Oak Grove and be out of her mind for good.

"You've been shot," Graham said. At Seth's silence, he continued, "I'm guessing you ran into whoever killed Mr. Davies and Dora."

Seth nodded. "I was scouting on the drive. Saw Davies's horse and investigated. It wasn't pretty. I rode right into Cal James foraging through their bags. I knew he worked with the railroad crew. I'm embarrassed to say he drew on me before I even realized he was there."

"I understand. I don't know a man worth his salt who hasn't been on the bad end of a barrel. I can't say I envy you facing your sister with that news, though." Graham jammed his hands into his pockets.

"Unfortunately, Cal got away," Seth said.

Graham pulled in a breath and tried not to be disappointed. "You know your brothers brought Stella to town."

"My condolences, Graham," Seth said. "I knew when we worked together down south that you had a sister, I just didn't realize James' wife was her. If I did, I would have found a way to get a message to you. were."

Graham didn't want Seth carrying a burden of guilt that didn't belong to him. "I know you would have, Seth." He adjusted his hat. "You're about the last person I expected to see here," Graham said. "I don't know why I didn't connect you with Fanny. Guess because you don't have quite the same coloring as her." Seth didn't have the red hair, or those same mossy green eyes that saw right through a man and unwrapped his secrets like a kid opening candy on Christmas morning. "Still, the way she shoots, I should have known."

"Can't say I was surprised." Seth led his newly acquired horse into the barn and began brushing him down. "I heard something about Fanny's shop being broken into. Mr. Taylor mentioned your name when it came to making the needed repairs. My thanks."

"No need." Graham told him all he knew and what had brought him to Oak Grove. He didn't tell his friend about his impending marriage to Fanny. He knew from their time spent together hunting down cattle thieves that Seth was mighty protective of his sister. Thing was Graham had pictured her much younger. Still a schoolgirl. And he'd never mentioned her name. Keeping their lives private was sort of a rule among them. They never mentioned where they came from, and they never mentioned the names of their families. It wouldn't do for that information to fall in the hands of the men they hunted.

Seth put the horse in the stall and leaned his good arm against the closed half door. "I'm sorry to hear about your sister, Graham. I can't imagine what I'd do if a scoundrel married Fanny and then killed her. But you've always been a cool head. I've never seen you act on your emotion."

Graham figured his lack of emotion had been due to the fog of grief he'd been living in. He didn't care one way or another what happened to a man once he brought him to justice, but he refused to spill blood unless it was necessary. "You must know Cal intends on coming for Fanny."

Seth's eyes narrowed to mere slits. "I don't like it, but we'll be ready. I wondered why you were still in Oak Grove."

"Well—" Graham scratched his beard "—seeing as how I feel Cal is my responsibility, I can't abandon Fanny and the twins."

"Mr. Taylor told me about those babies. What does my sister have to do with your niece and nephew?"

Graham's mouth twitched. No way to tell it but straight. "Stella had Mr. Davies give Lily Rose and

Sam to Fanny to protect them. Before Stella died, she asked Fanny to raise them as her own."

A myriad of emotions flickered on Seth's face before he settled on resignation. "Guess I should be thankful she didn't acquire another animal. If you haven't noticed, we have a menagerie of farm animals. Most aren't good for much other than talking to."

"That's part of your sister's charm," Graham said unintentionally. He might be having thoughts about holding her in his arms, but he didn't need her brothers to know his feelings were beginning to get involved. If they knew that, he might as well admit to himself that Fanny Ellis was weaseling her way beneath the armor he had cemented around his heart.

"Charm, huh?" Seth's eyebrow arched upward. "Never thought of my sister as charming. Irritating. Stubborn. Bossy. But not charming. Sounds like my little sister has pulled the wool over your eyes. Remember those stories I told over the campfire about sawing my biscuits?"

Graham nodded. He thought about the last several days whenever he chanced to have a meal. She'd made the biscuits, but he hadn't tasted them.

"Fanny can't cook. Not to save her life. Not certain how she'll feed those babies when they get older." Seth slapped Graham on the shoulder. "If you want your kin to survive, best convince her to give those babies over to you or marry her. As I recall, you cook up a good breakfast and make a better pot of coffee."

Graham gulped, wondering if Seth had encountered Nathan on his way home. However, he wasn't keen on bringing up the subject of marriage to Fanny's brother, especially since he had vowed to never take another wife. He wouldn't be doing so if he didn't feel the need to protect Fanny's reputation. Not to mention, he was fairly certain Nathan would push him down the aisle with the barrel of his rifle if he didn't readily volunteer to do the deed. The more he thought of marrying Fanny, the more the idea of marrying for convenience left a bad taste in his mouth. "Fanny will do just fine. I think Miss Gilbert has taken to her and offered to teach her a few things."

"Miss Gilbert?"

The door to the farmhouse swung open, and Fanny stepped out onto the porch. Her hair sprung from the tie at odd angles. Her apron and dress had seen better days, and dark circles draped beneath her eyes, but he'd never seen a lady look as pretty as she did at the moment. She was as wild and rugged as the Flint Hills, and more beautiful. "I should relieve Fanny. Let her get some rest from the babies before she decides to go blazing after Cal herself."

Seth rumbled with laughter. "You do know my sister well. Well, I suppose she won't rest until she hears about my time on the cattle drive. It's nothing grand, but still, when she hears about the mishap, she might not ever allow me to leave Oak Grove again, and a man has to let his feet roam. Especially men like us. Can't root us to one spot for long."

"Nope." Graham knew what he meant, and a week

ago he would have agreed with Seth. However, Fanny and the twins had him wondering what it'd be like to plant roots, to try once again to cultivate the land. To watch his wife flourish as she cared for their children, to watch those children grow. Those were dreams he'd had once. Dreams he'd lost and given up on ever having again.

Soon, if Nathan had his way, Graham would have a wife, and by all accounts he'd have two children to raise, but he wouldn't bring himself to hope for more, even if his heart was for the taking, Fanny Ellis knew his faults. Most of them, at least. She knew he'd failed as a husband and a father. In time, if he stuck around, he'd only disappoint her. He hadn't spoken to her about marriage. He'd admit he was a bit of a yellow-bellied coward when it came to that topic. It would be best if she found out from one of her brothers.

"Although, I think a man can get tired of roaming after a time. Restless legs get worn out, and it's good to have a fine nice hearth to kick your feet in front of, something to call your own."

Seth rocked back on his heels. "Never thought I'd hear you say that, Graham. You were always the first to talk about how having a piece of land was more risk than reward."

A sigh rushed over him. "I did."

It wasn't the land or the home that was more risk than reward. If his house burnt down, he could rebuild. If the crops succumbed to drought, he could replant. It was giving up his heart, allowing a claim to be staked on it and then having it ripped from him that was the great risk. He'd given his all. He'd given his heart and soul to Clea and Jacob. They were his sun and moon. The morning dew and a cool sip of water from a fresh brook. They'd given him a reason to put his boots on in the morning and had been the reason he rushed home from the fields. They had been everything to him, and he'd lost them. That was the reason he couldn't grow roots, even if he wanted to, right here in Oak Grove with Fanny.

"Sometimes a man's mind changes about needing to settle down," he said to Seth. Of course, his wouldn't.

"We should go to the house before Fanny drags us in by our ears," Seth said. "I am not sure how I'll tell her I was shot."

"I've learned she is straightforward with her thoughts. I imagine she'd appreciate you do the same."

Chapter Fourteen

Fanny chewed on the tip of her fingernail as she strode back and forth across the floor. Every now and then, she'd linger in front of the window and gaze at the man who'd held her in his arms yesterday and so thoughtfully seen to her well-being all while keeping his distance. She supposed it was his way of maintaining propriety, which no one, including Graham, had seemed to be concerned with since she'd yawned out of the bed this morning.

She didn't think it was too strange that Hiram and Nathan had left her alone with Graham and the twins until this moment. Now she wanted to rope Seth and drag him into the house. "What could be taking them so long?"

She would have paced enough in the last hour to wear a hole in the wooden floor, if her boots wouldn't have made too much noise and, risk another fit from Lily Rose. She just prayed the baby would sleep a while longer.

What could Seth and Graham possibly have to discuss?

Each pass by the window had Fanny glancing into the yard, hoping Seth would hurry up and make his way to the house. She didn't relish another brother harassing Graham. If the gunslinger hadn't intended on leaving before, he would when her brothers were done with him.

She peered over at the twins. "Thank you, Lord, for small blessings."

Maybe she could start on supper or at least the one thing she knew how to make. She dumped some flour into a bowl for some bread rolls and then added the rest of the ingredients, just as Eunice had shown her. Her fingers sank into the dough when she caught movement in the yard. The inside of her lip found its way between her teeth.

Graham Staddler was a fine-looking man, that was for certain. He swaggered as if his feet glided over the earth, caressing her with every step. Like a turtle held by the water as it floated on the surface. It was as if he was one with the elements surrounding him, smooth like her hand brushing the surface of a piece of finely woven silk.

As if he sensed her watching him, he lifted his eyes toward the window. Her breath suspended in her lungs. He adjusted his hat, revealing his shock of blond curls. Butterflies took flight in her stomach, and her knees felt as wobbly as if she'd just hit the ground after riding Daisy all morning. She clasped her hand to her chest and leaned against the counter. What was wrong with her? Surely, she wasn't taking a fancy to the gunslinger. Especially in the sort of way a woman fancies a man who was courting her. As soon as she thought it, she knew it to be true. "No, no, no."

Panic welled in her chest. He would leave Oak Grove, taking any opportunity she might have at finding a husband with him, because she now knew she couldn't settle for any man less than Graham Staddler. According to the papers, he was the most chivalrous gunslinger in the West. To her, he was even more, but she couldn't allow herself to acknowledge that.

"Oh, Lord, of all the men for me to fall for, why him? Why couldn't my heart desire the banker or the marshal's deputy? Why does it have to want to love Graham Staddler?"

The door was flung open, and before her brother stepped foot into the house, he said, "I was shot."

"What?" She spun around. Small bits of dough flung from her palms. She wiped her hands on a linen cloth as she glanced at her brother.

"Only a graze. Doc said a week or two, I'll be good as new."

Seth and Graham dipped beneath the doorframe and stepped closer.

She saw the spot of red seeping through his bandage and knew his injury had been caused by more than just a mishap, she just hadn't expected this news. "You were? By whom?" She hoped it was an accident, but given the events of the last day, she knew that was unlikely. Before her brother could respond, she held up her hand and said, "Do not tell me it was Cal?"

Seth and Graham held their tongues. Graham found his boots interesting. Seth just grinned at her like getting shot was equivalent to winning a ribbon during the harvest festival. She wanted to smack the smile from him. Being shot was serious, and if it was Cal who shot him… Well, she just wasn't sure what she'd do. Part of her wanted to find Cal James and give him what he deserved. The other part of her wanted to find a hole to hide in with the twins until Cal went away.

"Do not keep the truth from me. I know he killed Stella. I suspect he killed Mr. Davies and Dora for helping Stella." Fanny dropped to a kitchen chair and toyed with the loose stitches on the towel. All the bravado she'd chinked into place over the years began to crumble. She felt its absence distinctly. Her bravery and courage slipped between the cracks like smoke from a chimney, and she didn't think it was because she was frightened of Cal. She'd decided when she was little and at the orphanage to never huddle in fear again. She'd decided to always stand tall in the face of adversity and to never cower to bullies, but right now she wanted to shrink and hide. Men could be cruel. She'd known that the moment the intruder shot her father in the chest and then turned on her mother. She just never thought that people who acted in kindness would be punished for their deeds. She swiped at the hot tears racing down her cheeks. "All because they helped a woman in need. They were killed for their humanity."

If Cal came after her, would he cause her brothers and Graham harm if they got in the way? She knew the answer to that question, and she didn't like it. Her thoughts took her back to the day her parents were killed. She'd watched helplessly as they were murdered. She could not, would not, stand by and watch anyone else she loved meet the same end. Especially not at the hands of Cal James, and even more especially because of her.

She sensed Graham's attention on her, and she lifted her chin. They held each other with their eyes for a long moment, and it felt as if she were back in his arms, but that would never happen again. He was leaving, and she would not have any foolish notions that he might stay because he fancied her. Graham Staddler wanted nothing to do with holding her and everything to do with leaving her the first moment he could. He was a man who didn't want to hang his hat in any place for too long. "There is no doubt in my mind he is coming for me," she said.

Alone, she could face what would come, but Stella had entrusted her with her most treasured gifts this side of Heaven. She'd given the babies to Fanny to keep them from their father's cruelty, and Fanny had no idea how she would do that. Her earlier panic when she'd believed Cal had arrived proved as much.

The fact Seth had been shot by Cal James made her want to pack each of her brothers into the buckboard and carry them as far from Oak Grove as possible. And what of Graham? She'd hold him at gunpoint if she had to just to get him to go with her. She didn't want anyone else to get hurt, and she most especially did not want them to get hurt because a man was coming after her for revenge.

"I suggest," she said, "for Lily Rose's and Sam's sakes, that Graham takes them into town"

Graham narrowed his gaze, and for the first time, she saw the dangerous, deadly side of him, the keenness that earned him his reputation.

"I'm certain the Gilberts will offer you haven, and Eunice will be a great deal of help." She turned to her brother. "You'll be of little help with your shooting arm as it is, so you should go with him."

"No." That one word from Graham, cold as steel, was more effective at halting all movement in the room than a six-shooter firing off a shot.

Fanny pulled in a breath, rose from the kitchen chair and pressed her palms against the tabletop. She glanced at her brother, who shrugged. She pierced Graham with her sternest glare. "No?"

"No." Graham crossed his arms. "I agree there is some merit to the idea of moving the twins into town, but I. Will. Not. Leave. You."

"I am afraid you do not have a say in this matter, Graham." She straightened. "You are not one of my brothers, and you are not my husband."

"That can be remedied."

For the first time in as long as she could remember, no words came to her, none in her thoughts, and none on her tongue. She couldn't even utter a sound, no words of denial. If he thought to marry her, it was only out of duty to his niece and nephew or out of some sense of moral obligation to save her good name because her brothers might demand it of him.

She didn't know exactly what Nathan had been doing in the barn with his rifle pointed at Graham. She could guess, but she'd pretended otherwise, because she hadn't wanted to see Graham's reaction. She wanted a husband, but not one out of convenience, not even if the man was starting to own her heart.

She pressed her lips together and blinked back the tears threatening to make their presence known. Fanny could no longer deny what she suspected had started when she first saw the wooden sign on her establishment and discovered Graham had taken the time to do that for her. She was in love with Graham Staddler, a man determined to spend the rest of his life punishing himself for his perceived failures by roaming from town to town and never planting roots. It was just as well that he move on. She didn't relish competing with the lure of roaming. She'd seen it in Seth. He preferred sleeping beneath the stars rather than in his bed. Graham was the same. Another pull of breath into her lungs fortified her nerves and helped her find her voice. "That will never happen."

A muscle twitched at the top of his jaw. "I wouldn't be too sure about that, sweetheart."

Her eyes grew wide at the trill of excitement coursing through her blood at his confident tone. It was as if Graham wanted to marry her. Did he?

No, she knew better than to buy that bottle of watered-down concoction from the medicine man. If he wanted to marry her, it was only out of obligation, duty and morals. And she would not have that. She would not marry him and risk being on the receiving end of resentment. Her brothers had already set aside their lives for her; she would not allow Graham Staddler to do the same.

She moved around the table and, holding his steely gaze, jabbed the end of her finger into his chest. "There is no good reason or cause that I would ever vow myself to you, Mr. Staddler. None whatsoever."

One minute she felt defeated, ready to send everyone she loved and cared for away so she could face Cal James alone. Now all she wanted to do was wring Graham's neck, and then kiss him right smack on his full mouth.

Without a glance backward, she walked out of the farmhouse before the temptation to do either overcame her resolve.

She saddled Bellflower and climbed into the saddle. Frustration clung to her as she nudged the horse out onto the lane and rode hard. She rode until she no longer felt the sting of tears. Until she forgot that Graham suggested they marry. Hearing her hopes and dreams of being a wife and mother flippantly suggested due to his anger and sense of obligation was like eating charred biscuits. She sighed. The sooner Graham left Oak Grove, the sooner she could remove him from her mind and keep him from invading her heart. At least she had Lily Rose and

Sam. She sank into the saddle and closed her eyes. The babies. How could she have left them like that?

She turned Bellflower back to the farm and allowed her to keep a slow pace. She only had to make it through a few more days, and then he'd be gone. And then all would be right as rain, as Graham Staddler would say.

"Well, that went rather well." Seth kicked his legs onto the edge of the table. "I didn't realize you were sweet on my sister."

"I'm not," Graham said and felt the lie twist in his belly. He was sweet on her, more than sweet, but he couldn't follow his heart—he'd only fail her. And she knew it, if her adamant rejection of his botched proposal said anything.

He speared his fingers through his hair. Her rejection stung. She was probably the only single lady of his acquaintance since Clea's death who hadn't played coy and batted eyelashes at him, much to his discomfort. Come to think of it, she was the only woman he'd hoped would show him some sign of interest. But there was no artifice where Fanny was concerned. What you saw is what you got. "I'm just trying to protect her. Besides, if Nathan and Hiram have their way, it'll be a shotgun wedding."

Seth worked to keep a smile from spreading and Graham wanted to kick the chair out from under him. Seth lost the battle and burst into laughter. "Never known you to propose to any other damsel in distress before, even when prodded by a shotgun."

"I've never compromised one before."

Seth swung his legs down and jumped to his feet. His hand balled into a fist. "Best be getting the minister right away."

"Whoa!" Graham held out his palms. "It's not like that. Eunice Gilbert and her father were here the entire time." His mouth twisted to keep the next part from being uttered.

Seth, knowing him well, raised an eyebrow. "But?"

"We sort of fell asleep in the barn. Hiram and Nathan found us there when they returned."

"Like I said, better get the minister."

"I'll do right by her, but I fear Fanny might be the one needing a good prod with the barrel, and then you might need to protect me from her if you don't want her to be a widow soon after the vows are spoken."

Graham had a feeling Fanny wouldn't be happy being forced to marry him. In fact, he knew she wouldn't. A gal like Fanny Ellis liked to make her own decisions. She didn't like being corralled. He didn't blame her, either. After all, she wasn't livestock to be led around. She was a flesh and blood woman with a mind of her own. She'd made her thoughts clear on the matter of their impending nuptials before she stormed off to the barn to cool her heels. She didn't want a marriage to him, and not a single reason would compel her otherwise. Not even his love.

Seth burst into laughter and resumed his seat. "Fanny's a lot of bark."

"And I've seen her bite. She rescued me from a

rattler yesterday. Shot him dead-on. I think she might be a better shot than you."

"I know she's a better shot than you, Staddler."

Graham sobered. "That she is, Seth."

Graham couldn't deny the truth from his friend's mouth. However, after seeing what Cal had done to his sister, he did not want Fanny anywhere close to the wretch "Still, I wouldn't want her up against a man like Cal James, even if she is capable. He's as mean as they come and for no good reason."

Seth leaned back against the chair and picked at the edge of the table. "I agree, but short of tying her up and locking her in a room, I'm afraid there isn't much we can do to keep her from facing him."

Graham cocked his hip. "Guess there is no option but to keep her at my side and face him together."

"That's a big gesture, Graham," Seth said. "You ever fight beside a woman before?"

Yes, he had, and they'd lost. However, the enemy hadn't been a man, but an unseen sickness ravaging his wife's body. "I never encountered one capable."

"Not many men would see the value of my sister," Seth said as he stood up and held out his good hand. "It's an honor to welcome you to the family, and don't you worry about the wedding. I'll be right there behind Fanny in case she thinks to bolt.

"My thanks, although I'd much rather she was there of her own free will."

One of Seth's eyebrows rose high. "Like you will be?"

There wasn't a hint of sarcasm in his friend's tone,

only humor, and Graham knew he'd somehow re-vealed his feelings for Fanny, and there was no use denying it. Wagon wheels creaked into the yard, and a quick glance told him Nathan had returned with the minister. Hiram rode close behind them. Anx-ious to get his marriage to Fanny started, before fear grabbed hold of him by the boots and rushed him out of town. "Well, I guess I better go find my bride-to-be. I can't say she'll be too happy about a shotgun wedding, though."

Graham plopped his hat on his head and strode from the house to the barn with a quick stop to tell Hiram and Nathan he'd get Fanny. They could be married shortly before taking Stella to her resting place. He entered the barn, but Fanny was nowhere to be found and neither was Bellflower.

Fear tracked down his spine and gripped his chest. Memories of Clea's last days forced their way into his thoughts. This time, though, they weren't clouded with the guilt of failure. He'd done all he could to save her and their son. He knew that now. Thanks to Fanny. He thought of the tear-stained goodbyes and the tender words of love between him and Clea, words he hadn't spoken to Fanny due to his own stubbornness. Words Fanny deserved to hear.

He needed to find Fanny before Cal did. He needed to tell her what was in his heart before it was too late.

Chapter Fifteen

Graham ground his teeth together at the sight of Fanny nonchalantly riding Bellflower into the yard as if she'd been out for an afternoon stroll. He assessed her, looking for any hint of injury. A light dusting of freckles draped over the bridge of her nose and covered the curve of her cheeks. No scratches or bruises marred her skin. Her light lavender blouse ruffling in the soft breeze did not seem disturbed.

Relief washed over him like a deluge. His knees nearly buckled to see her good and well. Especially since his imagination had torn a trail of sheer terror through him when he hadn't found her anywhere on the farm. He traced her with his gaze once more, just to be certain she was all right. Strands of her fiery red hair floated around her with the breeze, and a pang of jealousy rode down his chest to the pit of his stomach. The way her locks sprung from its tie, he could nearly imagine she'd been out riding with a beau if it weren't for the pensive crease in her brow. She was deep in thought and hadn't noticed him standing there, armed and ready to pick apart every blade of prairie grass looking for her.

"Where have you been?" he asked as hot air pulled in and out of his nostrils.

Fanny jolted to alertness.

He wanted to holler and berate her for her foolishness at leaving unescorted. To throttle her for scaring every bit of sanity from his mind. However, he knew if she wasn't about to already, she'd quill up like a porcupine if he did, and it'd take even longer than he'd like to get the deed of their marriage over with. As soon as she was his wife, there'd be no more gallivanting around without him by her side. None whatsoever. He'd ensure whenever she took it upon herself to go to her shop, he would be right beside her. He'd even sit outside the door, beneath her placard, whittling a toy for one of the twins while he waited for her to conclude her business. She would never be out of his sight again.

Fanny didn't bother acknowledging his presence. Instead, she glanced at Hiram, Nathan and then Reverend Scott. She slowly took her time to meet each of their gazes. Did he imagine she lingered on the minister's a little longer than necessary? "Where is Seth? Is he all right?"

Concern furrowed her brow, and for good reason. Although Seth had been shot in the shoulder, any sort of wound could quickly inflame and do a man in.

"He's in the house with the twins," Graham said, motioning toward the house. His action didn't do any good, though, since she avoided looking at him. It was as though she hadn't heard him. He was about to repeat himself when her chin bobbed a little. Her avoidance told him she was either still mad or she believed he was mad. At least he thought that's what she believed. He supposed he could be wrong on the matter. It wouldn't be the first time.

He was angry. Well, not so much anymore, but he was upset about her prolonged absence while a crazed murderer was hunting her down. Of course, he'd gotten over it the moment she rode onto the lane dividing the farmhouse and the barn. As soon as he'd seen her, he'd wanted to pull her into his arms and kiss her.

He drew in a tentative breath, praying he wouldn't embarrass himself with tears now that his anger was beginning to subside. He took another draw of air and noticed it came without the hindrance of fear. If she would only look at him. He was zealous for their eyes to meet. For her gaze to linger longer on him than it had on the minister. He longed to see a flicker of recognition, a spark or even a hint of emotion. For them to sparkle like they had when she'd woken in his arms. "You mind telling us where you've been when there is a crazed madman on the loose?"

She shifted and nearly made the eye contact he longed for, but she stopped. Her throat worked as she swallowed, and he couldn't help wondering if she sensed the thrum of his heart. A heart that reached for her.

Fanny Ellis.

A woman worthy of all the goodness this world had to give, and Lord help him, he wanted to be the one to give it to her. But could she love him?

They'd only known each other a few days, but he couldn't be more certain about how he felt where she was concerned. He loved her. Spending the last half an hour worrying over her well-being while her brothers talked him out of rushing out to look for her without a plan had honed that to a sharp point, and there was no use denying it. It didn't matter if she loved him or not. Of course, he preferred she did, but marriages were made on less. Perhaps she would come to love him in time, and if she didn't, he would show her his love with everything in him, until their dying days, and God willing, they'd die together peacefully in their sleep so neither of them had to experience the agony of living alone after death.

Looking at her now, he knew without uncertainty that he wanted to be her husband, to stand beside her through each of her stubborn notions, such as riding off alone. He, Graham Staddler, wanted to hang his hat on a hook. He wanted to build a family with her and make a life with her. Until death parted them, which might occur before their nuptials were spoken given the high color of her cheeks.

The seconds ticked off as he waited patiently for an answer. Her refusal to do so pressed hard against his patience. He went to move to help her down from Bellflower but thought better of it when Nathan shook his head. His soon-to-be wife was headstrong and independent, and that was one of the things he loved about her and refused to curb, unless she did something so foolish again, then he might throttle her.

Fanny twisted out of the saddle and jumped to the ground. Her skirts billowed and swirled, and he nearly smiled at her competence of managing her dismount as good as any man in britches. She didn't need a husband, which made the task of convincing her to marry him all the more difficult. Lord help him, he wanted her to want a husband. To want him for her husband.

She tilted her chin, and with a slight drop of her dark lashes as she focused her attention on the minister, she said, "Hello, Reverend Scott. Thank you for coming all this way. I'm sure Mr. Staddler is eager to see his sister buried so he can leave town."

Her words stung, but even more so was the fact she did not tell him where she'd been. He opened his mouth to say something and felt a kick to his boot. He slid a sidelong glance at Nathan, who shook his head again.

Reverend Scott looked to Nathan and Hiram and then Graham before returning his attention to Fanny. He swept his black hat off and held it in front of him as if to shield himself from Fanny's wrath. The minister's lively purple vest beneath his claret-colored coat was a near perfect match to Fanny's shirt.

"Yes, of course. However, I understand there is to be a wedding first," Reverend Scott said.

Graham ground his teeth together.

"Who is getting married?" Fanny's gaze snapped to Graham's, and even though she was angry, he was thankful for the contact. The anger in her eyes was much preferable to her avoidance, and he couldn't wait to soothe it over with a good long touch of their lips.

He moved to open his mouth, but Nathan poked him with the end of his gun to keep him quiet.

"You can be mad enough at Mr. Staddler after the nuptials are done, Fanny," Nathan said. "We don't care how you go on from here as long as he doesn't lay a hand on you in anger, but he's going to do right by you and save your good name after his shenanigans in the barn."

"Nothing happened." She balled her fists at her sides as she looked to her brothers for help. "Hiram, you cannot mean to agree with this."

"I think if you consider the situation, you'll come to realize it's the right thing to do, Fanny," Hiram said as he kicked the toe of his boot into the dirt. "Think of the babies. They'll be better with two parents. You can raise them right and proper with Mr. Staddler's name."

Fanny's cheeks reddened and then lost all their color. She swayed on her feet and Graham thought she might faint, but she pulled her shoulders back and lifted her chin.

"I will be fine. The babies will be fine. Many women and children have persevered with less than what we have. And what good is two parents when one doesn't intend on sticking around?" Fanny stalked to Hiram and poked him in the chest. "I did fine without parents, and the twins will be just as good with only one. Me." She moved to walk around her brother, but Hiram reached out and snagged her arm. Graham was surprised at the oldest Ellis's action. Up to this point, he'd shown very little emotion and spoken very few words.

"Fanny, there is no better man than Graham," Hiram said. "Seth's known him a while and says he is as true as they come."

"That might be so, but I am not marrying him, and you can't make me." She turned to Graham. Tears quivered at the corners of her eyes, and he longed to pull her into his arms. "Say something. Tell them you won't marry me."

He shifted his weight. "I can't do that, sweetheart."

She fisted her hands "I'm seeing to Lily Rose and Sam while you figure out a way to convince my brothers we are not getting married."

"I will not do that," he said as she stomped past him. His eyes remained on her rigid back until she swung the door open and disappeared into the house.

Fanny threw herself against the door and crossed her arms. Hot tears sliced down her cheeks. Marrying a man for convenience's sake was one thing. She'd be more than willing to do it if she didn't love him. But she loved Graham Staddler, not the Graham she'd read about in the papers, but *the* Graham Staddler. The one who'd taken time to make a placard for her business. He was thoughtful and giving.

His heart was full of kindness. He was the perfect match to her heart, but she could not marry him. He was determined to live in grief, and there was no room in his heart for her.

She swiped the tears from her face and perused the room, wondering why Seth hadn't said a word to her. He was always the first to tease her whenever she cried, but he was also the first to help fight her battles. Surely, he'd make Hiram and Nathan see reason and call this whole charade off.

"Seth?" she called, finding it odd he wasn't in the kitchen or in the front room. She heard a noise and walked across the room. Her brother's wide gaze met hers. A trail of blood streamed down his brow. He was bound and gagged, lying on the floor next to their mother's old chest. She slid her gaze upward, halting on the arms of a trail-dust-covered dingy shirt holding the baby.

"Hello, Miss Ellis," Cal James said, flashing her an overexaggerated smile with various shades of yellowing and black teeth. "Seems you've been causing me all sorts of trouble since my wife started working for you."

Not wanting to cause Cal further irritation, she kept her lips pressed together. She shifted her hips, allowing her skirt to sway against her legs. The weight of her pistol bumped against her thigh, and she released the air held captive in her lungs. She flitted her gaze to her brother and then out the window to where Graham and her other brothers stood. She willed Graham to come to the house, to know she needed him, but his back was turned. She focused on the baby. Her stomach turned as Cal stroked a dirty finger over little Sam's face. Her heart thundered in her chest, pounding. Even if she could get to her pistol without Cal's notice, could she shoot him without harming Sam? Still, maybe the threat of her pistol would force Cal to put the baby down. Her fingers danced along the fabric until she felt the edge of the pocket containing the weapon.

Cal shook his head. "I wouldn't do that if I were you."

She opened her mouth to holler but clamped it shut when Cal shifted Sam in his arms.

"There will be consequences if you scream," Cal said, his voice low and hard.

"Put the baby down, Cal," she said, her voice wobbled with emotion as a tear slid down her cheek.

Cal motioned with his gun for her to move toward the back door. "Now, slowly remove your pistol and place it on the table. Don't do anything stupid, Miss Ellis, else I'll shoot your brother again, and this time he won't be breathing after."

Memories of Fanny's parents infiltrated her mind. Guilt fought for a foothold. She gulped. She knew she wasn't responsible for her parents' deaths, but if she didn't comply with Cal's wishes, she would be responsible if anything happened to her brother and the twins.

She looked to Seth and drew in a deep breath.

"I'm sorry." It was all she could say to her brother.

"I'm going to reach in my pocket and remove my

pistol." She reached in and grabbed the cool steel. Her hand trembled with the effort to not shoot Cal, but the risk of harming Sam was too great. She lay her pistol on the table and turned back to Cal.

"Now, move yourself to that door and open it. Without a sound."

Fanny moved toward the door. Her brother grunted through the gag in his mouth as he attempted to kick his feet.

"I'm sorry, Seth." There was no other way if she was going to protect those she loved. Her brothers. The babies. Graham. She prayed God would keep them well and safe. She prayed once Cal sought his revenge on her that he would leave Oak Grove and never bother them again. She turned the knob on the back door and quietly pushed the door open.

"Don't apologize." Cal's boot steps clattered behind her. "Your family will be grateful that I'm taking you off their hands. Can't be easy providing for a gal not earning her keep."

Fanny wanted to argue, to tell this man she did plenty to earn her keep. She did her fair share of chores and did what needed to be done. Her sewing brought in supplies for them to eat. Cal pressed a pistol to her back. Fanny drew in a shuddering breath a moment before Cal pushed her down the steps. She fell to the ground, and her skirts tangled around her legs, keeping her from quickly jumping to her feet. Cal followed behind her and yanked her up by her arm. Sam began to fuss, and her heart ached to hold the infant, to remove him from this scoundrel's grip.

"Holler, and I'll shoot you, then I'll go back and finish the rest of them."

She looked through the window. Seth struggled to free himself. Lily Rose remained sleeping in her bed.

"Don't get all weepy over the girl. She's worthless to us where we're going." He dragged her toward a pair of horses tied near an old shanty that had been left on the land by a previous homesteader when Hiram had purchased it. Cal tucked Sam into a makeshift saddlebag and then yanked some rope from the saddle horn. He looped the rope around Fanny's wrists so tightly the fibers bit into her flesh.

"Climb up." He nudged her with the end of his gun and motioned to the other horse.

She glanced to Sam and prayed Cal had him secure enough that the ride wouldn't jar him too much. If only Sam had been placed on the horse Cal intended for her, then she could have kicked free of Cal, but it wasn't to be. She held up her bound hands. "How am I supposed to do that?"

"Get yer foot in that stirrup, gal." He poked her with his gun.

She stuck her boot through the stirrup and began to grab hold of the pommel as Cal untied his horse.

"Fanny!"

Fanny snapped her head around, and her eyes widened at the sight of Graham stalking around the corner of the house. Cal spun, firing his gun wildly. Graham clutched his chest and fell to his knees. Fanny screamed. She threw her bound hands around Cal's neck and jumped on his back. She tightened her wrists around his neck. He turned in circles, clawing at her hands, but she held tightly. When Cal rammed his elbow into her ribs, she lost her air and her fight. He threw them both to the ground, and she kicked at him. He rolled off her, coughing and sputtering. Fanny rolled to her feet, and with every bit of strength she could muster, she threw herself up onto Cal's horse, careful not to kick or dislodge Sam. She turned the horse to ride to safety, and her eyes caught sight of Graham struggling to his knees.

She hesitated. She longed to run to him, but Cal remained armed. If she rode toward Graham, he'd fire toward her. *Toward Sam*, her heart whispered. Still, if she rode south, she'd keep the horse between Cal's gun and Sam. It would give her brothers enough time to get to Graham. To help him.

As if he read her mind, he yelled. "Fanny, no!"

"I love you, Graham Staddler," she hollered as she tapped her heels into the flank of the horse.

A shot ripped through the sky like a crack of thunder and Fanny slid to the side of Cal's bay and prayed the bullet missed its mark.

Chapter Sixteen

"That woman is going to be the death of me," Graham said, dropping Cal James at the feet of Nathan and Seth.

"That's Fanny," Seth said from beside him. "Seems to always have one foot on the edge of disaster."

Graham clutched his chest. A sticky warmth pulsed through his shirt, wetting his hand. He didn't feel like himself.

"Did she tell you she fell in the creek the other day?" Nathan asked. "She didn't say a word, but she came home looking like a drenched cat. Hiram made us keep quiet so as not to embarrass her. She can be clumsy."

Graham couldn't imagine Fanny as anything but sure-footed. He opened his mouth to saw so, but all he could say was, "She's a prize shot."

"Never said she wasn't." Seth pulled a length of rope from the buckboard tossed it to Nathan. "Guess you get to do the honors, brother."

Graham watched as Nathan trussed the scoundrel up like a calf.

"It's when she loses focus and starts gathering wool you have to watch out for her," Seth said as he watched Nathan wrap the thick rope around Cal's ankles.

"Always daydreaming about one thing or another." Nathan inspected his work and then scratched his head. "Funny thing is that didn't seem to be a problem until you started showing up in the paper. I imagine she was taken with those stories written up about you in the paper. She even started practicing her shot a little more."

Nathan jerked on the rope to tighten it. Cal groaned. Nathan tugged on the rope wrapped around Cal's ankles and stood, lifting Cal off the ground. Nathan dropped him with a thud. Cal yelped and his eyes flew open.

Graham pressed his lips into a fine line and crouched next to the good-for-nothing excuse of a man. "Best be thanking God I have a merciful heart or you'd be praying for a swift death."

A rider trotted into the yard and Graham stood. His heart fell a little seeing Hiram was by himself.

"I lost the trail," Hiram said, pulling Buttercup to a halt. Graham twisted on his feet and gazed in the direction Fanny had ridden. A new hot trail of blood oozed from his wound, sliding down his chest. A wave of dizziness assaulted him. "Where could she have gone?"

"I think we need to head back home before you

fall out of that saddle," Nathan said, and as if he knew Graham would argue, he said, "I wouldn't be none too happy if my sister's groom died of blood loss before he spoke his vows."

"I need to find her." Graham said, worry over her warred with the knowledge he was losing his battle with consciousness.

"We will," Nathan responded. "After what you did to Cal, she isn't in any more danger. She'll come home."

Every bit of him wanted to argue, but he knew he'd lost a lot of blood. He'd already pushed himself beyond his limits in hopes of finding her. He wouldn't last much longer.

"All right," Graham said as he turned Turnip back toward the farm. "I hope you're right."

They rode in silence until they entered the yard. Cal sat beside the wheel of the buckboard, his hands and feet trussed up, a bandanna tied across his mouth. Graham dismounted and nearly collapsed.

Hiram strode toward him and examined Graham's wound. "Not a clean shot."

That's what Graham feared. He only prayed the bullet would be easily extracted. They'd have to fetch the doc for him to dig it out. That wasn't going to happen until he laid eyes on his bride, no matter how much he bled. The confounded woman. She'd had the guts to tell him she loved him and then ride off like she was running from a pack of wolves. Didn't she trust him to rescue her? Probably not, given his track record of protecting those he loved.

"Well, at least you don't have to worry about him no more," Nathan said, nudging Cal James with the toe of his boot. "Don't know how you didn't kill him. I would have."

Cal shot him a gaze that would have sent the fear of God into a weaker man. "His death won't bring Stella back from the dead."

It had taken everything in him to not shoot the wretch dead, especially having witnessed the blows he'd laid on Fanny as she attempted to strangle the man. His bride sure was fierce, fiercer than any man he'd known. And brave. But she shouldn't have to be. "Trust me, I wanted to, but justice needs to be dealt by the judge, not by me."

"We should get you to the doctor and get this scoundrel to the marshal," Hiram said. "Reverend Scott offered to watch over Lily Rose."

"No," Graham said, wavering on his feet. He knew he needed to get to the doctor soon, but it'd wait. "I'm waiting right here for my bride."

"You're as stubborn as she is," Hiram said. "But I guarantee she'll be fine, especially with this one captured. She'll come home soon enough."

"That's what Nathan said, but she doesn't have her pistol."

Seth smiled. "Don't underestimate my sister. She probably has one or two tucked in her boots."

Graham began to laugh and was stopped short by the pain radiating through his chest. "Just like her brother."

"We taught her well," Hiram said. "When we chose

to break her out of the orphanage, we all agreed she would never again be at the mercy of a man, and if she ever was, she'd know how to put up a good fight. So we taught her all we knew about protecting ourselves and those we love."

"She couldn't have had a better upbringing," Graham said. Sadness and regret spilled from his eyes. "I wish I had given Stella the same opportunity."

"Your sister did what she could. Nobody could have known the type of man Cal James was." Hiram's quiet wisdom settled some of Graham's guilt. "He deceived a lot of folks. Stella just happened to be one his victims. You should be proud she broke free from the rascal to save her babies."

"Yep, you should be right proud of her," Seth said. "And you did right by her, coming after her when you knew she was in trouble."

"Thank you," Graham said, knowing it would take a long time, years maybe, before he could see the rightness of his actions. He wished he would have come for her sooner. He wished he would have found her before Cal James had killed her. "It'll be an honor to call you three family."

Seth nudged Graham's shoulder. "We ain't ever had anyone famous in the family before."

Hiram and Nathan laughed. Graham kept his laughter muted out of fear of succumbing to the weakness overtaking him.

"Now, let's get you into town," Hiram said.

Graham shook his head. "If you don't mind, I'd like to stay here and wait for Fanny. We've got things to discuss, and the sooner we get them done, the better."

"I suppose I can ride Mr. James to town and send Doc on out this way," Hiram said. "I'm guessing Nate doesn't want to take his eyes off you in case you take it in your head to leave town before the nuptials can be said."

"Naw," Nathan said. "I don't think we need to worry about the groom leaving town, but it would make me feel a mite better if I can track down Fanny and bring her back for her wedding."

This time, Graham did give in to laughter, but a wave of pain sliced through him. His vision wavered, and the world seemed to fall off its axis. He pulled in a few breaths to regather his wits. "I'd be much obliged as I'm not certain I have the strength to fetch her."

He glanced at his former brother-in-law and pulled his brows together. "It's a shame I can't take him in to the marshal, though."

Fanny slowed her pace to keep from jarring Sam too much as they approached the shell of Nathan's cabin. She dismounted as best she could with her bound hands and led the horse inside the cabin to keep from being seen by Cal if rode this way. She prayed Nathan would find her soon, for Sam's sake. Shutting the door behind them, she led the horse to the back corner and tied him to a post marking off Nathan's future bedroom.

She dug through the saddlebag, hoping to find

a knife to cut the ropes binding her wrists, but she came up empty. Her head fell against the saddle and tears streamed down her cheeks, leaving wet spots in the dirt floor beside her boots.

Cal had shot Graham. "My God, no!"

A keening wail tore from her chest and filled the cabin. He couldn't be dead. He just couldn't be. She loved him. She'd realized it the moment she discovered he'd made the sign for her sewing shop. Everything she'd heard and read about him had manifested into flesh and blood, the real man. Graham Staddler.

The recollection of Graham falling to his knees, clutching at the red spot staining his blue linen shirt sent her to the floor. She buried her face into her hands and sobbed. The blood staining his shirt had been so close to his heart. She could not see any way of him surviving. Had Cal's bullet taken the greatest gunslinger in Kansas down? All because of her. If Graham hadn't come looking for her, he'd still be alive. If he hadn't called out to her, Cal wouldn't have known Graham was there.

If she would have just let him go the night they said goodbye to Stella, he'd be alive, but she'd done what her brother's claimed women do and cried and begged him to stay. Why had she done that? Graham was dead because of her.

Sam began to fuss. She swiped at her eyes with the fist of her hand and rose to her feet. She peered into the saddle bag at his little round face, his sparkling blue eyes so much like Graham's. She stroked the soft round of his cheek with the edge of her pinkie. "Hello, little one."

She tugged at her ropes, but they only tightened. "Oh, Sam. What are we to do?"

They couldn't go back to the farm. What if Cal had made good on his word and killed all her brothers and Reverend Scott? What of Lily Rose? Could they remain here, waiting for Nathan to find them? What if he never came? What if Call killed him just as he'd killed Graham? "Lord, what am I to do?"

As if to answer her, Sam mewled. She had nothing here to feed him. She couldn't even pick him up with her hands tied the way they were. She needed help. The farm was closer than town or any of their neighbors. She risked running into Cal, but if Graham had gotten off a shot or her brothers had gotten to Cal before he'd come after her, then all would be well. She needed to see Graham, to know for certain that he was gone. To tell him she loved him, even if he couldn't hear her.

She didn't dare hope he was alive like she had with her parents. That hope had devastated her. If she hoped for Graham to be alive and discovered he was in fact dead, it would destroy her. It would destroy her faith. Especially since she'd only recently come to acknowledge God's plan for her life was much greater than she could imagine. If she hoped and prayed Graham was alive because he was part of the plan for her and she discovered he wasn't, she didn't know if she could ever bring herself to pray again.

She swiped at her tears once again and pulled in a

breath full of the scent of freshly cut wood. The smell reminded her of the door Graham had made, of the placard and the small intricate details he'd carved to give her something nice and beautiful.

Dare she hope Cal's bullet had missed Graham's heart? As much as she wanted to, as much as that tiny bit of faith called to her to trust God that all would be well, she didn't know if she could hope, because she knew sometimes God had a different idea of what was best for her. Still, she couldn't ignore that tiny spark spurring her to believe.

"All right, little one. I know you must be hungry." She brushed the tips of her fingers over his softy downy locks. "We'll go home."

She led the horse from the cabin and lifted her face to the warmth emanating from the sun. The sun kissed the tops of the prairie grasses, turning them a beautiful golden sea of color. Clouds embraced the rolling and ragged hills, changing the landscape before her eyes. It would be dark soon, sooner than she'd like, but thankfully she knew her way home. Although, it would have been better if she was on Daisy. The horse always knew her way home, no matter where they were coming from.

Feeling the hardness in her boot against her ankle, she knelt and fished out a small derringer. She lifted her face toward the sky in thankfulness. She'd forgotten she tucked it in her boot earlier in case she needed it. It wasn't much, would only give her a single shot, but she had confidence in her skills. If it came down to keeping Sam alive and killing Cal James, she'd shoot to kill.

Fanny slipped the derringer into her pocket, grabbed the pommel and tugged herself into the saddle. She nudged Cal's horse with her heels, and turned him toward home, where she silently and secretly prayed, Graham would be waiting for her. Alive.

Chapter Seventeen

Where was she? Graham paced from the east window to the west window, went to open the door and then paced once again. Nathanhadn't yet returned from searching for Fanny, and he'd left more than two hours before. Graham was itching to ride out and find her. He needed to see her, to see if any of Cal's blows had marred her beautiful sun-kissed skin.

Graham had woken after he'd passed out to find the bullet removed and an audience of six hovering over him. Reverend Scott had ridden into town and retrieved the doctor and the marshal while Seth and Hiram took turns keeping watch on Lily Rose and Cal James. Of course, word had gotten around town, and Eunice dragged her father back to the farmhouse, too. Soon, all of Oak Grove would congregate at the Ellis farm and witness the famous gunslinger's downfall. Not only had he been shot, but he was about to marry the woman he loved. If she ever came back home.

"Graham, you're supposed to be resting, not wearing holes in my floors," Hiram said.

"I've tried telling him," Doctor Harden said. "You lose any more blood, and you'll hit the floor, son."

"Here." Eunice set a hot cup of coffee on the table. "You should drink this. It'll calm you."

"Calm!" He rammed his hands into his pockets. "How do you expect me to remain calm when the woman I love is out there somewhere?" He speared his fingers through his hair and then collapsed in one of the kitchen chairs when he felt lightheaded. "They should be home by now."

"Nate will find her and Sam," Seth said. "He's the best tracker among us."

Graham growled and jumped back to his feet. "I know. You've told me that several times in the last fifteen minutes."

"Only to ease your worries."

"My worries will be eased once I see Fanny." Once she was in his arms. *Lord, please bring her and Sam home.* As soon as he saw her, he wouldn't let her out of his sight for days, a year even. He'd tie her to a chair if he had to, just to make sure she was safe.

"Graham, your wound is seeping through the bandage." Doctor Harden motioned for him to sit.

Graham's shoulders sagged, and he sank back to the chair.

"You're not going to do Fanny and the babies any good if you perish from your wound. Fanny is a strong woman, and she's smart. She'll be home soon."

"I know." That was all he could say. She was the

smartest woman of his acquaintance. However, his patience had been overtaken by fear for her well-being. What if Cal had an accomplice? What if she'd ridden right into a trap? Of course, all their threatening hadn't elicited a word from Cal. It was a good thing the marshal had taken him back to town, because Graham didn't know what he might do if the man had remained here at the farm.

Doctor Harden unbuttoned Graham's shirt and removed the bandage. He tsked and then replaced it with a new one. He redid the buttons and then tied around his neck and arm a makeshift sling made out of one of Fanny's shawls that had been hanging on the wall.

Graham drew in a breath and closed his eyes to relish in the scent so uniquely belonging to the woman he loved.

"You've got to keep it elevated. That bullet was too close to the heart. I still can't believe you're breathing."

"I'm hard to kill," Graham said, thinking about how he hadn't even caught the illness that had taken the lives of Clea and their son, plus most of the town. He thought surviving was a punishment from God, but he no longer recalled the pain of losing them, not the excruciating pain he'd felt for months after their deaths. Now, all he felt was the need to see Fanny, to know she was okay. To know Sam was okay.

He kicked out his feet and rested his head on the back of the chair. He'd barely closed his eyes when the sound of crying met his ears. He jumped up and looked to Lily Rose, but she was sound asleep. He scrambled to his feet and swung open the door.

Fanny!

Graham wasn't a fainting man, but the sight of her sitting on that horse made his knees wobble. He ignored Doc's call, tore himself free from Hiram's grasp, descended the stairs and rushed to meet his bride. Somewhere in the back of his mind, he heard footsteps following him outside, but his focus was solely on her, his beautiful, fierce bride.

"Fanny!" he said, reaching to pull her down. He tugged her into his arms. Ignoring the pain each movement caused him. He squeezed her and kissed her brow. His heart pounded between them as he drew his lips down to her mouth. Her lips, soft and full, pressed against his, and for several long seconds, he held her, their mouths connected. Her tears mingled with his. He pulled from her and trailed his mouth back to her brow, drying her tears as he went. "You're home."

"You're alive," she cried and buried her head against his shoulder. "You are alive."

"I am, Fanny," he said, pulling back to gaze into her mossy green eyes. "And I've never felt more alive than I do in this moment. Tell me, tell me again that you love me."

She opened her mouth, but before she said a word, Graham's world went black.

Fanny sank to her knees next to Graham. She rocked him with her bound fists, her hands numb from the ropes. "Graham! Graham! Please, please, please wake up."

His lashes didn't flutter, and his head lolled to one side. Sam quit his crying from the saddlebag, and a quick glance told her Eunice had him. Fanny knew he'd be taken care of. She lifted a silent prayer of thanks for friends like Eunice Gilbert and then laid her head on Graham's chest. "Please, Graham. Please wake up. I love you. You cannot die. I won't let you."

Doctor Harden appeared across from her, and she pleaded with her eyes. "Do something. Save him."

She felt Hiram's arm bend around her waist, and she was lifted to her feet. Seth appeared and cut the ropes from her wrists. She squirmed against her brother's hold, kicking at his shins. "Let go of me."

"Let Doc do his work."

"I need to move him back inside," Doc said.

Fanny fell limp against Hiram.

"We can't move him if you're in the way, Fanny."

She nodded, and Hiram loosened his arm. She pressed her fist against her mouth, the mouth Graham had so tenderly and lovingly kissed only moments before and muffled her sobs. Her tears flowed freely down her cheeks, just as they had when she'd seen him next to her. Alive. "Graham Staddler, I love you!"

She followed close behind them, but once they made it inside the house, she held back. Getting in Doc's way would only prolong the opening of her love's eyes. Hiram and Seth, with his one arm in a sling, carried Graham into Hiram's room off the back of the kitchen. The door closed behind them, and Fanny stared at that door for what seemed like hours.

"Fanny, would you like to hold Sam for a bit?" Eunice asked. "He might ease your nerves a little."

"Yes, of course." Fanny shuddered and then held her hands out. "I haven't thanked you for all your help. You are a good friend, Eunice. I hope I can be as good of a friend in return."

"You are, Fanny." Eunice wrapped her arm around Fanny's shoulder and hugged her. "Don't worry too much. Graham is in good hands. And, Fanny, that man in there loves you. He nearly shook the rafters over our heads saying as much."

More tears spilled over the rim of her eyelashes. She dropped her gaze to Lily Rose and swayed across the wooden floors. Was it possible? Did Graham love her? Enough to remain in Oak Grove? Her heart soared at the thought of them being a family, but her thoughts quickly crashed toward the ground. First, Graham had to stay alive.

She walked around the small area, rocking Sam in her arms as she fed him. Reverend Scott knelt in front of the fire, stirring something in a pot. Eunice fed Lily Rose more milk. Nathan stomped through the front door and nodded when he saw her. "Where'd you hole up, little sister?"

"Your place."

"Miss Gilbert. Reverend," he said, acknowledging them before he returned his attention to her. The corner of his mouth turned upward. "Figured so. It occurred to me that's where you might have been after

I'd check town and rode out to the railroad camps. I was on my way out there but decided to stop here first to check on Graham. How is he?"

Fanny's pulse raced. She glanced toward Hiram's room and shrugged. "I don't rightly know. He met me in the yard and seemed well enough for a bit, then he fainted. Doc, Hiram and Seth are in there with him now."

"He lost a lot of blood, and much to Doc's displeasure, Mr. Staddler refused to rest and keep his blood from flowing so hard through his veins," Eunice said from the kitchen.

"Did Doc retrieve the bullet?" Nathan asked.

"He did," Eunice said. "Said the wound looked clean."

Fanny hadn't even thought to ask those questions. A clean removal was good news, right? That meant he'd wake up, and she'd be able to look into his beautiful blue eyes.

"Still, he's lost a lot of blood," Reverend Scott said.

Fanny squeezed her eyes closed and forced the tears to cease. Graham would come through this. He had to. The babies needed him. She needed him.

The bedroom door swung open, and Fanny turned on her heel. Hiram poked his head through the door. "Good to see you came home, Nate. Doc says, Graham is going to be just find. Now, would you all mind coming in here, and Nate you might want to bring Fanny and the shotgun, seems we're going to have ourselves a wedding."

Fanny raced into the bedroom and eased onto the edge of the bed with Lily Rose cradled against her chest. "Graham."

His eyes flickered open, and his mouth curved into a smile. "Hello, sweetheart. How are you feeling?" He reached up and grazed the top of her cheek with his knuckle.

The metallic scent of blood filled her senses, but she didn't care. She was relieved to see his eyes were open and he was asking how she was doing. "I am well. Are you certain you want to marry me?" she asked him.

His laughter turned to a cough, and he clutched at his chest. "I wouldn't have it any other way, my love."

Her brothers, Eunice and the reverend crowded into the room. Nathan held his shotgun against his shoulder, but everyone knew it was only for show. When two people loved each other the way she and Graham did, there was no need of force.

They gazed into each other's eyes. His twinkled like a clear night sky. She twined her fingers with his. Their warmth intertwined, connected as one.

"Do you, Graham Staddler, take Fanny Ellis to be your wife, to love her, to honor her and to cherish her until death do you part?"

"I do, until death do us part."

"And do you, Fanny Ellis, promise to love, honor, cherish, and O—"

Fanny held up her hand. She shook her head, and then winked at Reverend Scott. "Do not say it, Reverend. I will not make a vow I cannot keep."

Graham burst into laughter. "As you shouldn't, sweetheart."

The reverend's mouth twitched. "Very well, Fanny, do you promise to love Graham Staddler until death do you part? "

"I do."

* * * * *

Get 3 FREE REWARDS!

We'll send you 2 FREE Books <u>plus</u> a FREE Mystery Gift.

FREE Value Over **$20**

Both the **Love Inspired®** and **Love Inspired® Suspense** series feature compelling novels filled with inspirational romance, faith, forgiveness and hope.

YES! Please send me 2 FREE novels from the Love Inspired or Love Inspired Suspense series and my FREE gift (gift is worth about $10 retail). After receiving them, if I don't wish to receive any more books, I can return the shipping statement marked "cancel." If I don't cancel, I will receive 6 brand-new Love Inspired Larger-Print books or Love Inspired Suspense Larger-Print books every month and be billed just $6.49 each in the U.S. or $6.74 each in Canada. That is a savings of at least 16% off the cover price. It's quite a bargain! Shipping and handling is just 50¢ per book in the U.S. and $1.25 per book in Canada.* I understand that accepting the 2 free books and gift places me under no obligation to buy anything. I can always return a shipment and cancel at any time by calling the number below. The free books and gift are mine to keep no matter what I decide.

Choose one: ☐ **Love Inspired Larger-Print**
(122/322 BPA GRPA)

☐ **Love Inspired Suspense Larger-Print**
(107/307 BPA GRPA)

☐ **Or Try Both!**
(122/322 & 107/307 BPA GRRP)

Name (please print)

Address _____ Apt. #

City _____ State/Province _____ Zip/Postal Code

Email: Please check this box ☐ if you would like to receive newsletters and promotional emails from Harlequin Enterprises ULC and its affiliates. You can unsubscribe anytime.

Mail to the **Harlequin Reader Service:**
IN U.S.A.: P.O. Box 1341, Buffalo, NY 14240-8531
IN CANADA: P.O. Box 603, Fort Erie, Ontario L2A 5X3

Want to try 2 free books from another series! Call 1-800-873-8635 or visit www.ReaderService.com.

LIRLIS23

Get 3 FREE REWARDS!

We'll send you 2 FREE Books plus a FREE Mystery Gift.

FREE
Value Over
$20

Both the **Harlequin® Special Edition** and **Harlequin® Heartwarming™** series feature compelling novels filled with stories of love and strength where the bonds of friendship, family and community unite.

YES! Please send me 2 FREE novels from the Harlequin Special Edition or Harlequin Heartwarming series and my FREE Gift (gift is worth about $10 retail). After receiving them, if I don't wish to receive any more books, I can return the shipping statement marked "cancel." If I don't cancel, I will receive 6 brand-new Harlequin Special Edition books every month and be billed just $5.49 each in the U.S. or $6.24 each in Canada, a savings of at least 12% off the cover price, or 4 brand-new Harlequin Heartwarming Larger-Print books every month and be billed just $6.24 each in the U.S. or $6.74 each in Canada, a savings of at least 19% off the cover price. It's quite a bargain! Shipping and handling is just 50¢ per book in the U.S. and $1.25 per book in Canada.* I understand that accepting the 2 free books and gift places me under no obligation to buy anything. I can always return a shipment and cancel at any time by calling the number below. The free books and gift are mine to keep no matter what I decide.

Choose one: ☐ **Harlequin Special Edition** (235/335 BPA GRMK) ☐ **Harlequin Heartwarming Larger-Print** (161/361 BPA GRMK) ☐ **Or Try Both!** (235/335 & 161/361 BPA GRPZ)

Name (please print)

Address   Apt. #

City   State/Province   Zip/Postal Code

Email: Please check this box ☐ if you would like to receive newsletters and promotional emails from Harlequin Enterprises ULC and its affiliates. You can unsubscribe anytime.

Mail to the **Harlequin Reader Service:**
IN U.S.A.: P.O. Box 1341, Buffalo, NY 14240-8531
IN CANADA: P.O. Box 603, Fort Erie, Ontario L2A 5X3

Want to try 2 free books from another series! Call 1-800-873-8635 or visit www.ReaderService.com.

*Terms and prices subject to change without notice. Prices do not include sales taxes, which will be charged (if applicable) based on your state or country of residence. Canadian residents will be charged applicable taxes. Offer not valid in Quebec. This offer is limited to one order per household. Books received may not be as shown. Not valid for current subscribers to the Harlequin Special Edition or Harlequin Heartwarming series. All orders subject to approval. Credit or debit balances in a customer's account(s) may be offset by any other outstanding balance owed by or to the customer. Please allow 4 to 6 weeks for delivery. Offer available while quantities last.

Your Privacy—Your information is being collected by Harlequin Enterprises ULC, operating as Harlequin Reader Service. For a complete summary of the information we collect, how we use this information and to whom it is disclosed, please visit our privacy notice located at corporate.harlequin.com/privacy-notice. From time to time we may also exchange your personal information with reputable third parties. If you wish to opt out of this sharing of your personal information, please visit readerservice.com/consumerschoice or call 1-800-873-8635. **Notice to California Residents**—Under California law, you have specific rights to control and access your data. For more information on these rights and how to exercise them, visit corporate.harlequin.com/california-privacy.

HSEHW23

Get 3 FREE REWARDS!

We'll send you 2 FREE Books plus a FREE Mystery Gift.

FREE Value Over **$20**

Both the **Harlequin® Historical** and **Harlequin® Romance** series feature compelling novels filled with emotion and simmering romance.

YES! Please send me 2 FREE novels from the Harlequin Historical or Harlequin Romance series and my FREE Mystery Gift (gift is worth about $10 retail). After receiving them, if I don't wish to receive any more books, I can return the shipping statement marked "cancel." If I don't cancel, I will receive 6 brand-new Harlequin Historical books every month and be billed just $6.19 each in the U.S. or $6.74 each in Canada, a savings of at least 11% off the cover price, or 4 brand-new Harlequin Romance Larger-Print books every month and be billed just $6.09 each in the U.S. or $6.24 each in Canada, a savings of at least 13% off the cover price. It's quite a bargain! Shipping and handling is just 50¢ per book in the U.S. and $1.25 per book in Canada.* I understand that accepting the 2 free books and gift places me under no obligation to buy anything. I can always return a shipment and cancel at any time by calling the number below. The free books and gift are mine to keep no matter what I decide.

Choose one: ☐ **Harlequin Historical** (246/349 BPA GRNX) ☐ **Harlequin Romance Larger-Print** (119/319 BPA GRNX) ☐ **Or Try Both!** (246/349 & 119/319 BPA GRRD)

Name (please print)

Address   Apt. #

City   State/Province   Zip/Postal Code

Email: Please check this box ☐ if you would like to receive newsletters and promotional emails from Harlequin Enterprises ULC and its affiliates. You can unsubscribe anytime.

Mail to the **Harlequin Reader Service:**
IN U.S.A.: P.O. Box 1341, Buffalo, NY 14240-8531
IN CANADA: P.O. Box 603, Fort Erie, Ontario L2A 5X3

Want to try 2 free books from another series! Call 1-800-873-8635 or visit www.ReaderService.com.

---

*Terms and prices subject to change without notice. Prices do not include sales taxes, which will be charged (if applicable) based on your state or country of residence. Canadian residents will be charged applicable taxes. Offer not valid in Quebec. This offer is limited to one order per household. Books received may not be as shown. Not valid for current subscribers to the Harlequin Historical or Harlequin Romance series. All orders subject to approval. Credit or debit balances in a customer's account(s) may be offset by any other outstanding balance owed by or to the customer. Please allow 4 to 6 weeks for delivery. Offer available while quantities last.

Your Privacy—Your information is being collected by Harlequin Enterprises ULC, operating as Harlequin Reader Service. For a complete summary of the information we collect, how we use this information and to whom it is disclosed, please visit our privacy notice located at corporate.harlequin.com/privacy-notice. From time to time we may also exchange your personal information with reputable third parties. If you wish to opt out of this sharing of your personal information, please visit readerservice.com/consumerschoice or call 1-800-873-8635. **Notice to California Residents**—Under California law, you have specific rights to control and access your data. For more information on these rights and how to exercise them, visit corporate.harlequin.com/california-privacy.

HHHRLP23

HARLEQUIN
PLUS

Try the best multimedia subscription service for romance readers like you!

Read, Watch and Play.

Experience the easiest way to get the romance content you crave.

Start your **FREE TRIAL** at
www.harlequinplus.com/freetrial.